MW01152647

Stillness, Storms, and Second Chances

A Novel

Lori Givan

To Marti –

Embrace the stillness

within –

Lori Givan

Luke 17:21

authorHOUSE®

AuthorHouse™
1663 Liberty Drive, Suite 200
Bloomington, IN 47403
www.authorhouse.com
Phone: 1-800-839-8640

©2009 Lori Givan. All rights reserved.

No part of this book may be reproduced, stored in a retrieval system, or transmitted by any means without the written permission of the author.

This book is a work of fiction. People, places, events, and situations are the product of the author's imagination. Any resemblance to actual persons, living or dead, or historical events, is purely coincidental.

First published by AuthorHouse   2/23/2009

ISBN: 978-1-4389-4240-7 (sc)
ISBN: 978-1-4389-4241-4 (hc)

Printed in the United States of America
Bloomington, Indiana

This book is printed on acid-free paper.

For Gene.
Thanks for sharing twenty-five of the best years of my life with me.

CHAPTER ONE

Annie had the Sunday night blues. This had been happening almost as long as she could remember in her thirteen years, but it seemed to be getting worse. No matter what she did, she couldn't seem to stop it. She couldn't really figure it out either. It wasn't like she hated school or anything. Sure, there was a lot of homework, special projects, and the constant stream of tests. Most of all she hated the standardized tests. They made her palms sweaty and her brain freeze. The only thing worse than the test itself was the day the results came. She knew the scores would never be as high as they should be, because she never felt like she'd done her best. Even worse was the look on her mother's face when she read the results. She tried not to even look, because the disappointment was almost too much to bear.

Of course her brother's tests always arrived around the same time, and her parents were always so proud of him. They had a lot to be proud of. Andrew was the shining star of the family—good-look-ing, tons of friends, great athlete, straight-A student. Even though they didn't expect as much from her, the disappointment on their faces was hard to miss. Was she just bound to be a let-down to them her whole life? She was even a let-down to herself. She felt like such a loser sometimes.

No matter how hard she tried, she never measured up. In fact, it seemed like the harder she tried, the greater the disappointment was later on. The worst thing was she knew she had the potential to be more. It was just that all the pressure got to her and she couldn't perform at the critical times, like with tests. Lately it was almost like her parents had given up on her. They still had high expectations for Andrew, but they seemed to have resigned themselves to the fact that she was just sub-par.

Now it was Sunday night again and the doubts were creeping in again, like storm clouds that quietly roll in to take over a clear sky. Sometimes she could distract herself by watching TV or texting friends. If she could trick her mind into thinking it was any other night of the week, sometimes she could forget, at least for a little while, that it was Sunday night and another week loomed large in front of her. But she'd already tried those things tonight, and the storm clouds were still rolling in.

She pulled the covers over her head in her bed, even though it was still early, and closed her eyes. She didn't consider herself a religious person, but she did believe in God, and she found herself praying. "What's wrong with me, God? Why am I such a loser? Nobody else seems to get like this on Sunday nights. I just don't get it." She started to cry and then wondered where the tears had come from. "I hate feeling this way. Can you make it go away? Will I always feel this way? Sometimes I just don't feel like going on. It all seems so pointless."

After crying a little more into her pillow, she sniffed, then became quiet and still in her bed, with her eyes closed. She wasn't sure what was happening, but she felt calmer for some weird reason. Then a voice, like no other she had ever heard, in fact not even like a human voice at all, said, "I am here, Annie. Come to me. Trust me."

Her eyes flew open to see who it was, but she was too scared to move. Her eyes scanned the room without moving her head, but she saw no one. The room was just as it had been, but somehow things had changed in a big way. Was she crazy, or had she just heard what she thought she had? She pinched herself to see if she was dreaming. Nope, not a dream. She felt a peace descend over her as she thought about the words she'd just heard. Could it have really been God answering her? It sure sounded like a voice, but she knew it wasn't anyone in her family. She had never heard a voice like this one before. Almost like it had come from a different world, but she knew it was real. It had spoken her name out loud, so she knew it was meant for her. She wrapped herself in its comfort and drifted off to sleep.

Ralph shifted to get more comfortable, but it was hard to do when you only had a small blanket and a piece of cardboard to cover you. He tightly re-folded an old sweatshirt to prop up his neck. He adjusted himself on the ground and closed his eyes. He didn't know how much longer he could stand this. He hated what life had done to him, but more than that, he hated himself for letting it happen. He remembered when he had a home, a wife, a family and a good job. What had happened to it all? It didn't seem like that long ago when he was a star on the corporate fast track. They thought he was brilliant and kept throwing him tougher assignments.

For several years, it seemed like he could take on anything and that his potential was unlimited. Senior management loved him and the promotions came quickly. But they stopped loving him quite so much when he started showing up late for work and began calling in sick more often. Damn the drink anyway. He couldn't believe he had let it get the better of him. He always thought he could stop whenever he wanted. But apparently not, based on where he was right now.

He couldn't blame his boss, or his wife for kicking him out. He despised what he'd done, and he despised himself. A tear rolled through the dirt on his face and he wondered what was left for him. He couldn't seem to stop drinking, nor did he really even want to. What was the point anyway? It wasn't like if he stopped, everything would get better. He wasn't going to get his job back, or his family, or his old life back. The drink had been his best friend, the only thing that was always there for him, ready to help him escape the daily pain of life.

But as he lay there unable to sleep, and the effects of the alcohol began to wear off, he shivered and wondered if he was ready to die. He wondered where he'd go if he did die. Would it all be over? Or was there a merciful God out there somewhere that would let him into heaven? He thought about all the money he'd donated to the church when life was better. Would that count for anything with God? Or all the money he'd contributed to charities at work? How much would be enough for God to overlook the man he'd become? Was there enough money in the world? He'd even been baptized when he was young. Would that help his case?

The tears streamed down his face as he thought, "God, what have I become? Can you even see me? Or am I too disgusting for you to even look upon? I hate myself, God, and I don't want to even live any more. Why am I here? I'm a loser, my family has turned me away, I have nothing to give anyone. Why don't you just take me now? Oh God, help me!"

His wracking sobs eased into the whimpering that is left behind when there are no more tears to cry. He sucked in a few gulps of air, and finally there was nothing left but the sound of his breathing, in and out. A voice spoke then, seeming to come from right next to him, though he was fairly certain there was no one else around. "Ralph, I'm right here with you. Come to me. Trust me."

He flung off the cardboard and whipped around. There was no one there. Whose voice was it? Who would say those words? Who would want him, a dirty, disgusting drunk, to come to them and trust them? He sat up, still waiting to see someone or hear something else, but there was nothing.

Rick Davidson sat in his study, reviewing his notes from that day's sermon. It just hadn't seemed to resonate with the congregation, and he couldn't figure out why. He'd preached from the Sermon on the Mount, and had thought it was a well-planned sermon. Read the scripture passage, break it down, tell what it's about, offer ideas for how it applies to their lives. But how did you tell some of the wealthiest people in the county that the poor and meek are blessed and that they would inherit the kingdom of God? He knew he couldn't afford to offend these people. They were building a new wing to the church and the expenses were adding up. To keep everything running smoothly, his sermons needed to uplift the congregation, and not ruffle any feathers. Still he wondered, "Is this really what God called me to do?"

He remembered back to a few years ago when he and Sarah were first married and he'd been assigned his first church in a small southern town. Even though everyone in the town knew each other, they were eager to welcome the young new pastor into their midst. They were a small congregation, maybe a hundred each Sunday on a good week, but they had a sincere desire to serve the less fortunate in their community. They donated the proceeds of their annual rummage sale and bake sale to the mission team at the church, and each Thanksgiving they hosted a free dinner for anyone in the community who wanted to come. Though it was a relatively poor rural community, the church members had given what they could and Rick was inspired by their willing spirit.

Eleven years later when the call came for him to leave and move to a large church in a suburb of Kansas City, he and Sarah were devastated. How would they ever make friends in such a big city? They'd both grown up in small towns and never imagined themselves fitting into such a place. But where the Lord led, he was supposed to be willing to follow. And he was, but sometimes he wondered if the Lord really knew what he was doing. So they'd followed the call, said painful good-bye's, picked up the roots they'd established, and moved here.

He set his sermon notes aside, took off his glasses, and sat back in his chair with a sigh. He closed his eyes, rubbed his forehead, and prayed, "God, I just don't know how to reach these people. I always thought I'd be somewhere where I could help people in need. But these people don't need me. All they need is a nice cushioned pew and someone to tell them what great people they are. Should I be doing something else, God? Helping the poor or the hungry? I just don't see the point of this. I don't know what to offer these people." He rubbed his eyes and sat for a while with his head in his hands.

He leaned back and as he stared at the ceiling, a voice seemed to whisper in his ear. "I am with you, Rick. Come to me. Trust me."

His whole body felt electrified, and his heart and mind went completely quiet, as if time stood still. He had never heard this voice before, but he had no doubt about whose it was. He held his breath, hoping to hear it again. But he heard nothing. Rick stayed in his chair and continued to feel the unworldly warmth long into the night.

There weren't many others with Carolyn at the gym on Sunday night. Most people either worked out earlier in the day or they'd skipped it and resolved to get started again on Monday. But Carolyn was unsettled and upset. Her husband was leaving town again Monday morning, and who knew how long it would be before she would have time to work out again. She figured she'd better take the opportunity while she could. She wondered if he secretly liked traveling more than he let on. Even though Eric said he missed the family when he was gone, it sure didn't seem like it. He almost seemed to look forward to getting away from them. But who could blame him, with two surly kids at home and a wife who nagged him more than she probably should. Heck, she'd probably get away too, if she were in his place. But she couldn't, since she was the one who stayed home and took care of things on that end. Why couldn't he appreciate her more, though? He expected her to do everything--pay the bills, keep the house clean, run the kids around, do the laundry, work a job herself, keep the yard mowed, plant flowers--with rarely a word of appreciation. She knew this was the life they'd agreed on, but somehow it seemed less ideal than when they'd first decided on it. Thank God for the gym membership though. At least this was one place she could go to get away and have some time to herself.

She found one of the empty treadmills, turned off the TV in front of it, and put the earphones to her MP3 player into her ears. Tonight she wasn't in the mood for inane television, she just wanted to zone out with her own music. She programmed the treadmill, started the music player and began her warm-up. But while she ran, her mind wouldn't settle down, and she kept thinking about her life, wondering why she felt so dissatisfied. Why did she feel so trapped and how could she possibly change it? She didn't want to leave Eric--she just wished he would more time with her and the kids. She didn't want to leave her home, yet cleaning up the messes day after day didn't appeal to her either. She loved her kids, but did they have to be so irritating and demanding?

Then she felt guilty for having any of these thoughts at all and she tried to push them out of her mind. She really was lucky to have the life she did. They were all healthy, most of the time anyway, they kept up with the bills, they had good jobs, and their kids did well in school. She kept trying to remember how much she had to be thankful for, but still the nagging thoughts came back. This just didn't seem like the life she'd ever imagined having when she and Eric walked down the aisle eighteen years ago.

While she jogged, she found herself thinking, "God, is this all there is? I love my kids, I really do, but is this really what I'm supposed to be doing with my life? I just can't face week after week of this for God knows how long." She breathed and ran. "I'm just so tired of it all. I hate my life. Sometimes I hate my husband, and sometimes I even hate my kids. What's wrong with me? What kind of mother am I? I'm not even worthy of being a mother to my kids. God, what should I do? Are you even there? Do you even care?"

As Carolyn continued to run, her MP3 player stuttered and then stopped. She looked down to see if the battery had gone dead, but the name of the song was still displayed on the screen. She jiggled it and adjusted the earphones in her ears. Still nothing. Then she heard a voice speaking through her earphones, only it didn't sound at all like a human voice. It permeated her whole body, though it wasn't really loud. "Yes, Carolyn, I am here. Come to me. Trust me."

She whipped around to see if someone was messing with the P.A. system. The few other people there were still working out, as if they hadn't heard a thing. She looked up at the speaker in the ceiling and looked around again, trying to keep up with the treadmill so she wouldn't fall off. But everyone else was just continuing as if nothing was out of the ordinary. She stumbled a little and grabbed the bars on the treadmill to steady herself. She jumped to one side before falling, pulled the earphones out and turned the treadmill off. She asked a guy across the room, "Did you hear something?" He looked around and said, "Hear what?"

"You didn't hear a voice, like, coming through the speakers or something?"

He raised his eyebrows a little and said, "No, sorry, I didn't hear anything. Is everything okay?"

Carolyn paused a moment, then said, "Actually, yes, I think it is."

Bob and Katie reclined on the hospital bed, Bob's arms wrapped around her as she convulsed with sobs. He was numb himself, but he knew he needed to be strong for her. Was this really happening? Just yesterday they'd finished painting the nursery and had carefully removed the painter's tape from the woodwork around the room. Everything had seemed so perfect as they prepared for their baby boy's arrival in a few weeks. When Katie started into labor, they both knew it was too early, but they hoped there was something the doctors could do. Everything had gone from being so perfect to being so horrible in just a few short hours. How could anything ever be right again? Where were they supposed to go from here? With every wracking sob coming from Katie's body, he felt himself dying a little more inside.

It had been two hours since they'd seen their baby boy born, and then got to spend a few short moments with him while he struggled to breathe. He was so tiny and yet so perfect – all his little fingers and toes were there and he even had some hair on his tiny head. But he was very premature and the doctor said his lungs were too underdeveloped to make it, yet he came anyway, breathed a few short breaths and then left them.

Katie had cried this terrible cry that would live in Bob's memory the rest of his life. Over and over she cried, "God, No! No! No!" And yet it had happened. As they held on to each other these past two hours, her cries had become, "God, why? Why?" He wondered the same thing. Why would God bring this perfect little being into their lives, only to yank him away before they'd even had a chance to get to know him? They had already fallen in love with their unborn son, gotten excited and prepared, only to watch him be taken from them. Where was the love in a God like that?

So he just held her, feeling the waves of her sobs begin to slowly recede. Finally she stopped and they lay there together, just breathing. He wanted to ask her if she was okay, but of course she wasn't. He wanted to tell her everything would be okay, but would it ever really be okay again? He wanted to tell her he'd take care of her, but he hadn't, had he? This terrible thing had happened and there hadn't been a thing he could do about it. Could he ever really take care of her? He felt completely powerless. Powerless as a husband, as a father, and as a man. So he just laid there holding her.

"What did I do wrong, Bob? I must have done something wrong." He could barely hear her as she whispered the words.

"Katie, honey, you didn't do anything wrong. Nothing at all." He pulled her tighter to him.

"I must have done something wrong, for God to hate me so much."

"Oh honey, God doesn't hate you. How could you think that? You would have been a great mother."

"He must hate me, to put me through this. I hate myself. He must be punishing me. I just want to die." She began to cry again.

Bob thought, *'I know, I feel the same way,'* but he knew he needed to comfort her. So he said, "Oh Katie, don't say that. We can try again. Things can be different."

"I don't ever want to try again, Bob. I just want this baby. If God hates me so much now, what makes you think he won't keep hating me and do this to us again?"

"Katie, God doesn't hate you. How could he? You're a sweet, loving woman who is someday going to make a wonderful mother, and he knows that. Maybe it just wasn't meant to be this time. Please don't give up. You've got to know…," but he couldn't finish. What could he say? You've got to know what? That God still loves you and will give you another chance? That God doesn't hate you? Was any of it really true? He felt the same way about himself, so who was he to offer these platitudes?

He felt himself getting angry. Now it was his turn to cry. But it was an angry cry. Dammit anyway, why did this have to happen to them? They would have been great parents. Why couldn't this have happened to someone else? Someone who wouldn't have loved their child so much? Was there such a person anywhere? He let the sobs come and this time it was Katie's turn to hold him. He turned away from her as he lied next to her, and she turned over to put her arms around him.

He cried, "God, why us? Why us? Why did you take our son? We already loved him so much. Oh, God, why?"

Then a voice spoke, "I am here with you. Come to me. Trust me."

Katie and Bob froze. The voice was like nothing either had ever heard before. It almost didn't seem real, yet it was clearly audible. There was no mistaking that it was a voice. The energy in the room felt different– buzzing, almost like an electrical current had passed through. Neither breathed, and they stayed where they were on the bed, Katie's arms still wrapped around Bob. A few seconds later, the energy seemed to return to normal.

Bob turned over to look at Katie. "Did you hear that?"

Katie's eyes widened and she breathed heavily as she whispered, "Yeah, did you?"

Bob sat up, looked around the room and back at Katie, wondering what exactly had just happened. They were both filled with a sense of calm and peace.

"What do you think it was?" Katie whispered, as she sat up, searching Bob's face.

"I'm not sure."

"It was amazing. You heard it, too? I thought maybe it was just in my head."

"No, I heard it, too." He looked around the room again, even though he could see there was no one else there.

Katie relaxed back in the bed, suddenly filled with a desperate urge to sleep. She was exhausted, and for some reason she couldn't exactly identify, she sensed that all was going to be okay, if she could just sleep. So she let go, and her breathing began to slow as she passed into sleep.

Bob sat up in the bed next to her, thinking about what had just happened. Whose voice was it? He had felt a tremendous power in the voice, almost as if he was a child again and the voice was his parent, making everything all right. A few minutes ago, he thought he would never feel at peace again, yet in the second the voice spoke, a peace descended over him like he'd never known before. It was almost like a miracle, except that he didn't really believe in miracles. But look what it had done for Katie. She had heard it too, and now she was resting, at peace.

Although they'd been to church a few times since they'd gotten married, he had never really been sure of the God thing. He went along with her to church to make her happy. When their baby had been taken from them tonight, he thought if there was a God, he sure wasn't someone he wanted on his side. What kind of a God would allow this to happen? But when the voice spoke, it was hard to deny that it had felt like God speaking to them. Or maybe it was an angel? It was definitely other-worldly and he didn't know what to make of it. When Katie woke up, they'd have a lot to talk about.

Robin felt like crap, so she poured herself another drink and took it to bed. Sunday nights were the worst part of the week. Well, Monday mornings pretty much sucked too, but sometimes the reality of just dealing with it was better than anticipating it on Sunday night. All week long she looked forward to the weekend, when she could finally be free again and have some fun. Sometimes she even managed to round up some friends for a happy hour during the week, which helped break things up a little. It was always more fun to drink with other people than to drink in her apartment alone. Friday and Saturday nights were the best part of the week—finally a chance to kick back and enjoy. Sunday mornings were for sleeping it off, staying in bed late, reading the paper and just hanging.

But man, she must have had more than her usual last night, because today had been pretty bad. She'd retched over the toilet more than once, and her churning stomach still wasn't sure if it was done.

She'd spent the day between her bed and the bathroom, trying to keep some aspirin down to take the edge off. She had a splitting headache and kept the curtains closed to keep her bedroom as dark as possible.

Lying in bed, she thought about the night before. It had started out promising enough. She loved dressing up in her party clothes— tight shirt, high heels, her favorite designer jeans. She loved watching the eyes follow her when she walked into Jackie's, her favorite night spot. The music got her going as soon as she walked in, and she worked her hips as she strutted across the room, finding her spot at the table with the regular Saturday night gang.

When her friends came in with a couple of new guys, she was quick to introduce herself to them. She wondered which one she'd like best. She'd have to dance with them to find out for sure. You could tell a lot about a guy by the way he danced. If he was uptight or relaxed, if he laughed and had a good time, or if he looked around, worried about who was watching him. By the end of the night, she'd danced with them all, but the new guy Rusty was the one who caught her eye. He kept the drinks coming and they'd had a great time laughing together.

Had she really fallen down when she got up that last time to go to the ladies' room? They'd all laughed it off like it was no big deal, but, how embarrassing. They probably thought she'd had too much to drink, and maybe she had, but she also knew how to hold her liquor. She had probably just tripped on something, but still, it was humiliating looking up at their faces while she was sprawled out on the floor and having them help her back up. She rubbed her knee, which she could now see was swollen and had turned purplish-blue.

As more of the evening came back, she wondered if some of those things had happened, or if her mind was playing tricks on her. Had she really given Rusty a lap dance in front of everyone after they'd all encouraged her to do it? Or was she imagining it? No, she was pretty sure she had done it. He'd seemed to like it at the time, and everyone was laughing and enjoying it. But now the thought of it was humiliating--especially when she found out later that he was married. Geez, what did they take her for? Some kind of slut?

She pulled the covers over her head, but couldn't help but wonder about herself. How had it come to this? She hated her life, except when it was time to party on Friday and Saturday night. Giving lap dances to married men, falling down in bars. If she didn't know herself better, she'd probably think she was a slut too. Was she? The thought repulsed her, yet she couldn't make it go away. The more she thought about it, the more disgusted she felt with herself. Why couldn't she just have a normal life? Find Mr. Right, get married and have children someday? Would she ever meet the right guy? It seemed like most of the guys she knew were either already taken or were players, not interested in getting tied down. She felt old and worn out, even though she was only twenty-five.

"There has to be more to life than this," she thought. "Is this all there is? Partying, then feeling disgusted with myself, over and over again? God, I hate my life." She began to cry, and then felt another wave of nausea coming on. She threw off the covers, ran to the toilet and hurled again. Was there anything left in there? She felt like she'd puked her guts out already. Finally she crumpled on the floor next to the toilet and sobbed.

"God, what have I become? I can't stand my life. I can't stand myself. I don't want this to be the rest of my life. Oh God, what do I do?"

After a while she stopped crying, but she stayed where she was on the floor by the toilet. She reached up to tear some toilet paper off the roll, wiping her mouth and eyes. She felt numb and sick of herself. Then a voice spoke: "I'm here, Robin. Come to me. Trust me."

She sat up and whirled around, looking for its source. No one was in the apartment with her, so who was it? It was so loud and real.

She croaked, "Who's there?"

She heard it again. "I'm right here, Robin. Trust me."

She felt a cloak of peace and love enfold her, and something deep within her wanted to trust this voice. She said, "Oh God, please help me."

CHAPTER TWO

When Katie woke up Monday morning, she looked around the hospital room for Bob. He was resting in an awkward position in the chair next to her bed, his eyes closed and his hair rumpled. She closed her eyes and slumped back in the bed. The realization of yesterday's events hit her and her heart sank. She wondered why she didn't feel more physical pain until she noticed the IV dripping through the line into her hand. But she also felt an odd sort of peace, and wasn't sure why. The worst possible thing had just happened, yet she felt at peace. Maybe it was the drugs doing a job on her.

Bob shifted in his chair and opened his eyes, slowly focusing on her. When he saw that she was awake, he rubbed his eyes, got up and sat on the bed. "How ya doin' sweetie?" He stroked her hair as he looked at her.

"Mmm, not bad, I guess." She scooted up into a sitting position on the bed. He adjusted the pillows to make her more comfortable. "What time is it?"

He looked at his watch and said, "Six-fifteen. Do you want me to have the nurse bring you something?" The sun was beginning to lighten the window through the blinds in her room.

"No, I don't think so. Can you open the blinds?"

"Sure," he said, walking over to the window and turning the rod to open them. The sun gleamed through, not quite bright, yet turning the room a different color.

"Did you sleep in that chair all night? You must feel awful."

"Oh, it wasn't that bad," Bob said, stretching his back and feeling a pop. "I wanted to be here when you woke up."

"Well, thanks. It was nice to see you here."

He sat back on the bed next to her and neither spoke. He held her hand and they stared ahead.

Finally Bob broke the silence. "I think I'll go out and get some coffee if you don't mind. You want me to bring you something?"

Katie sank back into her pillows. "No thanks. Go ahead though."

He got up, walked over to the sink in her room and threw some cold water on his face. He wiped it with a towel then ran a wet comb through his unruly brown hair. "Okay, I'll be right back."

He stepped out of the room into the hallway, letting the door close behind him, and leaned against the wall just outside. He couldn't remember ever feeling so tired and sore and empty. He thought back to the strange voice they'd both heard last night. Had it really happened or was it some kind of weird dream? Did she remember it too? If she did, why hadn't she said anything about it this morning? It had brought him a strange sense of peace, a feeling that somehow things were going to be all right. Even through the emptiness he felt, there was peace, somehow bringing a knowing that they would get through this.

He walked down the hall to look for the vending machines. The hospital looked different than it had last night. But then again, it felt like his whole life had changed since yesterday. A nurse looked up from the station and asked, "Can I help you?"

"Yeah, I'm looking for some coffee."

"The vending machines are around that corner there, but if you want the better stuff, the cafeteria's down on the first floor. Just take the elevator at the end of the hall."

He debated going down to the cafeteria, but decided to stay closer to Katie's room. "Thanks, I'll just get what's in the machine."

"Suit yourself. Are you Mr. Griffin?" She had seen him come out of Katie's room, but she had just come in for her shift, so they hadn't met yet. He nodded. "I'll be over to her room in just a few minutes to check on her. Is she awake?" the nurse asked.

"Yeah." He rounded the corner, deposited some coins and waited as the coffee streamed into the cup. He picked it up and took a sip in front of the machine. He heard some people talking in the waiting room on the other side of the vending alcove. They were speaking in hushed tones, but he could hear most of what they were saying.

"…heard a voice last night…." "…think she's crazy?" "Other people down in the cafeteria were saying the same thing."

Bob moved a little closer, trying to pick up more of the conversation. What was going on?

"She doesn't even believe in God, and now she thinks she heard his voice."

"Do you think she was out of her head? Was it the meds?"

"She wasn't even on any meds at that point."

"So who else is saying this?"

"Some nurses in the cafeteria. I was just down there, and I overheard one of 'em saying that a bunch of kids in the children's ward said they heard a voice speak to them last night, and they were convinced it was God."

"Well, what did God supposedly say?"

"I don't know. All I heard was they said they thought it was God."

Bob froze with his paper cup of coffee next to his mouth. What in the world was happening? Could it be true that other people had heard what he and Katie heard last night? Was it some kind of hospital joke they were playing with the intercom system? These people seemed pretty serious about it, not treating it as a joke at all. He wanted to hear more, but they got up from their chairs and he didn't want them to see him eavesdropping, so he walked back toward Katie's room.

He went inside and saw her lying on her side, facing the window. He sat down in the chair on that side of her bed so he could face her, and sipped his coffee.

"The nurse says she'll be here in a few minutes to check on you."

"Mm-kay."

They were quiet for a while, and he wondered if he should tell her about the conversation he'd overheard. Finally he said, "Katie, you won't believe what I just heard outside in the waiting room."

"What?" She looked up at him.

"Some people were talking about how some other people in the hospital heard God speak to them last night."

Katie raised her eyebrows. Bob wondered if she remembered what had happened, or if she was going to think he was crazy. He waited to see her reaction before saying anything else. Neither said a word.

Finally, Katie spoke quietly, "I thought maybe I'd dreamed it. The whole thing seemed like a dream. First the nightmare, and then that voice, which made it seem like less of a nightmare for some reason…."

Bob said, "I thought maybe I'd dreamed it myself." They looked at each other for a moment, then looked away.

"Bob, do you remember what it said? I can barely remember. I think I fell asleep right after that."

He was afraid to say the words out loud, afraid that he might not have remembered it correctly. It almost seemed that to say the words out loud would be to diminish them. They had seemed so profound at the time.

"What, Bob? Do you remember?"

After a long pause, he said, "I think it said, 'I am here. Come to me. Trust me.'" There. It was out in the open now. If she thought he was crazy, he hoped she'd just say it.

But her eyes grew wider, and she said, "Oh…yeah, now I remember. That's right. That's what I heard, too."

They were quiet as they each remembered. Katie was first to speak. "So you're saying other people heard it too?"

"Yeah. I think so."

"Well, what'd they say about it?"

"It sounded like they knew someone else in the hospital who had heard a voice last night, and they also heard some nurses in the cafeteria talking about some children who heard it too."

Katie took this in. "Wow. That's pretty freaky, isn't it."

"Yeah, it is." He scratched his head and looked out the window, noticing that the edge of the sun was appearing over the trees.

After a while she said, "Bob, whose voice do you think it was?"

"I don't know…maybe someone was messing with the hospital PA system. Maybe it was some kind of prank."

"It didn't sound like a voice on the PA system. It wasn't like any other voice I've ever heard before. I almost thought it was coming from inside my head. If you hadn't heard it too, that's probably what I would have thought."

"Well, then, whose voice do you think it was?" he turned from the window to ask her.

"I don't know."

They were considering this when the nurse opened the door and walked in.

"Hello, Mrs. Griffin, how are you feeling this morning?" She walked over with a tray, set it down on the counter, and began to check Katie's IV and blood pressure.

Carolyn needed to get up and start breakfast for the kids, but she just wanted to lie in bed a little bit longer. Eric had gotten up early to catch his flight, so he was already out of the house. She thought about what had happened last night at the gym. It was the weirdest thing, the words that had come through her MP3 player, and yet as she recalled it, she felt a peace she hadn't felt in a long time. It seemed to wrap around her like a blanket and she just wanted to enjoy it a little while longer.

She had grown up in the church, but hadn't attended in many years. Most of the time she thought she still believed in God, but sometimes she wondered, especially when catastrophic events happened that God could have prevented. But she couldn't help but think that the words she heard in her earphones had seemed like the kind of thing God would say. In fact, hadn't he even spoken them to people in the Bible? But why would he say them to her? If, in fact, that's who was even saying them? Maybe her MP3 player had just malfunctioned. But no, it was a completely different type of sound. It had electrified her whole body, and then she had immediately felt at peace. Now as she recalled it, the same peace embraced her like it had before. It felt so good and she wanted to stay in bed longer to hold on to it. What were the words again? 'Yes, Carolyn, I am here. Come to me. Trust me.'

But the buzzing of the alarm broke her reverie and she reached over to turn it off. She sighed and rolled out of bed to start the day.

She went into the kitchen to start a pot of coffee, and laid the placemats on the table. Then she went upstairs to make sure the kids were up and getting ready.

"Annie, you up yet?" She lightly knocked on the door. No response.

"Andrew, you up?"

"Yeah," was the sleepy reply, but she knocked on his door anyway, and then opened it. He was still in bed.

"You don't look up to me. Come on, get rolling."

She went back to check on Annie. "Hey Annie, time to get up," she said, opening the door to see that Annie was up, fully dressed and sitting at her desk.

"I'm up, Mom, okay?"

"Oh! What are you doing up so early?" Carolyn had never known Annie to be an early riser. She was usually the last one out of bed.

"I just wanted to review my vocab words before the test today."

Carolyn couldn't help but be shocked. Annie was a good student, but she usually had to be prodded to study or do homework. "Well…fine. That's great, honey. Come on down to breakfast in a few minutes."

"Okay, Mom."

Carolyn shut the door behind her, raised her eyebrows, and headed back downstairs to get breakfast started.

Annie stared at the vocabulary words on the paper in front of her. Celestial. It meant "other worldly" or "outer space." Sort of like the voice she'd heard in her room last night. She didn't know where it had come from, but it sure had made her feel better. She wanted to remember the voice always. She had written down the words last night, and she pulled that paper out to look at it again. "I am here, Annie. Trust me."

It had even spoken her name. She'd looked around, but she hadn't seen an angel or anything. She hadn't seen anything at all, but the voice had been real, there was no doubt in her mind about that. So whose voice was it? Did it mean she was crazy if she was hearing voices? She probably shouldn't tell anyone about it, just in case. She just wanted to remember the voice forever.

She'd stayed awake long after hearing those words, not wanting to let go of the new peace that had come over her, and completely forgetting her Sunday night blues. Now this morning, she couldn't believe it, but she was actually looking forward to going to school. She knew somehow that everything was going to be all right, and this made her calmer and lighter inside, without the usual sense of dread that Monday mornings brought.

She folded the vocabulary sheet and the notebook paper where she'd written the special words, put them in her backpack, and headed downstairs to breakfast.

Rick sipped coffee at the kitchen table with Sarah. He thought about what he'd heard the night before in his study, and wondered if he should tell her. He felt such serenity that he didn't want to ruin it by speaking about it out loud. Yet he wanted to share it with someone, too. He took a chance.

"Sarah, the most amazing thing happened to me last night."

She looked up from the newspaper. "Oh? What?"

"I was sitting there in my study, thinking about the sermon yesterday, wondering how I could have made it better, and then I heard a voice speak to me."

Sarah set down her mug of coffee and waited to hear more.

"Just as I was praying to God and asking him why I was having trouble reaching the people, I heard some words, quite clearly. Different from anything that has ever happened to me before."

"Words?" she asked.

"Yeah." He tried to think of how to explain it to her. "Usually when I feel the Holy Spirit speaking to me, it's sort of like words in my head that just come. But this time it was different. They were spoken words, out loud, as clear as anything." He looked over at her, almost afraid to see the doubt on her face, but he only saw a look of pure wonderment.

"Well, what were the words, Rick?"

He paused, and then decided to forge ahead and tell her, hoping she wouldn't think he'd lost his marbles.

"The words were, 'I am with you, Rick. Come to me. Trust me.' And that was it. Nothing else."

"And you heard them out loud?" She asked it more as a question to herself than to him. "Where do you think they came from?"

He paused a minute, then finally looked at her and said, "Sarah, I think it was God. Actually, I'm sure it was God. There's no doubt in my mind. There was no doubt in my mind last night, and there's no doubt now. It's hard for me to believe it happened, but I know it did." He looked away, and she waited for him to say more. Then he turned to her again.

"It felt like a big loving embrace of the power of God, as soon as the words were spoken. I felt tingly all over and it lasted a long time into the night. I've felt a similar feeling at different times in my life, when I knew I was feeling God's spirit."

Neither spoke. Sarah was the first to break the silence. "Wow. That's pretty cool, Rick."

"Yeah."

They were both quiet as they sipped their coffee and thought about what Rick had just said.

"Well, what are you gonna do about it now?" she asked.

"What do you mean? What is there to do about it?"

"Are you just gonna keep it to yourself then? You're not gonna tell anyone else?"

He got up from the table and walked over to the coffeemaker.

"I don't know." What would people think? He knew what they'd think. They'd think he'd lost his mind. His congregation didn't want their religion too far out of their comfort zone, and for him to say he had actually heard the voice of God would be pretty far out there. His mind raced ahead, imagining what might happen. They'd probably request a new pastor and he'd be kicked out, looking for another job. It could even become something of a scandal, if they wanted to get nasty about it. His experience last night was too sacred to let that happen. Maybe this was something he should just keep close to his own heart.

Sarah looked back at the newspaper. She'd known Rick since college, and they'd been through some incredible spiritual experiences together. It was his open heart and easy way with people that caused her to fall for him. She'd never met anyone else like him, a man who sincerely wanted to find God's will for his life, no matter what the cost. They had both been so idealistic, ready to do whatever it took to share God's love with people. They imagined themselves as missionaries, climbing mountains, forging jungles, rescuing orphans, preaching, whatever it took. What they hadn't counted on was ending up in an affluent suburb with people who enjoyed their cushy pews on Sunday morning, but preferred to leave their religion at church the rest of the week. It was hard to motivate people who claimed to be believers, yet didn't want to grow in their faith or stretch themselves. She knew Rick had struggled with this, just like she had, and secretly she'd been hoping that somehow God would see fit to move them to another community or church, where they could get back to what she thought their lives were supposed to be about.

But now God seemed to have spoken to Rick out loud, and she wondered why this would happen now. What did it mean? That they should just stay where they were? Or did God have something else planned for them? She was surprised at Rick's reluctance to tell anyone else about what he'd heard. But she figured he needed time to sort it out in his mind. She sat back in her chair and thought, 'We'll just have to wait and see, won't we?'

Rick rinsed his mug, set it in the dishwasher, and got his jacket out of the closet.

"I'm heading over to the shelter to help with the sack lunches."

This was something he did most Monday mornings, helping hand out sack lunches to people at the homeless shelter across town. He kissed her and left. This was at least one thing that made him feel connected to people who really needed help. Even though his work at the church kept him extremely busy, he wasn't willing to give up his time at the shelter working with the needy.

As he drove, he talked to God in the car—something he did often when he drove. "God, I'm not sure why I heard what I did last night, but I thank you for it. You knew how low I've been feeling. Sometimes I wonder if I'm even worthy of being a pastor. I just can't seem to get through to these people, and sometimes I just want to give up. God, help me know how you want to use me. I want to be your faithful servant, God, you know I do."

He felt the calmness and peace return that he'd felt last night, and so many other times when he prayed. He soaked it in as he drove. He still didn't have any concrete answers about what to do, but he knew he just needed to have faith. Trust him. That's what God had told him to do last night.

He turned into the shelter's parking lot and noticed several people shuffling in to the building to pick up their lunches. He parked, stepped out, pushed the remote to lock the car, and walked across the parking lot. It was a warm, sunny day, and he inhaled deeply. Something about birds singing always filled his soul.

"Hey, Pastor Rick, good to see you this morning!" One of the volunteers greeted him as he passed through the door.

"Mornin', Charlie. How's it goin'?"

"Pretty good. We've got alot of sacks to pass out today, and it's a good thing. We've already had about twenty people come in and it's not even nine o'clock."

Several area churches participated in the sack lunch program. Their members donated the items, assembled the sacks on Sunday afternoons, and then someone delivered them to the shelter on Monday morning to be shared with the needy. More than a hundred sack lunches were usually distributed.

Rick slipped off his jacket and hung it on the coat rack. He walked over to the table that held all the filled sacks. His heart filled as he read the messages people had written on the sacks, some with children's drawings and stickers. Rick recognized a man coming through the door and picked up a lunch for him.

CHAPTER THREE

"Hey, Ralph. Good to see you," Rick said, handing the man a sack. The man took it, mumbled his thanks, and glanced around the room.

"How have you been?" Rick tried to catch his eyes, but they were darting around the room as if looking for someone. "You okay, Ralph?"

"Yeah, I'm okay. I guess." Ralph looked at Rick then, and started to say more but then he stopped.

"What's up, Ralph?" Rick sensed something different about him this morning. Most people were quick to take their sacks, mumble a thanks and head for the door. But Ralph shifted from foot to foot, trying to work up the nerve to say something.

"Pastor, is there some place we could talk for a minute?"

"Sure, let's go over here," Rick said, and he led Ralph to a small break room in the shelter, where there was an old kitchen table and a few folding chairs. "Here, have a seat," and he pulled a chair out for Ralph. They both sat down, and he waited for Ralph to say what was on his mind.

Ralph looked him in the eyes, then said, "Uh, well… I'm wondering somethin'. Do you think God ever speaks to people, like out loud?"

Rick stopped breathing and stared back at Ralph. Did he just hear what he thought he heard? How bizarre.

Then Ralph started to get up, saying, "Whatever. You know I was just wonderin'."

Rick jumped up and said, "No, please, sit back down. I'm sorry. Let's talk about this."

Ralph continued toward the door.

"Actually, yes, I do believe that God speaks out loud to people."

Ralph stopped and turned around. "You do?"

"Yeah, I do. The Bible is filled with stories of God speaking to people."

"Yeah, sure," and Ralph started out of the room again.

Rick wanted him to stay and tell him why he was asking this question, so he quickly added, "And I think he still talks to people, even now."

Ralph paused and looked back at Rick.

Rick continued, "I think it's entirely possible that God speaks out loud to people. Even today. Why do you ask?"

Ralph's face softened. He walked back to the chair and sat down. "So you don't think people are crazy if they say they heard God speak to them?"

Rick knew he should be careful. "Well, Ralph, I think it can happen. But I also think there are some people who think they've heard voices that weren't the voice of God. So I guess it's kinda hard to know when it's real and when it's not."

"Wouldn't a person know if it was real or not?" Ralph asked.

"I think most people probably would. But there are probably some people that think they heard God and they probably really didn't."

Ralph considered this, and then said, "So would you believe me if I told you I'd heard God's voice?"

Rick leaned back in the chair. He sure wasn't prepared for this one. He'd noticed Ralph at the shelter several times, and sometimes they'd even chatted a little. He knew Ralph had once been a successful businessman with a family and home, but that alcohol had finally gotten the better of him. Ralph had even come into the shelter inebriated on occasion, though he'd never caused a problem. But today Ralph's eyes looked clear, and he was speaking coherently.

"Yeah, Ralph, I'd believe you," he said quietly, looking him in the eyes. "Why do you ask?"

Ralph seemed to be debating whether to say more while he stared at the floor. He looked around to make sure no one else could hear him, then looked back at Rick and whispered, "Because I think God spoke to me last night, that's why."

Rick tried to find his voice, and finally squeaked, "Really? What did God say to you, Ralph?"

"I was just layin' there, tryin' to get comfortable, thinking about my life and how I'd screwed everything up so bad, and I cried out to God. I was just feelin' so damn bad, y'know?" He looked up at Rick, and Rick nodded for him to continue. "And then…well, then I heard a voice, and it wasn't like a regular voice, but it wasn't in my head either. I know it wasn't in my head," he said adamantly. He knew he hadn't been 'hearing voices,' and he didn't want Rick to think he was crazy.

Rick said, "What did you hear the voice say?"

"First it said, 'Ralph, I'm right here with you.' Then it said, 'Come to me. Trust me.' And then I just felt this amazing thing come over me, a peace like I haven't felt in years. It was like I could feel God's love, right there with me, and I never wanted it to end."

His eyes stared into space while he recalled what had happened. Then he focused on Rick again. "Do you believe me, Pastor?" He searched Rick's face to see what he'd find there.

Rick could hardly breathe, but he forced himself to take a deep breath. "Yeah, man, I believe you."

What was going on here? Could God really have spoken to this homeless man last night the same way he'd spoken to Rick in his study? His mind didn't know how to process this and he searched for something to say. Finally he found his voice again, "So what'd you do then, Ralph?"

Ralph's eyes brightened as he looked back at Rick.

"I just laid there, soaking it all up, this feeling that had come over me. Like I said, it was just so peaceful. I just wanted to love God back and I didn't even know how. So I just said, 'I do want to trust you, God, I do, please don't give up on me.' And the peace stayed with me until I finally fell asleep."

Rick was amazed that Ralph had just described the same experience he'd had last night, the incredible serenity and an overwhelming desire to place his trust in God. He mumbled, "Amazing…," and he and Ralph just sat there a while.

Should he tell Ralph that he'd heard the same thing last night? He wanted to, but he just couldn't do it. Who knew who Ralph might tell, and he wasn't sure he wanted anyone to know about it yet.

Ralph rose to stand up, and said, "Well, I better be goin'. I just wanted to see what you thought about it."

"I think it's amazing, Ralph," was all he could think to say.

As Ralph headed out of the break room, he turned around and said, "You know what the most amazing thing about it is? For the first time since I can remember in a long time, I don't even want to drink. It's the damnedest thing…," and he walked out the door, carrying his sack lunch with him.

The clock radio buzzed again, and Robin reached over to hit the snooze one more time. She groaned as she checked the time and flopped back onto the pillow. Her head still hurt, but she knew she had to get out of bed and get ready for work. She pushed herself up, looked out the window by her bed and held her head. Mondays were the worst, but as she remembered what had happened on the floor of the bathroom last night, her sense of dread turned back to the peaceful feeling she'd felt then.

Had she imagined the whole thing? Sometimes she wasn't sure whether some of the things she'd said or done had really happened, especially when her friends told her about them later. She hardly knew what to believe about herself any more. But last night was different, not something she had said or done herself. There had been another voice there, and she remembered the love and peace she'd felt when she'd heard it. It was almost like how her mother had comforted her as a child, the few times her mother was sober. The same kind of feeling, but even better.

The more she thought about it, the more the memory filled her and warmed her again. But then she realized it was getting late and she'd better get moving if she was going to make it to work on time. She couldn't afford to be late any more, since her boss was keeping a closer eye on when she came in and when she left. He used to be a pretty nice guy, but lately he'd turned into a real control freak. She wished she could tell him where to put his stinkin' job, but until she found something better, she'd better just hang on to this one.

She got up, left the bed unmade, and started some coffee while she got in the shower. Forty minutes later she was in her car, crawling along the highway in rush hour traffic, wondering if she was going to make it on time. She was sipping coffee from her travel mug, and barely paying attention to the radio when she heard a news reporter say, "Some Tibetan monks claimed that last night they heard the voice of God speak to them out loud. They were in the United States, visiting a monastery in New York and were in the middle of a meditation session, when they say they heard a voice that they claim was God. At this time we don't have details about what God reportedly said to them, but they were all quite certain that it was in fact, God, and they claim to have found great comfort and encouragement from it."

Robin spit coffee from her mouth, and looked for a tissue to wipe it up with. Did they just say what she thought they said? She turned up the volume. Now the deejays were chattering.

"So, what d'ya think, John? Do you think those monks really heard the voice of God?"

"Well...I'm not gonna argue religion with a bunch of Tibetan monks, I know that much. What do you think, Sammie?"

"I think it's kinda cool, if it's true. I'd sure like to know what God said to them though."

"Yeah. Like, did he say, 'You guys should start eating meat, you need the protein,' or maybe 'Go get yourselves some wives and have a little fun for a change'."

"Yeah," Sammie laughed. "Probably something profound like that. Maybe we'll hear more about it later."

They chattered about other news and Robin was left to her own thoughts. Weird. Did other people hear the same voice she'd heard last night? Was it really God? She wished there was someone she could talk to about it, but she couldn't think of anyone who wouldn't laugh at her or think she had lost her mind. So she decided to just keep it to herself for now. But she planned to check the internet when she got to her desk at work to see if there was more on this Tibetan monk story.

CHAPTER FOUR

Carolyn was in the kitchen Wednesday night fixing dinner while Annie and Andrew were upstairs working on homework, or doing whatever they could find to do instead of working on their homework. The TV was on while she cooked, and when she had the meal ready, she called up to them. "Hey guys, come on down, dinner's ready!"

She poured the drinks, put the salt and pepper shakers on the table, and ladled the chili into each of their bowls. Annie came down the stairs first and sat at the table.

"Did you get your homework done yet?" Carolyn asked.

"Most of it. I just have a few more math problems, but they shouldn't take long."

"That's great, honey." Carolyn bustled around the kitchen, putting some veggies and dip on a plate that she set on the table, along with a plate of crackers. Annie watched the TV while she waited for her brother to join them.

"A decision was made today to re-locate some of the U.S. troops, and we'll have more on that story later. Before we break for a commercial, just a quick note to say that tomorrow on the 'Hailey' show, Hailey will be interviewing some Tibetan monks and others who claim to have heard the voice of God. This reportedly happened Sunday night, when some people say they heard the audible voice of

God. Join us to hear more about this unusual event on the 'Hailey' show tomorrow." Then they broke for a commercial.

Annie stared at the TV. Her mother was still clattering around in the kitchen and didn't seem to have heard the story. Carolyn placed a few more things on the table and yelled, "Andrew! Are you coming? We're ready to eat!"

"Yeah, yeah, I'm coming," he hollered back from his room.

Annie decided to see what her mom would say about they story. "Mom, did you hear what they just said on TV?"

"No, honey, what'd they say?"

"They said that tomorrow on 'Hailey,' she's gonna talk to a bunch of people who said they heard God speak to them last Sunday night."

Carolyn fumbled the dish she was carrying, but got hold of it before it fell. "What did you say?"

Annie noticed how shaken her mom seemed and thought it odd. "Hailey's gonna have some people on her show tomorrow talking about hearing God," she said again, now watching her mother close-ly. Carolyn walked over to the table and looked at the TV which was still running the commercial break.

Andrew bounded down the stairs, pulled out his chair and said, "Hey, what's for dinner? Chili? Great. I'm starving."

Annie continued to watch her mother, who was trying to act like nothing was different, but Annie could see that something about the story had shaken her. She wondered what it was, but she didn't want to bring it up again in front of Andrew. He'd think the whole thing was stupid and she knew she wouldn't be able to have a serious con-versation with her mother about it in front of him. She'd wait until later. As they began to eat, Annie tried to figure out how she could get home early enough tomorrow to watch the 'Hailey' show.

Rick finished his dinner with Sarah, and then drove back up to the church for Wednesday night choir practice. He liked to sing along with the choir whenever he could make the practice. Since hearing what he believed to be the voice of God on Sunday night, he had continued to feel a surreal sense of peace, especially when he was praying or singing, so he looked forward to the opportunity to sing with the group tonight. He pulled up in the church parking lot, and walked into the choir room where choir members were assembling and chatting with each other.

"Hey, Pastor Rick, how's it goin'?" the music director, Dean, greeted him.

"Great, Dean, how are you?" He took a music folder out of the storage bin and walked over to take a seat with the choir. But before he could sit down, a couple of women were chatting and they stopped him.

"Hey, Pastor Rick, did you hear that story on the news about the people who say God spoke to them?" they said, facing him expectantly. He was caught off guard and felt a little stunned. He didn't usually listen to TV news or read newspapers, since the stories tended to depress him. How many ways could people find to hurt each other? It seemed like that's what the news liked to focus on.

"No, I haven't heard about that," he said.

They were quick to fill him in. "Apparently there were some Tibetan monks here in the U.S., and they say they all heard God speak, and a bunch of others are saying they heard it too."

"Hmm…really…." He tried not to let anything show on his face.

"Yeah, Hailey's doing a show on it tomorrow and I'm dying to see what these people have to say. What do you think about it?"

"Well, I haven't heard anything about it, so I guess I'll have to reserve judgment."

"Are you gonna watch the show tomorrow?" one of the ladies asked.

He thought about it. "When is it on?" He'd only seen the show a handful of times and thought it was probably one of the better talk shows. Maybe he would tune in.

"Tomorrow afternoon at four. I hope you watch it, 'cause I want to hear what you think about it. Maybe you can talk about it in your sermon this Sunday."

Ugh. Now he was annoyed. He didn't mind when people came to him with ideas for sermon topics, but this one in particular sounded like a can of worms. Still, he didn't want to offend them, so he said,

"Yeah, well, we'll see." He took his place in the choir among the tenors.

Rick could hardly keep his mind on the songs, as his thoughts kept turning to what the ladies had said. He usually found it hard to believe people who said they heard the voice of God. Most of the time it either meant someone was off their meds, or they were trying to justify their actions by saying God told them to do something. A bunch of monks from Tibet? He wondered if there was some political agenda attached. But then why couldn't God have spoken to them?

He knew in his heart that he himself had heard God's voice Sunday night. In fact, the more he thought about it, the more sacred the whole event had felt to him. He just wasn't sure how he could ever share it with anyone besides Sarah, and especially not with his congregation. Now the fact that a bunch of other people were saying they'd heard the voice of God almost made it feel less sacred. But maybe he should withhold judgment and see what they had to say. If they were crackpots, which they probably were, he'd be able to spot it right away. He would need to denounce this quickly to the congregation so they didn't get caught up in some crazy New Age idea.

But if it was in fact true, then what would he say? That thought sent a wave of fear through him, because he had no idea how to deal with something like that. He would have to pray about it and hope that God would guide him. And he was definitely going to tune in and watch the 'Hailey' show tomorrow.

Thursday morning, Bob and Katie were back at home, sleeping late into the morning. The hospital had released Katie the day before, after making sure she'd stopped bleeding and that there was no infection. Bob's boss had given him the rest of the week off, and with Katie still feeling weak, he was glad he could be there for her. It had been hard to get to sleep last night, and he knew that even though neither of them had spoken, they'd both lain awake long into the night. It was nice to sleep in this morning, and be in no rush to go anywhere or do anything.

Katie was still asleep and Bob tried to be as quiet as possible as he rose to make some coffee. He got dressed and walked into the kitchen. The sun was shining, the birds were singing, and it seemed almost an effrontery to the pain they still felt. He looked out the window while he waited for the coffee to drip into the pot.

Sometimes life seemed so unfair. There were people all over the world that didn't even want their babies, and here they were, ready to be great parents, and God had taken their baby away from them. Was he just a cruel God, messing with people's lives this way? Didn't he care about them? Why would he allow babies to be born into homes where they wouldn't be taken care of, and then refuse to give people like Katie and him a chance?

Yet there was that voice that they'd both heard, which had comforted them and brought them peace, if only for a little while. In spite of it, he couldn't help but feel somewhat bitter about what had happened. He wasn't really sure what he felt. One minute he felt bitter, and the next he felt at peace, as he recalled the voice that had spoken, and the two feelings battled back and forth inside him.

He poured a cup of coffee and sat down at the kitchen counter. He turned the TV on to take his mind off his problems for a little while. As he sipped coffee and zoned out, his ears perked up when he heard the TV news anchor mention God.

"It's a pretty strange thing, all these people claiming they heard God's voice at the same time on Sunday night. Are you going to watch the show later today, Mark?"

"I don't know. I'd like to, but my son has a baseball game this afternoon, so I'll probably miss it. How about you? Are you going to watch?"

"I wouldn't miss it. I think it's fascinating and I want to hear what God said to them."

"I'm sure you'll tell me all about it tomorrow. We'll be back in a moment."

Bob heard a quick intake of breath behind him. He turned around to see Katie standing there. She said, "Did you hear that, Bob?" she said, staring at the TV.

"Hey, are you all right?" He was worried about her being out of bed.

"I'm fine… but did you hear that? What they just said? What's going on, Bob? Did other people hear what we heard?"

He pulled out a chair for her and she sat down. "There's going to be some show on later today and they're gonna talk to people who heard it."

"What show? Did you hear?"

"No, I don't know. Maybe they'll mention it again." He went to the counter to pour her a cup of coffee.

"We have to watch it, Bob. Wouldn't it be freaky if other people heard the same thing we did?" They both sat quietly as they absorbed this piece of news. They'd been pretty out of touch with the world since her stay in the hospital. They hadn't turned the TV on in her room much, since she had slept a lot of the time.

Bob said, "I'll get on the internet and see what else I can find out about it." He handed her a cup of coffee and went to get his laptop out of his bag. It seemed like ages ago when he'd last gotten on his computer, almost another lifetime ago. He'd been a different person then, full of hope for the future and excitement about the baby on the way. Now he felt like a much older man, one who moved slower and looked at life differently, maybe with a little more skepticism. He wondered if he'd ever feel joy again, or allow himself to trust any moment of joy, since it could be taken away so quickly.

He set the laptop on the kitchen counter and plugged in the power cord. After it started up, he went to his favorite news site, but saw nothing there about the God story. He found the TV station's web site and clicked on the morning show program and saw the story there. He scanned it as Katie got up to read it too.

"Looks like it's going to be on the Hailey show later this afternoon. She's gonna interview some people who say they heard God speak to them."

Katie said, "Wow…" and then walked back to the bedroom to lie down again.

CHAPTER FIVE

Hailey wasn't sure what to think of the story she was about to air, but it intrigued her and from what she could tell about the people she was going to interview, they believed what they were saying. Who knew whether it was the truth or not, but she knew it would make a good story, and if there was a chance they weren't telling the truth, by God, she'd do her best to expose them. She was a believer in God herself, though she preferred to think of herself as a spiritual person rather than a religious one. She'd been raised in the church, but had turned away from it in later years because their dogmatic approaches to some things didn't match what she felt in her own heart to be true. She would try to keep her own beliefs out of this conversation today as much as she could. She didn't want her own biases to interfere with getting at the truth of this story.

She reviewed her notes while she met with her key staff members to prep for the show. Some of them had tried to discourage her from even airing this topic, especially since it had thrown their regular schedule into an upheaval. They thought it might discredit her, or make her look too exploitive. But she had her own private reasons for wanting to air it, and she thought she could manage the discussion in a way that would be professional and respectful. The last thing she wanted was to look like a predatory tabloid reporter on a story that practically everyone was talking about. She was determined to remain unbiased and detached and to avoid influencing her viewers either way. They could decide for themselves. It was her job to bring the story forward, get people talking about it, and then to probe any weaknesses or cracks in the story, if they were there.

Annie tried to pay attention to her teacher, but her eyes kept moving involuntarily to the clock on the wall. The teacher was assigning a new science project, which they were supposed to work on in pairs, and Annie knew she better try to focus. Science was her least favorite subject, and so far, her lowest grade. She had to do well on this project to bring up her grade before the end of the year.

"Are there any questions about this project? This will be worth 100 points, so it would behoove you to start as early as possible and give yourselves plenty of time to do a good job on it. You'll need to find a partner to work with, and if you don't have one by the end of the day, see me and I'll assign one to you."

Annie looked over at Kendra and raised her eyebrows. She and Kendra had been best friends since first grade, and except for a few times when they got on each others' nerves, their friendship had grown even stronger through the years. They often worked on homework together, and Kendra was the only person Annie would even consider partnering with on this project. Kendra nodded her silent agreement. When the bell rang at the end of the day, they hurried out of class and down the hall to their lockers.

"Finally..." Annie mumbled as she prepared her things to go home. Kendra waited for her and they walked out of the building together toward their school bus waiting outside.

"Can you come over after school today?" Kendra asked her.

"No, I have to go home today. Maybe tomorrow," Annie replied. Sometimes she rode the bus home with Kendra after school and they hung out together. Kendra's mom was usually home, but Annie's mom didn't get home from work until later on.

"Oh, come on... we haven't hung out all week," Kendra said. "Can't you come over for a little while?"

"No, I have to go home." Annie wanted to get home as quickly as possible to watch the Hailey show. If the bus wasn't running late, she'd be able to catch most of it if she hurried home from her bus stop. She hadn't mentioned anything about what she'd heard to Kendra or anyone else, and she wanted to watch this show alone. She wanted to see what the other people said they'd heard, and if it was like her own experience.

"Well, fine, be that way." Kendra looked put out.

"It's just that I have some stuff I have to do at home," Annie said, trying to ease her friend's feelings. "How about tomorrow?"

"Oh, I guess." Kendra still didn't look happy with her, but they walked out toward the busses together. "See ya," Kendra said as she turned in the direction of hers.

"Yeah, see ya." Annie climbed onto the bus, took her seat and hoped the bus would get on the way soon.

When she got off at her stop, she hurried up the street to her house. She didn't want to run. Anyone who saw her would think that was so un-cool, but she walked as quickly as she could without breaking into a run. When she got into the house, she dropped her backpack, and grabbed the TV remote to turn it on. The show was already in progress, but she had only missed the first few minutes.

"So where were you when you heard this voice?" Hailey was posing the question to a bunch of bald headed guys in robes.

"We were in the middle of our evening meditations at a monastery just outside New York City," one man began.

"So you were sitting there, meditating, and then what happened?" she asked.

He took his time continuing. "Yes. We were in various forms of meditations, and a voice spoke to us."

"A voice spoke to you. To all of you?" she repeated.

"Yes. It spoke and we all heard it."

"Was this voice something different than a normal voice? I mean how did you know it was a 'voice'?"

"It's very hard to explain, but we just knew. It was not like any other voice I had ever heard in my life. It was audible, but it was not like a human voice."

"But it was audible? So it wasn't just a voice you heard inside your head?" she asked.

"Yes, it was an audible voice. As soon as we heard it, we stopped chanting and the room became completely silent. Except for the voice."

"Except for the voice... and what did the voice say?"

He hesitated and took a deep breath, searching Hailey's eyes to see if she truly wanted to know, or if she was somehow going to try to make him look like a crazy man. Her eyes seemed to reflect a genuinely open spirit, as if she actually wanted to believe him.

"It said, 'I am with you all. Seek me. Trust me.'"

Annie gulped as she watched. It was the most astounding thing. This group of monks had heard almost the very same thing she'd heard. Maybe she wasn't crazy. Or if she was, then they were too, and they were all crazy together. She held her breath as she waited to hear more.

Hailey didn't seem to know what to say next. Finally she said, "Really... did it say anything else?"

"No, that was all."

"And everyone in the room heard this voice?"

The monk looked a little uncomfortable then. "Well, almost everyone, yes."

"So some heard it and some didn't?" Hailey asked.

"Most heard."

"Most heard..." she said. "So who didn't hear? Did all of y'all hear?" She directed this question to the other monks. They all nodded their heads. "So you all heard? Okay, so who didn't hear it?"

The monk who had been responding to her questions answered slowly again. "There were at least two in the room who didn't hear it."

"So why didn't they hear it, do you think?" Hailey was probing.

"I don't know why," he answered. "All I know is that I heard it, and I knew what I heard. There was no doubt in my mind."

"Well, did you know whose voice it was?" she asked.

"I was sure it was the voice of God."

Hailey knew she needed to tread softly here. If she was too quick to accept this story, her viewers would think her gullible. But if she was too skeptical, the monks would feel discredited and that wouldn't be fair to them. She tried to walk a careful balance.

"The voice of God. How did you know it was the voice of God?" she said, keeping her facial expression as neutral as possible.

"I think when one hears the voice of God, there is just no mistaking it," he said. "I felt a peace descend over me like I have felt rarely in my life. It was a feeling of complete and utter peace as I wanted to surrender myself wholly to God."

"Hmm," she said. She looked to the other monks. "Did you feel this too? Did you know whose voice it was?" They all nodded and smiled. She directed her question to one of them, "How did you know?"

"I just knew," he said. "I have never heard anything like it before, but I have felt the same spirit before. I recognized it as God's spirit in the room with us."

"God's spirit," she repeated. "Well, I find this all very intriguing." She turned to the camera. "In a few minutes, we'll be talking with some others who also claim to have heard the voice of God Sunday night. We'll be back after this break."

Annie could hardly believe it. She realized she'd been holding her breath, and when the station cut to the commercial, she finally exhaled and breathed. She knew her own experience had been real, and the monks had just described the exact feelings she'd had herself. She was remembering the peace she had felt afterward when Andrew came bounding through the kitchen door. She'd been so focused on the show she hadn't heard his car pull into the driveway. He threw his stuff on the floor, opened the refrigerator, took a gulp of milk straight out of the container, then glanced her way and said, "Hey, what's up?"

She tried to appear disinterested in the TV. "Nothin'."

He grunted and grabbed a bag of chips out of the pantry. She hoped he'd go away soon. She didn't want him to see the program she was watching and she didn't want to talk to him about it. She looked at a book when the show came back on, trying not to let on that she was watching it, but he was still standing there. He was making a lot of noise with his chips, and she wanted to turn up the volume, but that would tip him off. So she did nothing and tried not to look at the TV. Though her eyes were directed at the book she was holding, her ears were tuned to what Hailey was saying. Andrew crunched loudly, and looked over at the TV as Hailey introduced another person who said she'd heard the voice Sunday night.

"What is this garbage," Andrew said. "Why do you watch this crap? People will say anything just to get on TV."

"How would you know?" Annie retorted, a little quicker than she'd meant to.

"What, don't tell me you believe this stuff," he said.

"I didn't say that."

"Geez, you are one gullible chick if you think there's any truth to any of this. Don't waste your time."

"Yeah, well maybe you shouldn't waste your time with potato chips either."

"Bite me," he said, taking his bag of chips and his backpack to his room.

Thank goodness he was gone and she could hear the program again. She turned the volume up a little. The other people on the show echoed what the monks had said. They had heard a similar voice, also on Sunday night, and had the same sense of peace from it that the monks described. As Annie sat and watched, she wondered how many other people had heard the same thing. Why did some people hear it and some didn't? She wondered if Hailey believed it. Maybe she should call in to the show or email them and tell them that she had heard the same thing. But then someone might find out and that would be too weird. She still wanted to keep it to herself, for the most part. She wished there was some way for them to know that it had happened to others, but she wasn't ready to go public with it. For now anyway, she'd keep it to herself. She could still recall the same peace she felt when it happened Sunday night, and she didn't want to tell anyone else for fear of ruining the whole experience. God only knew what Andrew would say about it. He'd never believe her in a million years, and she wasn't going to let him make a mockery of what had happened.

Rick left his church office early on Thursday afternoon. He wanted to watch the Hailey program, but he didn't want the others in the office to know he was watching it. He wanted to watch it in privacy by himself, to digest it and decide what he thought about it without the pressure of others standing nearby. He pulled into the driveway and pushed the remote to open the garage door. Good, Sarah's car was gone, and he remembered that she said she was going to spend the afternoon shopping. Even though he'd talked with her about his experience, he still would rather watch the program by himself so he could think through it alone. He parked the car, put the garage door back down and walked into the house.

He went to the TV in his study and flipped it on to wait for the program to begin. He had only seen parts of the Hailey program a handful of times, but she seemed like one of the better TV talk show hosts. At least it seemed like she was trying to do something good in the world, instead of encouraging and promoting bad behavior like so many other talk shows. He wondered how she would treat this topic and the guests on the show. He sat down in his comfortable leather chair and waited for the program to begin.

When it was over, Rick turned off the TV and sat back down in his chair. What was he going to do now? He knew the people in his congregation would be talking about this show, and they'd ask him what he thought about it. The truth was he wasn't sure what to think about it. It shouldn't be up to him to decide whether the people on the Hailey show were telling the truth or not. For all he knew, she could have rounded up a bunch of sideshow freaks. But if that was the case, how was it that they heard the same thing he had heard, and at the same time? It was so bizarre. But without revealing his own experience, how could he talk about what he truly felt with anyone? What if he told them about what had happened to him? What would they think of him? Should he even care what anyone else thought of him? If God had really spoken to him, and he was quite sure that he had, then wouldn't God want for him to share what had happened with others? But if this had happened to someone else and not him, would he have believed it? He could imagine what they'd say. "How can you know for sure?" "How long have you been hearing voices?" "Are you sure it wasn't just thoughts in your own head?" "He's just jumping on the bandwagon with everyone else who says they heard God." There was no way to prove it. It was just that he had a very strong sense of a Godly presence when it happened, and the voice had been out loud, not at all in his head.

The more he imagined their questions and doubts, the more he felt sure that his only recourse was to briefly reference the Hailey show in his sermon on Sunday, but to not make it the focus. He'd try to cover it, so they'd have his opinion, and then maybe it would just go away. He would keep his own experience to himself. After all, the voice spoke to him, and presumably to some others, but nowhere did it say to tell everyone about it. He'd leave that to the people who felt a strong need to share it. He knew he was playing it safe, and a part of him was disappointed in himself. But another part of him was convinced it was the best way.

When Carolyn had hustled Andrew and Annie off to school Thursday morning, she cleaned up the kitchen, did some vacuuming, took her shower and drove to the library to work. Her part-time job there gave her flexible hours that allowed her to be home most evenings with the kids, and she could usually make it to their after-school activities. Since Eric travelled so much, she was the one who kept everything going at home, and showed up at the school functions. She didn't mind it, in fact she got more pleasure out of watching her kids in their activities than just about anything else in her life. She only wished Eric felt the same way and that he could be there more often. She knew he probably wished he could, but the demands of his job just wouldn't allow it. Sometimes she knew she nagged at him, urging him to turn down a trip once in a while, but she knew he couldn't, so then she'd back off and just try to deal with it. Most of the time she kept her resentment buried, but sometimes, especially if she hadn't been able to work out for a few days, she got crabby about it, okay, even bitchy sometimes. It just hurt to see so many of the other dads at baseball games and PTA meetings. Why couldn't Eric have a normal eight-to-five job like other men?

As Carolyn made the short drive from her home to the library, she thought back to Sunday night at the gym, and what she'd heard. She'd been thinking about it all week, and when she'd heard people at the library talking about people hearing God speak Sunday night, she was shocked. From what she gathered from the research she'd done online, the other people had heard the same words she'd heard. At first she wondered if it was some electronic virus type of thing, since she'd had her headphones on at the time and it had come right through them. Maybe some kind of big public broadcast had come on and that's how people had heard it. Most of the headlines implied that this was more of a tabloid-type story than a real one. "Man claims to have heard God." "Monks hearing voices." "Did God really speak?" She scanned the articles and read that other people claimed to have heard the same words she'd heard, also on Sunday night. Some were even from other parts of the world, but the timing lined up to Sunday night in her time zone. She wondered what these people had in common, and what she had in common with them. Were they all the same religion? The same age? Doing the same thing? Nothing lined up. She couldn't find an obvious connection, except that they all were searching for something when it happened, as if they really wanted to hear something from a higher power somewhere.

She knew that's how she had felt that night on the treadmill. She often zoned out during her workouts, and while she wouldn't call it praying, she did often talk to God while she ran. Not that she ever expected to hear anything in return. It just made her feel better to express herself, to say all the things she had bottled up inside. That's what she'd been doing Sunday night, and it seemed like that had been the experience of others in the articles she read. Everyone seemed to be at a low point, or seeking, calling out to God in some way. But why would it happen now? She'd done the same thing many times before, and had never heard anything then. Why would God choose to speak out loud this time? When she let herself be quiet enough to recall what had happened, she could feel the same sense of tranquility come over her. It was so reassuring to think that God really was there, that he could be trusted to take care of things.

She wished she could hold on to that feeling forever. But she was a woman used to taking charge of things and it was hard not to be that person all the time. But where had it gotten her? Yes, she was a good mother, involved with her kids, keeping up their home, keeping everything together. But was she keeping it together? If that was true, why did she feel like she was about to fall apart so much of the time? God, if it was only true that she didn't have to constantly be in charge of everything.

When Carolyn finished her shift at the library Thursday afternoon, she swung by a fast-food restaurant to pick up dinner. She wasn't in the mood to cook and they hadn't had fried chicken in a while. The kids always liked fast-food better than her cooking anyway, though she tried to keep it to a minimum. She pulled into her driveway and then the garage, picked up her purse and the bag of food from the car and stepped out. As she opened the door to the kitchen, she yelled, "Hey kids, I'm home!" She set down her purse, put the chicken on the kitchen table, and washed up at the kitchen sink.

Andrew came down the stairs, peeked into the bag, and said, "Awesome. Fried chicken. I'm starved." He started to grab for a piece of chicken.

"Wait a few minutes and I'll get everything ready. You can wash up and set the table," Carolyn said, without turning around from the sink.

He started to argue, but put the chicken down and walked over to the sink.

"How was your day," she asked him.

"Okay, I guess." He washed up, then grabbed some silverware out of the drawer and tossed it on the table.

Carolyn pulled some leftover potato salad out of the refrigerator and set it on the table, along with the salt and pepper. "I'll pour the drinks if you'll call Annie to come down."

Andrew went to the bottom of the stairs and yelled at Annie as Carolyn poured milk into their glasses. Annie joined them a minute later and they sat down at the table together.

"Anything interesting happen at school today?" Carolyn asked, while they ate.

"Not really," Andrew answered. "Trevor says he's dropping off the team."

"Oh? Why?" Trevor had been the best first baseman the last two years.

"He wants to keep working. He says he needs the money to pay for his car insurance."

"Well, that's too bad. Who do you think will play first base then?"

"I don't know. It sucks. We don't have a good back-up first baseman."

They continued chatting about baseball, and Carolyn turned to Annie. "So how was your day, honey?"

"Fine."

"Anything interesting happen to you today?"

Annie thought about it, and wished she could tell her mom about the Hailey show. But she resisted the impulse, shook her head and said, "Not really." Then she added, "We got a new science project assigned today. I'm gonna work with Kendra on it."

"Great, honey. I hope it goes well. Let me know if you need any help."

They continued to eat in silence, then Andrew said, "Hey Annie, tell Mom about that dumb show you were watching when I got home today."

Annie didn't want to talk about it, so she just said, "It was nothing. Just a dumb show."

Andrew continued, "Hailey had a bunch of psychos on her show today that were talking about how God spoke to them. Geez, what'll they come up with next."

Carolyn looked from Andrew back to Annie, but Annie's eyes were down, focused on her chicken. Carolyn asked, "This was on the Hailey show?"

"Yeah, she sure picked a bunch of whackos this time. Ask Annie about it, she was the one watching it, not me."

She looked back at Annie, whose head was still down. "Annie, what about it? What were they talking about on the show?"

"I wasn't really watching it. It was just on while I was doing homework, that's all." She still didn't look up from her plate. Carolyn could tell she wasn't going to get much out of her with Andrew around, so she dropped it. But she intended to talk with Annie about it privately as soon as she got the chance.

Bob wasn't sure if he should be leaving Katie alone yet, but by Thursday she insisted that she'd be fine at home by herself and he should go on back to work. She told him she was feeling fine, physically anyway, and would call if she needed him. So he went in to the office on Thursday, trying to remember where he'd left off on his project before everything that had happened on Sunday. It was hard to concentrate on work, and he thought maybe a cup of coffee would help, so he walked over to the break room. Robin was pouring herself a cup.

"Hey, Robin," he said, as he walked into the room. She turned around. "Oh, hi, Bob." She finished pouring and stepped over to a different counter to add cream and sugar. "Gosh, I am so sorry to hear about what happened." She wasn't sure how much to say about it, but she wanted to say something.

"Thanks, Robin. I appreciate it." Bob poured his coffee.

"How's Katie doing?"

"She's better. She told me to come on in today."

"Well, that's good to hear. We were all so upset when we heard what happened, and... well, I'm just so sorry." Robin looked down as she stirred her cream and sugar. She felt so awkward and didn't know what else to say. But she really liked Bob, and she didn't want the moment to pass without expressing her sincere sympathy, even if it felt a little awkward.

"Thanks," he said. He followed Robin out of the break room back to his office. He sat down in his chair, pulled up a spreadsheet he'd started last week with the financials for the latest marketing plan, stared at it and tried to remember what he'd been doing before his world turned upside down. Did any of this even matter in the long run? Last week it had seemed so important and pressing, but now it just seemed like a pointless exercise. He took a deep breath. He'd better try to get his mind back in the game. Katie needed him now more than ever, and part of being needed was being a good provider.

They hadn't talked much more about what they'd heard in the hospital last Sunday night, but that didn't mean it wasn't affecting their lives. Katie was taking things pretty well, and didn't seem as devastated as she might have been otherwise. He knew her peace with the situation was a direct result of what they'd heard that night. He felt the same peace, most of the time anyway. All he had to do was stop, close his eyes, breathe, and recall the words of the voice and it was like he was back there again, as if he could trust in a higher power to take care of things, and that made him feel like everything really would be all right.

Ralph hadn't had a drink all week, and he was having some withdrawal symptoms. He couldn't remember the last time he'd gone this long without a drink. Even though it felt weird, and his body could have used something to take the edge off, he just didn't want to give in to it. The drink had brought him nothing but heartache and had pretty much destroyed his life, and after his experience Sunday night, he felt like a different man somehow. He had no question now that there was a God, even a merciful God, because he knew what he'd heard and what had happened to him as a result. He carried a deep sense of peace inside and he didn't want to screw it up by drinking again. God only knew he'd screwed up just about everything else in his life, but here he was, being given a second chance. He wasn't sure exactly what he was going to do with that chance, but he was damn sure he wasn't going to drink it away.

He'd risen early each morning this week, and instead of having a headache and feeling groggy, he had gone for a walk and watched the sunrise for the first time in years. What a glorious sight it was, and it almost seemed made just for him, like God saying, "Hey Ralph, this one's for you, now go and start this day anew." Even though he'd only heard the voice that one time Sunday night, he still carried the memory of it inside, and often found himself praying throughout the day. No big flowery prayers or anything, just thanking God for being there, for not giving up on him. He felt like he owed the big guy something in return, but wasn't sure what that would be.

It helped take off the jitters when he walked and stayed busy, so he started picking up trash in the park as he watched the sun rise each morning. A small thing, perhaps, but maybe that was all he was capable of right now. As long as he didn't walk past his old favorite liquor stores, he could pretty well keep his mind off the urge to drink.

As he made his way to his favorite park bench this Thursday morning, the one with a great view of the morning horizon, he thought back to his conversation with Pastor Rick at the shelter earlier in the week. It had been hard to talk about what had happened, and he was afraid Rick would laugh at him or crack a joke about him being crazy. But Rick had listened and even seemed to believe him. Rick seemed like a good guy, and Ralph had always liked him when their paths had crossed at the shelter. Rick treated everyone there with dignity and was willing to take the time to sit down and listen to them, even some of the crazies that wanted to blame God or the government for all their problems.

Ralph thought about maybe talking to Rick again. Even though he felt like a new man, he wasn't sure how to get his life on a new track. Would it even be possible for him to re-enter society as a productive human being? He felt like God had given him a second chance and hope for a better life, and he didn't want to disappoint him. He had disappointed so many others in his life—his employer, his friends, his wife, his daughter, and most of all, himself. He had wasted so much of his life, all because of the stupid booze. How had he let it get the best of him? He hated to think of how it had wrecked his life. But today was a new day, with an amazing sun rising in the sky before him, birds singing, and he was determined not to waste it. After a while, he got up from the bench, stretched, picked up his backpack, and began the several block walk to the shelter.

CHAPTER SIX

Carolyn knocked quietly on Annie's door. "Honey?"

"What?"

Carolyn opened the door and peeked inside. "You ready for bed? Is your homework done?"

Annie was lying on the floor with her earphones in, surrounded by books and papers. She took out the earphones, looked up and said, "Yeah, pretty much."

Carolyn sat down on the bed and tried to approach what was on her mind. "So tell me about that Hailey show you were watching today…people were talking about hearing God?"

"Yeah."

"Well, what did you think? Do you think they were telling the truth?"

"I dunno." Annie looked at a book in front of her, open on the floor.

"Hmm." Carolyn wasn't sure how to continue. It wasn't easy trying to communicate with a thirteen-year-old. "I used to think that when people said they heard God speaking to them, they were either crazy, or it was just their own voice in their head, which they took for the voice of God."

Annie looked up with no reply. She waited for her mother to say more.

"Now I'm not so sure."

"So you don't think that any more?"

"Well, I don't know. I guess now I think it's possible that people may actually hear the voice of God."

"Really? Why do you think that?" Annie scrutinized her mother's face.

"I just think we need to be more open-minded about it. I mean, God spoke to people back in Bible times…why wouldn't he do it again?" She waited a minute. "What do you think?"

Annie looked down and shrugged. "Sure. Why not."

"Did you think the people on Hailey were sincere? What did they say they heard?"

"They said they heard God speak to them. On Sunday night. And he said the same thing to all of them." She looked back up at her mother.

Carolyn tried to quell her nervousness. "What did he say to them?"

"He said, 'I am here. Trust me.'"

"Oh…and they all heard this on Sunday night?" The same night she had heard the voice in the gym. "Why do you suppose they all heard it at the same time?"

"I dunno. Some of them were praying or meditating when they heard it, like the monks. Some of them said they were upset about something and then it happened."

Carolyn needed time to process this. She wanted to hear more about what Annie heard on the show, but she didn't trust herself to not say more than she was ready, so she kissed Annie on top of the head and said, "Well, you better get to bed soon. Lights out in five minutes, okay? Love you."

"Okay. Love you too, Mom."

Carolyn walked across the room and was about to close the door behind her, when Annie said, "Mom?"

She looked back in the room. "Yes, honey?"

Annie's face had a look of innocence and purity, but then she looked back down at her books and said, "Oh, nothin'. Good night."

Carolyn closed the door and stood in the hallway, wondering what Annie wanted to say, but had suddenly changed her mind about.

Robin sat alone in her living room, curled up on her couch with the remote. She had just watched her recording of the Hailey show and she could hardly believe what she'd heard-- other people claiming to have heard the same thing she'd heard, all at the same time on Sunday night. When her parents had taken her to church as a kid, she used to think she believed in God. But she had to admit, God wasn't someone she'd thought about much recently, that is, until this past Sunday night. Now here she was thinking about God almost every waking minute. She knew she'd heard something that night, but was it really the voice of God? She had wondered a lot during the week if it wasn't some alcohol-induced hallucination. There had been times she couldn't remember things she'd said and done when partying. But in this case, she had a very clear memory of it, and it was unlike anything that had ever happened to her before. Still, she couldn't help the little voice inside that said, "Yeah sure, another voice in your head, that's probably what it was. There's plenty of room for all those voices."

But while she had watched the Hailey show, and heard the people describing the exact experience she'd had, to the point of even hearing the same words at the same time, she knew this was something beyond her typical alcoholic haze. She thought about how her concept of God had changed over the years--from some big "being in the sky" who watched over everything from afar, to more of a vague idea or a concept. Then finally wondering if there even was a God, because if there was, and he really cared about people, how could he let such awful things happen, like hurricanes and tsunamis, or even Bob and Katie losing their baby? Wasn't he supposed to be all-powerful and loving? She didn't know how to reconcile this concept of God with the peace she'd felt on Sunday night. Did he only choose to speak to a few people? Why not everyone? Didn't everyone need to feel that peace? She wondered if anyone else she knew had heard it too. How could she even bring it up with anyone?

It seemed like most of her friends were just going about their lives, as if nothing out of the ordinary had happened. Maybe it seemed to them like she was doing the same thing. So how would they know that she'd heard? Could she take a chance with anyone and ask them? Who would it be? She ran through a quick list of her friends, her partying buddies, her work friends. But she quickly dismissed all of them, unable to even imagine bringing it up without them thinking she was crazy. So she decided to keep it to herself, at least for now, unless an opportunity presented itself.

She clicked the remote to turn off the TV, sat in the quiet of her room, and closed her eyes. "God, are you really there?" She waited, heard nothing, but as she breathed deeply, she felt a deep sense of something present in the room with her, so she just kept breathing, willing it to stay just a little while longer.

CHAPTER SEVEN

Ralph had walked over to the shelter on Thursday, but Rick hadn't been there, and Shauna, one of the social workers, told him Rick would be there Friday to conduct a prayer service at noon. So Ralph had come back a little before noon on Friday to try to catch him. While the center was non-denominational, it had a strong spiritual focus as they tried to help people get back on their feet. Many of the homeless only came to stay during the most extreme weather, but they often dropped in for the free meals, as Ralph also once did. But he'd begun to strike up friendships with some of people he met there, and now he often helped with clean-up after the meals, or offered to put away chairs, or whatever needed to be done. Ralph especially enjoyed visiting with Rick when he was there.

Rick wasn't a stereotypical pastor, someone who wore suits or cleric robes and talked down to people. No, he was more of a buddy, someone you could imagine shooting hoops with or sitting down and having a beer with. Not that he'd ever done any of those things with Rick, but he could imagine them. Rick's penetrating blue eyes seemed to look into a person's soul, not in a judgmental way, but in a compassionate way, as if to say I love you just the way you are. He'd most often seen Rick wearing jeans, and depending on the weather, either a t-shirt or flannel shirt, and almost always a ball cap. Someone who didn't know better might even mistake him for a homeless person, except that his clothes were clean.

What Ralph most liked about Rick was his belly laugh. When Rick got tickled about something, which was often, he'd laugh from way down deep in his gut, which couldn't help but make a person smile. When Rick was serving meals, he could often be heard laughing with one of the men about something. It didn't take much to get him started. He knew most of them by name, and last week Ralph heard him ask Paul how his back was feeling. Paul had said, "My back said we're sleeping in today, but my stomach said we're going in for a hot meal," and Rick could be heard laughing clear across the building. He'd thrown an arm around Paul and said, "Well, I'm glad your stomach won that time, Paul, but I hope your back gets to feeling better." He seemed to mean what he said, looking you right in the eye when he spoke to you.

Ralph asked Shauna if Rick was there yet, and she looked at the clock and said, "No, I haven't seen him yet, but it's almost eleven forty-five, so he should be here soon."

"Do you need help setting up chairs or anything?" he asked her.

"Sure, Ralph, that'd be great. Go on back and see if Lauren needs help with that."

Ralph walked back to the large gathering room where they held the Friday prayer session. He saw Lauren, one of the newer social workers, making coffee in the back of the room. There were only a few chairs set up, and most were standing folded against the walls.

Lauren looked up as he came in. "Hey Ralph, how's it goin'?" She measured the coffee and put it into the filter.

"Pretty good, how are you, Lauren?"

"Just fine." She smiled. "You here for the prayer service today?"

"Yeah. I was hoping to find Pastor Rick and talk with him."

"Oh, well I haven't seen him yet, but I'm sure he'll be here soon."

"I can set up the chairs if you want. Might as well make myself useful."

She looked around. "Yeah, that'd be great. Just put 'em in a big circle. Thanks a lot, Ralph."

He busied himself with the chairs while she went to get the water for the coffeemaker. He was arranging the chairs when Rick walked in. "Hey buddy! I heard you were looking for me." Rick walked over to pat him on the back.

Ralph shook his hand, finished straightening the chairs and then said, "There's something I'd like to talk to you about. Do you think we could talk for a few minutes after the meeting today?"

"Sure, I don't have to be anywhere until later this afternoon. I'm always happy to talk with you, Ralph."

When the meeting was over, Ralph helped pick up the room and waited for the others to leave. Finally after Rick was finished visiting with people, he turned to Ralph and said, "How about we go into another room?" They walked down the hall to an empty office and stepped inside. "I think Ryan is out sick today, so let's just talk in here." Rick flipped the light switch and they both took a seat.

"What's on your mind, Ralph?" Ralph seemed different, and Rick noticed that he even smelled different. He was still dirty, but the smell of alcohol was gone, and his eyes seemed brighter.

Ralph fumbled around for a moment, shifted in his chair, and said, "Remember what we talked about earlier this week?"

Rick's expression changed to a more serious one. Ralph tried to read him to see if he remembered and if he thought Ralph was crazy. He wasn't sure what he saw in Rick's expression yet.

"Sure, I remember, Ralph." He waited for Ralph to say more.

Ralph took a deep breath. "Well, here's the thing. After what happened to me last Sunday night, I feel different. I don't know how to explain it exactly, but I used to feel like I was dying this slow death, that nobody really cared, not even me. Most of the time I think I even wanted to die. But then Sunday night, that changed. I don't want to die any more. I feel like a different person. I want a different life." He waited for Rick to say something.

"Well, Ralph, you can have a different life. It just takes a leap of faith. I don't mean to make it sound easy, because it's not easy, but if you can take that leap, your life can change."

"Well, that's just it. I do feel ready to take a leap of faith. Since I heard that voice say, 'Trust me,' I've felt for the first time in years that there was something bigger out there looking out for me, that maybe God is really there."

Rick swallowed. It sure sounded like the same voice he'd heard, but he wasn't sure what to say next.

Ralph looked at the floor and almost whispered, "Do you think I can believe it? Do you think it was real?"

"Yeah, Ralph, I think it was. You felt it was real, and it's obviously had an impact on you. I don't think it gets more real than that." He wondered if Ralph knew about all the other people who said they too had heard the voice on Sunday night. He figured probably not, since Ralph didn't have easy access to TV or newspapers. "Ralph, I don't know if you're aware of this, but there are other people who say they heard it Sunday night too."

"What? You mean they heard the same voice?"

"Yeah, a voice that sounds a lot like the one you've been talking about."

"No kiddin'. What'd it say to 'em? Did they hear the same thing I heard?"

"Yeah, at least that's what they say."

Ralph sat back in his chair and stared off into the room. Finally he said, "So what do you think about all this, Rick? Do you believe 'em?"

"I don't know, Ralph. I know I believe you. I'm not sure what to believe about all the others. I don't know them like I know you."

"But why would God start just talking to people, all at once like this, do you think? Do you think this happens a lot?"

Rick took off his hat and scratched his head. "I don't know. I've never heard of it happening before. Of course there have always been people who say God spoke to them or whatever, but who knows? But I've never heard of God speaking to a whole bunch of people at the same time, and saying the same thing."

"Has it ever happened to you?"

Ralph's question took Rick off guard and he squirmed in his seat. "To me?"

"Yeah, has God ever spoken to you?"

"Well...there have been times when I felt God's presence with me, sort of a strong urge to do or say a certain thing." He wasn't sure if he was ready to tell Ralph about his own experience Sunday night. But Ralph had been so open with him, why couldn't he do the same? It just wasn't the same though. He was in a position where people looked to him for truth and he just wasn't sure what to think about all this yet, so he stalled.

"But have you ever heard...out loud, words...that you knew were the voice of God?" Ralph pressed.

Rick looked away and stammered, "Well...I'm just not sure, Ralph."

Ralph sensed that Rick was holding back, and he started to worry again about what Rick thought of him. Maybe he thought Ralph was a crackpot after all. Had he just been patronizing him this whole time? He stood up and headed for the door.

"Hey, where ya' going?" Rick stood up. "Do you want to talk any more about this?"

Ralph opened the door and looked back at him. "Nah, that's okay." He walked through the door and down the hallway. It didn't matter what Rick thought. He knew in his heart that what he had heard was true, whether Rick believed it or not. He knew his life was headed in a new direction. He wasn't sure exactly how yet, but he felt it as certainly as anything he'd ever felt.

Rick stood in the doorway, yelled good-bye to Ralph and watched him as he walked down the hall. Why hadn't he had the courage to tell Ralph he'd heard it too? Why was he so worried about what other people would think? Was he worried what they'd think about his mental state? Was he worried about losing his job? The words of Jesus came back to him, "He who shall lose his life shall find it." Is that what it was going to come down to, losing what he knew as his life, his job and his reputation? Was that fair to his wife?

He put his ball cap back on and walked down the hall and into the meeting room. No one was inside, so he sat in one of the chairs, leaned over and held his head in his hands. He prayed in his thoughts, "God, I know it was you who spoke to me, but why did this happen? What am I supposed to do about it now? Did you really speak to all the other people too? Why just some of us, God?" He stayed quiet with his eyes closed and head bowed, half hoping that God might even answer his questions out loud. His breathing slowed after a while and the questions slowed down in his head. After a while, he felt the familiar peace of God descending upon him that he had come to recognize over the years. He immersed himself in it without thinking, without any words at all. When he finally opened his eyes, he knew what he needed to do. He just hoped God would give him the strength to do it.

Friday afternoon drug by, and even though Bob had a lot of catching up to do from his days out earlier in the week, he couldn't help watching the clock, anxious to get back home to Katie. Physically she was a lot better, but emotionally she still seemed so fragile. Maybe he'd stop on his way home from work and pick up some flowers for her. He had one more meeting this afternoon, and then he'd try to get out of the office for the weekend.

He picked up his notebook and a water bottle a few minutes before three o'clock and walked to the conference room. The lights were on and a couple of his colleagues were already seated, talking about their plans for the weekend. He set his things on the table and sat down. He took a sip of water and listened while they waited for the others to join them in the room.

After Robin and another woman came in and sat down, Cal said, "Looks like we're all here. Why don't we go ahead and get started." Bob did his best to concentrate on the topic, but it was a long hour. When the meeting was finally over, everyone stood up and Robin turned to Bob.

"What are you and Katie gonna do this weekend?"

"Nothing much. I don't know what she'll feel up to doing, to tell you the truth. I might get some carryout dinners for us or something, so we can stay home. What are you doing this weekend?"

Robin looked away. She still wasn't sure what she was going to do. She usually went to Jackie's on Friday night for happy hour with her regular gang, often staying into the wee hours of Saturday morning. Then on Saturday night someone would pick one of their favorite clubs, usually based on which one had the best band or the lowest cover charge, and they'd close the place down. But after what had happened last weekend, she just didn't feel like doing the same thing again. She felt different somehow. What had happened in her bathroom as she was lying on the floor had become a defining moment in her life. She didn't feel like doing the same things any more, but she wasn't sure yet what she did want to do. All this passed through her head quickly, and then she realized Bob was still waiting for a response, so she shrugged, "Um, I don't know. I don't really have any plans."

CHAPTER EIGHT

Rick was stumped as he sat alone in the church office on Saturday morning. All week he had struggled with a sermon topic for Sunday. He had first planned to start a new series on the Beatitudes, beginning with the poor in spirit. But he tried to come up with a new angle or something original to say, he kept recalling his experience last Sunday night, and then his conversation with Ralph, and then he just couldn't get his mind focused back on the Beatitudes, no matter how hard he tried. He scribbled some words on a tablet and stared at them for a while.

Finally he sat back in his chair, closed his eyes and prayed. "God, what do you want me to say this week? How do you want to use me? You know I am your servant, and I want to be willing to do whatever you need." He waited, felt nothing, and began to pray again. "God, I know it was you that spoke to me last weekend, is it something you want me to talk about? Or was that just for me?" Rick wondered if God would ever speak to him again. He didn't hear audible words, but he did feel the same sense of God's presence that he had felt before, and he felt comforted. He also felt a strong urge to re-direct his sermon in a different way for Sunday. He knew better than to fight this urge, so he began to make new notes. The Beatitudes could wait for another Sunday.

Robin woke early on Saturday. At least it was early for her. She couldn't remember the last time she was out of bed before nine o'clock on a Saturday. She also couldn't remember the last time she hadn't first reached for the aspirin bottle next to her bed to ease her aching head. But her head didn't ache this morning and she realized she felt pretty good. She picked up the newspaper outside her apartment door, and walked into the kitchen to make coffee. She stepped out onto her balcony while she waited for it to brew. The sun was shining brightly, the birds were singing, and the world seemed different somehow. Is this how other people spent Saturday mornings, getting up early, reading the paper, having coffee? She stepped back inside to pour a cup and took it along with her newspaper back outside to sit down at her small table.

She turned to the lifestyle section of the paper, the first place she usually looked on Saturday, to see what bands were playing at her favorite clubs that night. Even though she recognized some good ones, she'd heard them all before. She took a deep breath and looked away from the newspaper, sipping her coffee. She didn't feel like going to the same clubs, hearing the same bands, drinking the same drinks, feeling like hell the next morning. She was ready for her life to be different. It already felt different this morning. She wasn't sick, lying in bed with a headache or on the bathroom floor. She liked how she felt for a change.

She thumbed through the newspaper, noticing the religion/spirituality section where a headline caught her eye. 'Does God Really Talk to People?' She set down her mug to take a closer look at the article. It was the same story Hailey had done on her show Thursday, about the monks and other people who said they'd heard God speak last Sunday night. Her eyes were glued to the paper as she read their stories. They described the same experience that had happened to her, but she had still told no one about it. How could she? Her friends would have laughed at her, and she didn't know anyone else well enough to even think about telling them. But she knew that what had happened was real, and she wanted to trust the voice that said, "Trust me." Each time she'd re-played the experience in her mind this past week, she'd felt calm and at peace, but she was afraid that if she told anyone, somehow it would all fizzle away into some figment of her imagination.

The listings for area churches were on the opposite page of the article she'd just read. Wouldn't it just be crazy to pick one and go tomorrow? She could hardly remember the last time she'd been to church. Her family used to go together, but when her parents got divorced, they'd stopped going and she couldn't say she missed it. It had always seemed like a boring ritual to her, loaded with too much fear and guilt, and she usually left feeling worse about herself than when she'd come in. She couldn't imagine why anyone would choose to go, and when her mother picked up an extra job on Sundays, she and her brother slept in and that was the end of the church thing. But now she felt curious about it. Maybe things had changed in churches, or she could even try a different denomination. She found the name of the church that was just down the street from her and noted its service times for Sunday. Maybe she'd make it to one of them.

Katie didn't tell Bob about the Hailey show she'd watched on Thursday. Neither of them had talked any more about what they'd heard in the hospital, since they'd been home. There were so many other things on their minds, relatives to call, thank you notes to write for flowers sent, and then dealing with all the baby things in their nursery at home. Katie didn't know what to do with it all. Sometimes she wanted to keep everything, the next minute she wanted to give it all away. As the days passed, she found herself feeling madder at God than she'd ever felt before. When Bob was gone, she often broke down and cried for hours. She knew Bob was going through his own private hell, but she was unable to do anything to help herself, much less him. Sometimes she even screamed and yelled at God, "Why us? Why me? What did I ever do to deserve this? What did our baby do to deserve this?" But no answers came. When she stopped long enough to remember the "voice" last Sunday night, she wondered now if she'd made it up in her head. Everything that happened that day seemed so unreal, like some kind of nightmare. But then the reality would hit her again, that it was real, and it was almost too much to bear. How could the world ever feel right for her again? Was it even possible to get through something like this?

But when she'd watched the Hailey show, something deep inside her connected to it, and she felt calm during that hour. She felt a connection to the people who talked about hearing the same words she'd heard. She realized then that it hadn't been a dream or something she'd imagined. She wondered why it had happened to her and Bob, and to the others on the show, but not to everyone? What singled them out? Had there been other times when God had tried to get through to her, but she just hadn't listened? Would it ever happen again?

When the show was over, she turned off the TV and sat down, thinking about what she'd just heard. She wondered if she should mention it to Bob. Since neither had talked about it again, it seemed awkward to bring it up.

Saturday morning Bob and Katie slept late. It had been an exhausting week, and sleep was the one place they could escape the painful reminder of losing their baby. When Bob realized that Katie was awake, he turned over and put his arm around her.

"Hey, how ya doin," he said, pulling her closer to him.

"Pretty good, I guess."

"You want to get up yet?"

"Not really. Let's stay here a few more minutes."

So he held her a while longer and wished there was some way he could mend their broken hearts. Somehow a spark was gone. Something precious had been taken from them both and they would never have it back. He felt like he'd aged about ten years in one week.

They got up a few minutes later, made the bed together and shuffled into the kitchen. As they ate breakfast and read the newspaper at the kitchen table, Bob wondered how Katie would feel about attending church on Sunday. They were somewhat sporadic about church attendance, just going on the big holidays and whenever the mood struck. But maybe the church would provide some sort of comfort for them now, so he broached the idea.

"Katie, what would you think about going to church tomorrow?"

She hesitated. "Hmm....I don't know."

"I just thought maybe it would help us," he said with a shrug.

"Yeah…" She paused. "I'm just not ready to see people we know and have to answer a bunch of questions. I don't think I could deal with that."

"Well, what if we went late and slipped in the back? We could even slip out early and we wouldn't have to talk to anyone."

She hesitated but finally said, "Well, I guess we could do that. Do you really want to go?"

"Well, yeah, I guess. Maybe it'll help."

CHAPTER NINE

Annie woke to a quiet house Sunday morning. It was nice to have one day a week to chill out and not have to get up early. After snuggling back under her covers for a while, she realized she wasn't going back to sleep, so she picked up the remote to her TV, flipped it on and channel surfed. One station caught her attention when she heard, "Does God really speak out loud?" It was a TV preacher she thought she may have seen before, but she'd never listened to him. She scooted up in her bed to listen.

"We know that in the Old Testament God spoke out loud, several times to Moses as a matter of fact. There are other instances of where he spoke out loud as well. But does he speak out loud to people today? That is the question." He paused and the camera scanned the audience, which looked mostly skeptical, but they were waiting to hear what he'd say. "I believe there may be a few, but a very few, instances of God speaking to someone in this day and time. But who would he speak to, and what would he say?" Annie sat up a little more. "I'm not sure, but here's what I do know. I know what God would not do, and that is be made a spectacle of, which is what much of the media this week has done. God has never spoken to a large group of people at once, he speaks to people individually. What's happened this week has been a media circus, and it's been a sacrilege to our God." The camera scanned the audience again and they were nodding their agreement with furrowed brows. The preacher got louder. "We cannot tolerate this behavior, people. We have to put our foot down and say 'No!' You will not treat our God this way! We won't have it." This brought many loud 'Amens' from the audience.

He continued in a gentler tone. "We know how God speaks to us, and it's certainly not in the way these people have talked about this past week. God speaks through the Holy Spirit, not in an audible way, but through our hearts. What's happened this week is a travesty and a mockery of our religion, and we must turn away from it and renounce it."

Annie grew tired of his narrow-minded tirade, so she flipped to another channel. She found a different preacher, and she watched to see what he might say about God speaking to people. His style was more laid-back, and he wasn't yelling like the last preacher.

"So my good people, I ask you this today. What will it take for you to do the will of God? It may be hard to discern, but God will reveal it to you if you really want to know. Now, the next question you may be wondering is, 'Why can't God just speak out loud to tell me what he wants me to do?' You may have heard stories this past week of people who claim to have actually heard God's voice." He smiled, but it seemed fake. His tone turned patronizing then. "Do you believe these outlandish claims?" The camera scanned the audience and heads shook as people mouthed no. He continued, with the smile still plastered across his face. "Well, I don't know about you, and you certainly have the right to believe whatever you want, but as for me, I'm not going to buy into every media trick they try to play on me. If God really spoke out loud, wouldn't he have spoken to good people like you, or like me? Wouldn't someone in this audience be able to say they heard it too?" The camera scanned again, and people's eyes and lips were tightened as they nodded their agreement.

Annie switched to another channel. She found a news program where the host was interviewing someone and debating whether the claims that people had made about hearing God were true. The caption at the bottom of the screen read: "A speaking God? Why or why not?" She got tired of listening after just a couple minutes and finally turned off the set and sat back in her bed.

Why did everyone have to argue so much about this? Did they think it was that far-fetched, that God could speak out loud to people? What was so hard to believe about it? But then she thought, 'If it hadn't happened to me last Sunday night, and someone else had just said this to me, I wouldn't have believed it either. But it did happen to me, so I know it could have happened to other people, but why didn't it happen to everyone? Why didn't it happen to some of these so-called religious people? It must not have, or they wouldn't be making fun of it the way they are.'

She wished she could talk about it with someone, but she knew she couldn't mention it to Kendra or any of her other friends, especially not her church-going friends. If this is what they were hearing at church today, she didn't want them to treat her like some kind of liar or attention-getter. She had almost told her mom about it, but now she was glad she hadn't. If her mom heard all these stories on TV too, and the way the religious people were bad-mouthing it all, she'd probably think Annie was just making it all up. God only knew what Andrew would say about it. She shivered at the thought.

She pulled the covers up over her head, closed her eyes, and decided to go directly to the source. "God, are you there? What should I do about this, God? I don't understand why you said what you did to me. Was it meant just for me? Am I supposed to tell anyone about it?" She waited then, but heard nothing. But that was okay, because she began to feel the way she had last Sunday when she'd heard the voice. So she surrendered to it, and immersed herself in the satisfying sense of peace.

Bob and Katie were first out of the church doors, leaving before the service was even over. Without a word to each other, they made their way through the parking lot to their car. Bob opened the door for Katie, carefully closing it behind her and walked around to the other side to get in. When he'd started the car, backed out, and turned out of the church parking lot, he looked over at Katie and asked if she wanted to get something to eat somewhere.

Katie looked out the window on her side of the car. "No, I don't think I could eat anything right now. I just want to go home."

He said, "All right," and drove in that direction. The church idea had backfired on him, and now he remembered why they didn't go very often. He'd hoped maybe there would be something encouraging there, something to give them hope or to help them understand why bad things can happen to good people. But if Katie was feeling at all like he was, they both felt a lot worse than they had when they had gone.

"I still can't believe the self-righteousness and smugness of that guy," Katie said. "It's like he thinks he knows everything, and anyone who believes something different is just wrong." Bob nodded and kept his eyes on the road. "How can he condemn people who think God spoke to them? Just because God didn't speak to him? If it doesn't happen to him personally, then it doesn't count? Who does he think he is to make that call for everyone?"

She was ranting, but Bob agreed with her. "Yeah, who died and left him Pope anyway?" He smiled and looked over at her.

"Really," Katie said, still looking out the passenger window. Neither spoke the rest of the way home. But when they'd gone inside, Katie brought up the topic again.

"Bob, what do you think about everything that's happened this past week, all the news shows and reports of people saying they heard God's voice?"

"I don't know what to think." He looked over at her. "What do you think about it?"

"I don't know either. I mean I know what I heard, or what we heard. But it's weird to think other people may have heard the same thing, and at the same time."

"Yeah, I know. It is weird."

"Do you think they really did?"

"I don't know. Maybe some of 'em did. Maybe not all of 'em. I think some people just like to jump on a bandwagon if they think it'll bring them attention somehow."

Katie thought about that. "But what about that preacher? Why do you think it didn't happen to him?"

"I don't know. Maybe his heart wasn't in the right place or some-thing."

Katie sighed. "But why do you think it happened to us? It's not like we're religious or anything. We hardly ever even go to church."

Bob looked away and said, "Maybe God just knew we needed some looking after. Or that we needed a sign of some kind."

Katie began to cry. "What we really needed from God was our beautiful baby boy. That's what we needed. Not some sign." The bitterness rose up inside her.

Bob went over and put his arms around her. "I know," he mur-mured in her hair. It tore him up inside to see her this way. He felt so empty inside and so helpless to do anything to help her. Would he ever feel joy again? But even through his bitterness and sorrow, sometimes he could still draw on the same sense of calm he had felt when they'd heard God's voice. He only had to close his eyes and recall the moment, and it came back to him, as if it was all happen-ing again. If he just let go and went with it, he felt like he didn't have to try to figure everything out, that he could just sit back and let God take control and work things out. Unfortunately this only lasted as long as he could stay in that moment, which usually wasn't long. As soon as he opened his eyes, the realities of the world crashed in again and he felt the pressure again to be in charge and to take care of everything.

Robin was disoriented when her alarm went off Sunday morn-ing, and at first she thought it was a work day. Sunday was usually her day to sleep until noon and work off the hangover from the night before. But last night she'd gone to a movie with a friend instead of partying, and she was home by eleven--the earliest she'd been home on a Saturday night in years. She reached for the alarm, shut it off and rolled back over in bed. Although she was tired, her head didn't hurt and she thought it was actually kind of nice to wake up on Sunday morning without a major headache. Two mornings in a row without a headache. What was the world coming to? She figured she could stay in bed a little longer and still make it to the church service down on Cherry at ten-thirty. Did she still even want to go?

She sort of did and sort of didn't. But the more she thought about it, she figured what did she have to lose? If she didn't like it, she'd just get up and leave. But maybe there would be something interesting there for her. So she got out of bed to put on some coffee.

Robin felt apprehensive as she pulled into the church parking lot. What was she doing here? She didn't know a soul here, and she wasn't even sure she was dressed right. She glanced at people walking in from the parking lot to see what they were wearing. Some were dressed up, but others were in casual clothes, and then she saw a couple wearing jeans. She figured she'd be okay in her khaki pants and sweater. She was losing her nerve, though, as she drove through the lot and she almost kept driving, thinking she could still just go back home.

Someone waved then and smiled at her from the parking lot. She waved back, and looked closer to see if she knew the woman. She didn't recognize her, but at least someone was trying to be nice. So she swallowed, pulled into a parking space, took a deep breath, grabbed her purse and got out of the car to make her way into the church. She told herself if anything happened that made her feel uncomfortable, she could turn right back around and go home. She didn't have to do this if she didn't want to, and this bargain with herself kept her moving forward. She wasn't exactly sure where to go, so she just moved in the same direction she saw everyone else moving.

Once inside, she looked to her left and saw the doors to a large sanctuary, so she headed toward them. Someone greeted her with a "Good morning" and handed her a program. She walked into the room and looked for an open seat in the back. There were plenty, so she headed to one.

The first thing that surprised her as she walked inside and sat down was the music. It was loud and had a great beat, and gave the place a fun atmosphere. While she waited for the service to begin, she watched the singers and musicians, who sang and played so joyfully she couldn't help but smile too. She looked around and noticed the stained glass windows, the high ceiling, the muted lighting, the tan carpet, and the pews beginning to fill as more people streamed in. She started to relax a bit as she took it all in. 'So far so good,' she thought. There was something about the place that seemed almost comforting, but she wasn't sure what it was. 'Let's just wait and see,' she told herself.

As the service began, Robin felt suspended in time. She didn't recognize the songs, but she found herself humming along. She was surprised at herself when one of the songs brought tears to her eyes. She didn't remember church being like this when her parents made her go with them. She remembered it as being serious and boring. This was entirely different. She felt uplifted and something about it moved her deep inside.

She was surprised again when the sermon began, because the man delivering it (was he the pastor?) was dressed so informally, in a polo shirt and khaki pants. She looked at her program to see his name. Rick Davidson. Where had she heard that name before? She watched him closely as he spoke. She thought she'd developed a pretty keen sense of judgment over the years for people who weren't sincere. So far he seemed like the real deal.

The title for the sermon intrigued her--"Are You Listening?" He was talking about how over-stimulated our society is with all the things coming at us, from the TV, newspapers, radio, internet, everyone telling us what to do or trying to influence us in some way.

"So we've learned to filter, haven't we? Most of the time we probably don't even realize we're doing it. There's just so much coming at us, there's no way we can take it all in, so we learn to filter and just let in what we want to hear, and let the rest go. Do you get those emails that people like to send, you know, the jokes, stories, warnings about this or that? Or maybe you're one of those people who like to send those emails." He smiled and the audience chuckled. "Not that there's anything wrong with it," he said, putting his hands up. "But after a while, I have to admit I just start deleting some of them without even reading them. But what happens if we miss an important message? What if someone we love sends us an email with an important message and we mistake it for something else? We run the risk of missing out on something we wished we'd seen, right?" He paused and lowered his voice. "Could the same thing happen with God? What if God tried to send us an important message, and we missed it?" Robin's heart skipped a beat. Was he going to talk about what had happened to people last Sunday night? Was he one of the skeptics? She held her purse closer, ready to bolt. If he started discounting it, she was out of there.

"Many of you have heard a lot on the news this past week about how God seemingly spoke to some people. If you haven't heard about it, then let me fill you in. Many people throughout the world, people of all faiths and all walks of life, claim that God spoke to them last Sunday night. This was not like the Holy Spirit speaking inside their soul. They say God actually spoke out loud, words they could hear, and that there was no mistaking what He said."

The congregation seemed to be collectively holding its breath, waiting to hear what he'd say about this. Robin was holding hers too. He continued, "So what are we supposed to think of this story? Is it just a story? Or did God in fact speak to these people?" He paused and scanned the audience, looking directly into their eyes. "Well, I'm not going to stand up here and tell you what to believe or what not to believe about this. You'll have to decide that for yourself. But I will share a couple of thoughts with you. The first one comes from the Gospel of Matthew, chapter seven, verse one, where Jesus said, 'Do not judge, or you too will be judged.'" He paused to let the words sink in. "As a matter of fact, I spoke with someone this past week who told me that God had spoken to him last Sunday night." Several people in the audience gasped. Robin leaned closer.

"Now this was not a man who is here with us today, and he had no idea that other people had reported a similar event happening to them. In fact, this man doesn't even own a TV set. But he knew that God had spoken to him, there was no question in his mind. So I'm not going to sit back and judge him, or what God said to him. That's not my job here today. I believe my job is to ask you this: if God spoke to you, would you be ready to listen?"

Robin finally released the breath she didn't realize she'd been holding. She glanced around to see what others were thinking about this. She saw a mixture of expressions—some scowls, as if they'd expected the pastor to take a firmer stance on all this, some contemplative looks, wondering about what they'd heard, wondering what they'd do if God spoke to them. She looked around, trying to see if anyone else felt like she did--sure that God had spoken to them already. But what would a person look like if this had happened to them? She paid close attention to the rest of the sermon and decided that Pastor Rick Davidson was someone she'd like to talk with more.

Later that afternoon Rick and Sarah sat down at their kitchen table for an early dinner. Sometimes they joined other members of the congregation for lunch after church, either going to a restaurant or to someone's home. But yesterday Rick had specifically told Sarah he didn't want to make any plans with anyone. She didn't ask why, but she wondered if it had something to do with him sharing in his sermon about hearing God's voice. After being married to Rick for 28 years, she had learned when not to probe for more information, which was actually most of the time. Rick would talk when he was ready, after he'd had plenty of time to reflect. Today's meal was a simple one, a slow-roasted pot of beef with garlic, potatoes, carrots and celery, one of Rick's favorites. It had roasted all morning while they were at church and when they pulled their car into the garage, the aroma floated out to meet them.

Sarah passed him the plate with the roast, and he sliced through the tender meat with a carving knife, placing a piece on each of their plates. "Mmm, this looks great," he said, as he picked up the vegetables.

"Thanks," Sarah said, straightening her chair under her.

He asked God's blessing on the meal and they ate quietly for a while. Finally she said, "I enjoyed your sermon today," without looking up. He didn't respond at first and she wondered if she should say more. But she kept quiet, waiting for him.

"Sarah, I just couldn't do it," he finally said, almost apologetically. She didn't need to ask him what he was referring to. "I just couldn't tell them it had happened to me too, at least not yet." She chewed and nodded her understanding.

After she swallowed her bite, she asked, "So someone else came to you and said it had happened to him too?"

"Yeah, a man at the homeless shelter."

"Really? What'd he say?"

"He came up to me last Monday when I was there to help pass out the sack lunches. He said he had a question for me and wanted to talk privately. So we went into another room and he asked me if I thought God still spoke out loud to people today." Sarah raised her eyebrows. "Yeah, I could hardly believe it either."

"So what'd you tell him?"

"I didn't know what to say at first, I was just stunned. So I told him about the many accounts in the Bible of God speaking to people. But he pressed me and wanted to know if I thought it still happened today. So I said yeah, I thought it probably did."

"Did you tell him…"

"That it had happened to me too? No, I didn't. I tried to let him know that I thought it could happen, but I just wasn't ready to talk about my own experience with anyone."

"Hmm," she said as she chewed.

"He was there again at the shelter on Friday and we talked again. He says this experience has changed his life, and I could tell he was different. For one thing, he didn't appear to be drinking any more. At least I couldn't smell it on him, and I always could before. His eyes were clear, he spoke coherently. He seemed like a completely different person."

"Wow."

"Yeah, it was pretty cool. So when I was working on my sermon for this week, I felt like God wanted me to address what had happened to people and all, but I just wasn't ready to tell them it had happened to me too. I just wasn't sure they were ready to hear that. So I thought maybe they'd find it easier to accept if I shared Ralph's story, instead of my own. I wanted them to realize that it's not up to us to judge whether people actually heard God speaking, but that the words are true…God is there and he just wants us to trust him. And I wanted them to think about whether they'd even listen if he did try to speak to them."

The phone rang then, startling them both. Rick got up to answer it. Sarah continued eating while he spoke with the person on the other end. She could tell the conversation was about today's sermon, but wasn't quite sure what the other person was saying. When he hung up, he sat back down at the table, and said, "Sorry about that. That was Betty Thompson. She was calling to tell me there's been a lot of discussion about the sermon today."

"Oh?"

Betty Thompson was one of the church's charter members, and considered it her job to inform the pastor what people were saying and thinking. While sometimes Rick found it interesting to know what was going on behind the scenes, he also found it annoying at times. But he figured it was usually better to know than not to know.

"Yeah, apparently a group went out for lunch after church today and had quite a spirited discussion, some of 'em giving me the benefit of the doubt and some of 'em ready to ask me to resign if I don't denounce the blasphemers who say they heard God speak to them."

After a minute, Sarah said, "Well, did you expect anything different?"

"No, I guess not." He took another bite and they finished their meal in silence. Rick wondered what the rest of the week would bring, and it made him tired to think about it.

CHAPTER TEN

On Monday morning, Rick headed back to the shelter to help with the sack lunches. He greeted Shauna as he walked in the main entrance

"Mornin' Rick, how ya doin'?" she asked, chewing her gum.

"Great, Shauna, how about you?"

"Doin' fine." She waved with a smile and continued down the hall. He walked over to the table where Ryan was already handing out lunches to a few early arrivers. "Hey Ryan, you feelin' better?"

"Yeah, better, but I've still got this cough."

"Well, I hope it gets better soon."

Rick picked up a lunch and handed it to a woman who had just come through the front door. "God bless you."

"Thanks," she mumbled as she turned and left.

He and Ryan were continuing to hand out the sacks to people coming in for them, when he looked up to see Ralph standing in front of him. "Hey Ralph, how are ya, man?" Rick came around the table to shake hands and to throw an arm around him.

Ralph smiled. "I'm doin' alright."

Rick noticed again the marked changes in him. "Well, it's good to see you. You're looking good, Ralph."

"I feel good, Pastor. Better than I've felt in a long time."

"Do you want a lunch?" Rick asked, offering a sack to him.

Ralph hesitated for a second, then said, "Sure," and took it from Rick. "Actually I came in today to check the job posting board."

"Did you find anything on it?"

"Yeah, a couple things." He paused, then he added, "But I'd sure like to get back into the kind of work I used to do."

"What kind of work was that?"

"I was in marketing. Worked on publicity campaigns, advertising, that kind of stuff."

"So you wanna get back into marketing again?"

"Yeah, I had a pretty good career before I threw it all away on the booze. I always thought I could handle it, but I guess everybody thinks that. Turns out I couldn't."

"Yeah, sometimes it can really get a grip on people and strangle them before they even realize it. I've seen it happen to a lot of good people." Rick wasn't against having a drink now and then himself, but from what he'd seen, alcohol created a lot more problems than it had ever solved for most people.

"You got that right, brother. It sure had a grip on me."

"Ralph, I gotta say it…you've seemed different these last couple of times we've talked." They had walked over a few feet away from the table where Ryan was still handing out lunches.

Ralph smiled. "Yep. Haven't had a drink now in a week."

"You mean, since…"

Ralph looked around and lowered his voice. "Yeah, not since last Sunday, when I heard what I told you about."

"That's great, Ralph. God can do some amazing things, huh."

"Yep, he sure can. I kinda thought he'd given up on me. I never would've believed it, but it's been a week now. I'll admit, sometimes I've wanted one…bad. A couple times I almost caved, but then the whole thing came back to me, and I was able to walk away. Man, something happened to me that night and I feel like a new person."

Rick could see the change in Ralph's eyes and face. Even his hands weren't trembling. He looked like a man who was thinking clearly, one who now had hope. Before, Ralph would barely make eye contact with anyone. Rick was filled with a sudden urge to want to help Ralph however he could.

"Ralph, I've got an idea. We could use some help at the church. We need someone to help get bulletins ready for Sunday, stuffing inserts into them, folding, and a few other odd jobs. It's just one day a week, on Friday, and it doesn't pay much, but the job is yours if you want it. I know you're way over-qualified for this job, but we could sure use your help, at least until you find something else."

Ralph scratched his head, looked up at Rick, and said, "Seriously?"

At first Rick thought he might have offended him, so he back-pedaled, "I know it's not much, and I didn't think you'd be interested. Just thought I'd..."

Ralph interrupted him. "No, no. I mean, yeah, I'd love the job. If you're serious..."

"Sure I am. Well, great. Then come on over to the church this Friday morning around nine and we'll get you started. Do you know where it is?"

"The one down on Cherry, right?" They firmed up the plans, and Ralph departed with his sack lunch. Rick waved as he left and went back to the table to help Ryan, thinking about how good it felt to finally help someone who needed it.

Bob hadn't slept well and when his alarm sounded Monday morning, he groaned and hit the snooze button. He knew he could go one more round before he had to get up, and he pulled the covers back up and closed his eyes. Katie turned to curl up beside him. When the snooze went off nine minutes later, Bob turned it off, stretched and rolled out of bed. While he was in the shower, Katie got out of bed and started some coffee brewing. He came into the kitchen a little later and picked up the mug she'd poured for him.

"Thanks, hon."

"Sure."

Katie knew she'd have to go back to work at some point, but she just didn't feel ready yet, physically or emotionally. Martha, her boss at the florist shop, had told her to take as much time as she needed. She appreciated Martha's offer, but she also knew it would leave her under-staffed, since Martha hadn't yet hired her replacement while she was on maternity leave. She took a sip of coffee and looked out the window.

The doctor had told her to ease her way back into work, to take at least a week off to heal physically, then maybe start back part-time, as she felt up to it. It had been a week, but she still didn't feel ready. She kept imagining how it would be to have everyone asking her about it. But it would be worse if they acted like nothing had happened. She wasn't even sure what she wanted them to do. There was no "right" way to be or act. It was going to hurt, no matter what. The longer she put it off, the worse it would be, so she thought about maybe going in for a few hours later in the week.

Bob came back into the kitchen then, ready for work, rinsed his mug and set it in the sink. He walked over to her and embraced her.

"You gonna be okay today, hon?"

"Yeah, I'll be fine. Don't worry about me." She forced a smile, looked up at him and returned his kiss. "I thought I might even call the shop today and see about going back later this week."

He looked a little alarmed. "Are you sure you're ready?"

"I've gotta go back sometime, don't I? It won't be full-time yet or anything. I was just thinking about a few hours later this week."

"Well, don't push yourself too hard. You've been through a lot." He still didn't look convinced.

"Go on to work, Bob. I'll be fine. See ya tonight." He gave her another kiss before leaving. When he'd pulled his car out of the garage, she sipped her coffee and thought about what a good guy she'd married. She'd never known love like his growing up. Her family was what most people would call dysfunctional. Her parents had divorced when she was young, and she hadn't seen much of her dad since. She knew her mother probably loved her and her brother, but she'd been too busy with her string of boyfriends to spend much time at home with her kids. Katie and her brother Kyle had practically raised themselves.

Katie tried to stay in touch with her mother, but it was hard. Her mother moved around a lot and seemed more interested in pursuing new adventures than anything else. When Katie had told her mother about her pregnancy, her mother had expressed excitement over the phone, but then they didn't talk for weeks afterward, and when they finally did talk again, Katie had to bring it up first, which made her wonder if her mother had forgotten about it. Their phone conversations consisted mostly of Katie's mom telling her about her latest adventure, like riding motorcycles on the beach or living in some commune. Katie had always felt more like the adult in their relationship than the child.

Katie hadn't heard from her mother in about three weeks, so her mom still didn't know what had happened. She wondered if her mother would even remember that she'd been pregnant the next time she called. Maybe she wouldn't even answer the phone if her mom's number came up on the caller ID. The last thing she wanted to do was remind her mother that, oh yes she'd been pregnant, and that oh, by the way, she'd lost the baby. She could only imagine what her mother would say. 'Well, it's probably for the best,' or 'There was probably something wrong with the baby and this was nature's way of taking care of it.'

But as Katie thoughts turned back to Bob, she realized, as she had so many times before, how lucky she was to have found him. Without any kind of role model set before her, it was amazing that she could have found such a good man, and that they had such a healthy relationship. Even if she wasn't always sure how to create a good marriage, she knew what she didn't want to be, as a wife and mother. She was determined to be a caring and loyal wife, and an involved mother. That is, if she ever got the chance.

When Annie stepped off the bus at school Monday morning, she saw Kendra looking for her.

"Hey, Annie!" Kendra yelled, waving at her near the front doors. She waved back and hurried to catch up with her. They walked inside and turned down the hall that led to their lockers. The aroma of food from the cafeteria wafted through the hallway. They moved along with the crowd in the hall and caught up on each other's weekends.

"You'll never believe who texted me Saturday night," Kendra chattered.

"Who?"

"Mike Murray."

"No way! What'd he say?"

"Nothing much, just 'what's up,' that sorta thing. Back and forth practically all night. Oh, and he says Trevor likes you."

"Shut up!"

"Yeah, that's what he said."

"Did he 'say' that, or did he text it?"

"He texted it. He said Trevor wanted your cell but I wouldn't give it to him without asking you first. I kept texting you but you never answered."

Annie didn't say anything.

"So…do you want me to give it to him or not?"

"Well…I guess."

"What do you mean, 'you guess'? Don't you like him?"

"Duh, of course I like him. It's just that I have a limited number of texts and if I go over, my mom takes it out of my allowance."

"That stinks. Well, don't pass up your chance. A guy like Trevor will move on if you don't let him know you're interested."

"Yeah, I know. Go ahead and give it to him then."

"Cool. You're really lucky he likes you, you know. This could open up a whole new world for you." Kendra was such a match-maker, but Annie didn't mind. She'd had a crush on Trevor since fourth grade, but he'd never paid any attention to her. They dropped their bags in their lockers, got out their books and walked to their first class together.

"So what'd you do this weekend?" Kendra asked.

"Not much." Kendra wasn't listening anyway, so Annie didn't think she wanted much of an answer.

"Hey, Kendra," Allison said with a smirk, as they passed in the hall.

After she'd walked past, Kendra made a face to Annie, and whispered, "I can't stand her."

"Why?'

"Well, her dad's the preacher at our church, and yesterday after church, she comes up to me and says the dumbest thing. She goes, 'Hey, Kendra, are you one of those people who hears voices?' There were all these other kids around, you know, like guys and stuff, and she just wanted to embarrass me in front of them."

"So, what'd you do?" Annie asked.

"I just ignored her and started talking to some friends. I wish I'd thought of a good come-back though."

The bell rang then, but Annie couldn't wait to ask Kendra more about what Allison might have been talking about. She wondered if her dad had preached about God speaking to people.

After school they met outside and Annie brought it up. "So why do you think Allison was asking you about hearing voices, anyway?"

"Cuz she's weird. Her dad preached about these people who said they heard God speak or something. She was just using that to make me look bad in front of her stupid friends."

"What did her dad say about those people?"

"What, you mean the ones who say they heard God?"

"Yeah." Annie didn't want to appear too interested, but she really did want to know what was being said in church about it.

"Oh, he just said there were a bunch of crazies running around saying that God spoke to them and stuff. It was even on the Hailey show last week."

"Crazies, huh…"

"Yeah."

"So he doesn't believe 'em?"

"What, that God really did speak to them?"

"Yeah."

"No, he said the whole thing was bogus."

Annie thought about this. Then she asked, "Well, what do you think?"

Kendra looked to see if Annie was asking what she thought she was. "You mean, do I think God really spoke to people?"

"Yeah, do you think it could happen?"

"Sure, why not. He did it before. Why couldn't he do it again? Hey, wait up, Jenny!" Kendra yelled at one of her friends that rode the bus with her. "Gotta go, see ya, Annie."

Annie walked to her own bus, thinking about what Kendra had just said. She was glad her friend thought it was possible that God could speak to people. But what would she think if she knew that Annie had been one of them?

Robin decided she needed a break, so she got up from her desk and headed to the break room. Sometimes it was hard to focus on work Monday mornings, though it had been a little easier these last couple of weeks, since she hadn't gone out partying over the weekends. It was actually kind of nice to not have a hangover on Monday morning. She poured coffee into her mug, and was adding the cream and sugar when Bob walked in.

"Hey, Bob," she said, looking up as she stirred.

"Hi Robin."

She didn't know if she should ask about Katie again, but decided to go ahead. "How's Katie doing?" She looked up, to let him know she wasn't just making casual conversation, but that she genuinely cared. "I've been thinking about you guys."

"She's doing okay, I guess, all things considered."

"I guess it'll probably take a while."

"Yeah. We did get out of the house yesterday to go to church."

"Oh? Well, that's good," Robin said.

"Yeah, I thought it might help her to get out, and maybe hear something inspirational or encouraging. Too bad it didn't quite work out that way."

"Oh? Why not?"

Bob glanced around to see if anyone else was nearby. He felt comfortable with Robin, but he didn't want to say anything about religion at work that might offend someone. Since he didn't see anyone, he said, "Oh, it's just that the sermon yesterday really ticked her off. We made a beeline for the door as soon as we could."

"Yeah? What was the sermon about?"

Bob lowered his voice. "Did you hear on the news last week about how some people said they heard God speak out loud to them?"

Robin almost spilled her coffee. "Yeah, I heard about that."

"Well, that's what the sermon was about."

"What was upsetting to Katie about that?" Robin set her mug down on the counter.

"The pastor called it all a big hoax. Said people were making it all up and we shouldn't believe any of it. We were both pretty upset about how he talked about it."

"Hmm," she nodded. How much should she say to him? "That's interesting, Bob, because I went to church yesterday too, for the first time in years, and the preacher I heard also spoke about that."

"Really? What did he say?"

"He said it wasn't up to us to judge whether it happened to people or not, but that what we should be thinking about is whether we'd be ready to hear him if he did speak to us."

"No kidding. That sounds a lot more open-minded than what we heard." Neither spoke for a minute, thinking about the differences in the two sermons. Finally Bob broke the silence. "So what do you think, Robin? Do you think God really spoke to those people?" As soon as the words left his mouth, he couldn't believe he'd asked it, but now he was curious to hear her response.

Robin paused before answering. Could she trust Bob? Even though he'd always seemed like a nice guy when they talked, she didn't know him all that well. But how could it hurt if she just expressed an opinion? So she said, "Yeah, Bob, I think it's possible."

"You do?"

"Well, yeah…I do. What do you think?"

He looked down, but then said, "Yeah, I do too."

Robin wasn't sure why, but she was surprised. Bob had always seemed so grounded and practical, not like a person into spiritual stuff. "You do?" she asked.

"Yeah," Bob replied, and then Ted and Dave walked into the break room, talking about the weekend baseball games. Robin and Bob took their coffee and walked out of the room. "Well, see ya," Bob said, turning down the aisle toward his office. Robin returned to her office, sat down, took a deep breath and felt a smile come over her face. Monday morning didn't seem as hard as it had just a few minutes ago.

Hailey McCoy was in her dressing room sifting through the piles of emails her assistant had printed off for her. There were hundreds of postings on her web site in addition to the emails, all about the show last week when she'd interviewed the Tibetan monks and the others who said they heard God speak to them. She'd never done a show that had generated this level of interest afterwards. She read through some of the emails that praised her for being open-minded enough to air the show and to treat the topic respectfully, and then she read through the larger stack of emails from outraged viewers, accusing her of exploiting God for ratings, and even for outright blasphemy. It was disheartening to see that many of the most hateful writers were church pastors. Even though she knew she'd face criticism when she'd agreed to air the show, she never imagined the full extent of it. Some churches were calling for boycotts of her shows' advertisers and many had created letter-writing campaigns to the network. She couldn't have created this kind of publicity if she'd tried. It was strange the things that got people's undies in a bunch.

She set the papers down, sat back in her chair and breathed deeply. She thought back to last Thursday's show, and the people she'd interviewed. She'd been doing this job for a long time, and she took pride in her ability to spot the fakes. Her staff was good at sorting through them too, but she always had the final say as to who made it on the show and who didn't, and there had been a few times when she'd seen through someone they had missed. But she'd found herself very intrigued with the guests last week.

The authenticity of the monks seemed to have set the tone for the rest of the show. She'd watched a tape of the show later on, something she didn't usually do, but she wanted to see if the camera picked up what she'd felt sitting next to them. The light in their eyes had shined through on camera just the way it had in person, as if they knew without a doubt that what they'd heard had come from God. The other guests on the show had shared similar stories, and she'd seen the same light in their eyes. Clearly these people weren't putting on anything; they were the real deal. So it distressed her to read the hatred spewing forth in some of these letters. Couldn't these people see the truth when it was right in front of them? How could they be so blind to it? They were so intent on maintaining their rigid belief system, which said that God only communicates through certain means, that they were unable to accept anything that departed even the slightest from that.

It had been her life's mission to make the world a better place by being interested in people, being a good listener, being open-minded, and helping people come to a deeper understanding of each other. She knew her mission was in direct opposition to those whose mission was to hold firm to certain belief systems, and that she was bound to raise some hackles. But she didn't care, and she remained committed to making a difference for at least the ones who were ready to hear. She knew for a fact that the people on last Thursday's show were telling the truth. Because she had heard God's voice herself.

CHAPTER ELEVEN

By Tuesday afternoon Katie was feeling better and starting to get bored at home, so she picked up the phone and called the florist shop. Martha answered.

"Hi Martha, it's Katie."

"Katie! Oh, how are you, sweetie?" The compassion in her voice was sincere and Katie tried not to choke up.

"Well, I'm doin' pretty good."

"I've been so worried about you and I'm just so sorry, Katie."

"Thanks, Martha," she said, trying to keep her emotions in check. She cleared her throat. "Actually the reason I'm calling is I wondered if I could come back to work this week, maybe just a few hours?"

"Oh…are you sure you're ready for that, hon? We're handling things here, if you're not quite ready. Don't feel like you have to rush back if it's too soon."

"Thanks, but I think I'm ready. I'm not ready to come back full-time yet, but I'm getting bored at home and I think it's time I get my mind on something else for a change."

"Did your doctor say it was okay for you to work again?"

"He said to ease back into it as soon as I was ready."

"Well, I'd love to have you back any time, sweetie. Whatever you want to do, you can come back and do."

"If it's all right with you then, could I come in tomorrow morning for a few hours?"

"Sure, that'd be great. You just come in whenever you want. I'll be here by nine, but come in any time after that."

"Okay, then. I'll see you tomorrow. Thanks a lot, Martha."

Katie hung up and stared out the window. Was she really ready to face the world again? It seemed like the entire world as she knew it had changed, and now she was just going back to her old life as if everything was still the same. But it never would be. She knew she was lucky to have such a great boss. Martha had been more of a friend to her than a boss, and even though she could make more money working somewhere else, she just liked being in the shop with Martha. It would do her good to get out of the house tomorrow, even if just for a few hours, and get busy again. She actually looked forward to the aroma of fresh flowers that would greet her as she walked into the shop. She turned away from the window and walked through the house to her bedroom to look through her closet for something to wear to work tomorrow. She couldn't stand the idea of wearing any of her maternity clothes, but she wasn't sure any of her pre-pregnancy clothes would fit either.

Carolyn pulled her car into Kendra's driveway and came to a stop. As Annie opened the door to get out, Carolyn asked her, "When do you want me to pick you up?"

"A couple hours, I guess. I'll call you."

"All right. Good luck on the project. See you in a couple hours."

"Bye, Mom," Annie said as she slammed the door and walked to Kendra's front door. Carolyn backed the car out of the driveway, watching to make sure someone let Annie into the house.

The front door to Kendra's house was standing open, and before Annie could ring the bell, Kendra's little brother came to the door. "Hi, Annie," he said, opening the screen door for her.

She smiled at him as she walked in. "Thanks, Davey. Is Kendra around?"

"Kendra!" he yelled up the stairs. "Annie's here!"

Kendra yelled back, from upstairs. "Tell her to come on up!"

Davey pointed upstairs, as Kendra's mother came out of the kitchen. "Oh, hi Annie. I thought I heard someone come in."

"Hi, Mrs. Reynolds."

"Do you want something to drink before you go upstairs?"

"No, I'm fine, thanks," and she turned to go up the stairs.

Kendra was on her bed, shuffling through her MP3 player. "You've gotta hear this song, Annie, listen…" she said, plugging the player into the speakers and pushing a button. Annie sat down next to her on the bed.

"I like it, who is it?" she asked, as it played.

"This group called Wicked Monkeys. I saw them on TV the other day, and I just downloaded some of their songs."

They listened until the song finished, and Annie said, "Well, we better get started on the project. I can only stay a couple hours." She had come over to work on their science project. "It's due Friday and I have stuff every other night this week, so we should try to get it close to finished tonight."

"Yeah, I know," Kendra said, turning down the volume on the player. They sat on the floor with their science class notebooks open in front of them. "What are we gonna do it on?"

"Well, I looked over some of the topic ideas she gave us and here are a couple I thought might work," she said, showing the list to Kendra.

Kendra looked at it and groaned. "Geez, I don't like any of this stuff. It all sounds either boring or too hard."

"I know, but we've gotta do something." She looked at the list again. "What about a polygraph?"

"A polygraph? What's that?"

"It used to be called a lie detector test, but now they call it a polygraph."

"A lie detector test, huh? That sounds kinda cool, but how would we do it? I mean, aren't those things really complicated and expensive?"

"I don't know, but look, it's on the list. Maybe she just wants a simpler version of the real thing."

Kendra looked at the list again and said, "Let's search it on the computer and see what we come up with."

They spent some time reading about polygraph tests on the computer, and how they use changes in blood pressure, breathing rates, pulse rates and perspiration to detect deceptive responses to questions.

Annie said, "I think we could do this. Do you know where we could get a blood pressure cuff?"

"Yeah, my parents have one. We could use that."

"Cool. Maybe we could measure breathing rate by watching and counting. How would we measure perspiration though?"

"Yuck. I don't even want to think about that one. I'll go get the blood pressure thingy."

"Okay. I'll start making some notes, and I'll see if I can find ideas online for how to measure perspiration." Annie got busy writing down the description of their project.

Kendra came back with the blood pressure monitor and said, "Here it is. Did you find anything on perspiration?"

Annie looked up from the computer. "Yeah, it says here they usually measure it through the fingertips, like with these fingerplates. Hmm." She showed Kendra the web page she was reading.

"I've got an idea," Kendra said, as she read about the fingerplates. "What if we used facial blotting papers? My mom has a bunch."

"Facial blotting papers? What are they?"

"They come in these packages and you take one to use it to blot the oil on your face throughout the day. We could set people's fingertips on them and see if they perspire. I don't know if it'd work, but we could try it."

"Sure, why not. You think your mom could loan us some?"

"I'll go ask." Kendra left again while Annie wrote more about how they planned to take measurements using the blood pressure monitor and by observing breathing rates.

Kendra came back, "Got it! She said she didn't mind and we could have as many as we need. Annie, do you really think this'll work? Do you think we could actually use this stuff to tell if someone was lying?"

"I don't know. From what it says on the internet, there's a lot of disagreement about polygraph tests. They're not allowed in court, but people are still using them for other things. I guess we'll just have to practice on ourselves and see."

Kendra had watched her parents use the blood pressure cuff many times, so she knew how to operate it. "Let's try this thing out first. Here, I'll hook you up with it, then put your fingertips on these things and I'll ask you some questions. Let's see what happens."

Annie gave her arm to Kendra, who wrapped the cuff around it and tightened it. She watched the readouts as she squeezed.

"I think the numbers are finally staying in place. Hold still. Now put your other hand over here and set your fingertips on these papers." She laid out four pieces of the blotting papers and Annie complied. "Now I'll ask you some questions. Try to lie about something along the way so we can see if there's any difference, okay?"

"Okay."

Kendra cleared her throat and began. "First, what is your full name?"

"Ann Marie Stockton."

"Good." She was watching the readouts on the cuff. "What is your brother's name?"

"Andrew David Stockton."

"Okay. What is the name of your school?"

"Bridgeton Middle School."

"What is your favorite color?"

"Blue."

"What is your favorite food?"

"Tacos."

"Who was your first boyfriend?"

"Conor."

Kendra raised her eyebrows, but kept going as she watched the blood pressure monitor and the fingertip papers. "How many boys have you kissed?"

Annie paused and said, "One."

"Who do you wish would kiss you?"

"Kendra!"

94

"Come on, Annie! You gotta answer so we can see if this thing works." She looked back at the monitor.

Annie sighed and sat back. "Fine."

Kendra repeated in her tester voice, "Who do you wish would kiss you?"

"Trevor."

"What do you want to be when you grow up?"

Annie thought and said, "A teacher."

Kendra paused a minute, then released the cuff and said, "Annie, I think it works! Look, the blood pressure reading was the same up until that last question, and then when you said 'teacher,' your blood pressure increased and fingers started perspiring!" She pointed to the moist papers. "Did you lie when you said teacher?"

"Yeah, I lied about the teacher thing. I really want to be a doctor or a sports therapist."

"Awesome! It works, Annie!"

Annie was glad they'd come up with a science project. "Cool!" She hugged Kendra. "Now let's try it on you and I'll come up with some other questions." They went through another round of questions with Annie asking Kendra, and again the readings changed when Kendra lied about how many boys she had kissed.

Annie checked her watch. They had about fifteen minutes left before her mother would expect her to call to come and pick her up. "Okay, how can we get this ready for Friday? We need to write a list of questions we can ask when we have to demonstrate this to the class, and we need to write up the project description page."

"How about if I take the questions and you can work on the description part?"

"Okay," Annie agreed, and they both got busy on their sections.

CHAPTER TWELVE

Robin couldn't get the words from Sunday's sermon out of her head: "Would you be ready to hear God speak?" She couldn't have been the only one in the room who had actually heard God speak, could she? Did that mean she was ready? Rick's attitude about the whole thing had surprised her, especially when he'd said, "It's not up to me to judge whether God speaks to someone or not." She wondered what it would be like to talk with Rick in person, but it just seemed so weird to call him up out of the blue and ask if they could talk, after only being at the church that one time. She'd gone to the church's web site and come close to calling a couple of times, but she kept losing her nerve. Finally by Wednesday morning, while she was sitting at her desk at work, she thought, 'What the hell…what's the worst thing that could happen…that he'll say no?' She made the call before she could talk herself out of it.

The person who answered transferred her to Rick, and he seemed friendly enough, and agreed to meet with her later that day.

When she hung up, butterflies twirled in her stomach. What was she going to say? Could she actually come out and tell him it had happened to her? That God had spoken to her, like the other people? She almost wished she hadn't called then, but she had, so now she had to go through with it. She hoped she wouldn't regret it.

As she pulled into the church parking lot after work, her stomach was so knotted she could hardly breathe. She forced herself to inhale deeply and thought, 'You can do this.' They had agreed to meet in his office, so she parked near the main entrance and walked inside to find it. She'd just play it by ear. She'd ask him a few questions and see what he said, and then decide if she would tell him any more about her experience. If it didn't go well, she'd just politely thank him for his time and leave. One more deep breath, and she smoothed her hair back from the wind, and walked up to the office window. She didn't see anyone, so she knocked on the door next to the window and waited.

No one came to the door, so she looked around, wondering if she was in the right place, then she saw someone come from around the corner. "Hi! Are you Robin?" he asked.

"Yes. Hi," she said, offering her hand.

"I'm Rick Davidson," he said shaking it warmly. "It's nice to meet you." He took some keys out of his pocket and opened the door. "Come on in and we can meet in here." He held the door open for her, and she followed him into the reception area. He opened another door, and pointed to the table inside his office. "Here, have a seat. Would you like some coffee or something?"

"No, thanks," she said, sitting down at the table. He tossed the keys on his desk and took a seat opposite her at the table.

"Are you new here at the church? I'm sorry if we've met and I'm not remembering you," he said, trying to place her.

"No, I came this past Sunday for the first time."

"Oh. Well, I hope you'll be back." He smiled.

"I haven't been much of a church-goer since I was a kid, but yeah, I'll probably be back."

The moment became awkward, but then he said, "Was there something in particular that brought you to worship with us on Sunday?"

She took a deep breath. She'd planned to be the one asking the questions, but she wasn't sure how to start. "Well, actually, yes, there was. I guess I've been looking for something more in my life, and I wasn't sure what that was. I thought maybe I'd find it here, I guess," she said, shrugging.

He nodded and waited for her to continue.

"I guess I wanted to see what you'd say about this whole thing about the people hearing God speak to them." She noticed that he sat up a little straighter in his chair as he nodded. "Well, what do you think of all that?"

He chose his words carefully. "I think that God speaks to people in all kinds of ways, and if someone says God spoke out loud to them, then who am I to say any different?"

"So are you saying you believe them? That God spoke to them?"

"I don't know, Robin. I guess I'm saying it's not for me to judge. What do you think?"

She looked away. "I don't know...." She waited, then looked back at him. "You said in your sermon on Sunday that a man came to you and told you that it had happened to him, that God had spoken to him."

"Yes..."

"Well, what did you say to him when he told you that? Did you believe him?"

Rick considered what he could reveal about his conversation with Ralph without violating his privacy. "I told him I thought it was entirely possible that God had spoken to him. There was no doubt in his mind God had spoken to him, and he said he heard the words quite clearly, and there was no one else around. He said he was sure it was the voice of God, and so I tend to believe him. He's a changed man because of it, that's easy to see. I think that when God speaks to people, it has an impact. How can it not?"

Robin thought about how her own life had changed since that Sunday night a week and a half ago. She didn't want to do a lot of the same things, like partying with her friends, and she found herself a little adrift, like she was seeking a new life, but she hadn't figured out what it was going to consist of yet. She still wasn't sure how much to tell Rick, but she'd come this far--why not go for it.

He seemed like a good man, not quick to judge, a good listener. So she dove in.

"Here's the thing…I heard it too." Her eyes met his, gauging his reaction.

A moment passed and then he said, "You…heard it too," meeting her eyes.

"Yeah, I did."

"Tell me about it."

He asked like he was truly interested, not like he was going to judge her one way or the other. So she told him everything. She told him about how she'd been a major-league partier, about being sick on the bathroom floor and crying out to God, and then hearing his voice. As she told the story, he nodded and listened. When she finished, they sat quietly.

"So now I don't know what to think about all this. I mean, what am I supposed to do now? I don't want to keep living the way I was, but those are my friends, and now I don't even feel like I have any friends, but I can't tell them. I haven't told anybody, until you today. I know people would think I'd lost my mind. You know what I mean?"

"Yeah," he nodded. He knew exactly what she meant. "Robin, I can't tell you what you should do. I wish I could, but I really don't know what you should do. But I will say this. From what you've told me, it sounds like you've had a deep spiritual experience, one that few people ever have in their lifetime, and you should believe in it and trust what you know to be true about it. If you know that God spoke to you, then it doesn't matter what anyone else thinks about it, or even whether you decide to tell anyone about it or not. Just embrace it like the sacred experience that it was, and let God take it from there."

She thought about this. "Yeah, but how? It's not like he's said anything else. It was just that one time."

"Maybe you don't have to know what comes next. Just live one day at a time. It might help you to spend some time being quiet, in meditation or prayer. I think God will give you the answers you want, if you keep seeking him."

She sat back in her chair and wondered how exactly that was supposed to happen. Seek God? Yeah, right. She looked at her watch, and decided she'd taken enough of his time. She stood up and said, "Well, thank you so much for your time, Pastor."

"Please, call me Rick."

"Okay, Rick. Well, thanks. You've been very helpful, and I appreciate it." They shook hands again, and she turned to leave.

"You're welcome, Robin. Please call me any time if you want to talk more. And I hope to see you again at church."

"Yeah, maybe," she said with a smile, as she walked out of his office.

Rick sat back down in his chair and thought about what she'd just told him. It was remarkable. First it had happened to him, then Ralph had shared his experience with him, now Robin, all three of them hearing the same message at the same time on the same night. He wondered how many more had heard it and were too afraid to come forward and tell anyone. Had others in his congregation heard it? Who was God trying to reach? Was it only meant for a few, or was it meant for everyone? He felt blessed to have been one of those who heard God that night. Now he just needed the wisdom to know what to do with it. He admired Robin for her willingness to come in and meet with him and tell him her story. Why couldn't he have shown the same kind of courage she displayed? What was it about her that had seemed so familiar? He felt like he knew her from somewhere.

CHAPTER THIRTEEN

Thursday night when Bob got home from work and pressed the garage door remote in his car, he was surprised to see Katie's car already there. He knew she'd gone back to work at the florist shop on Wednesday for a few hours, and that she'd planned to go in again today and stay until closing at six. He'd been planning to surprise her before she got home by having dinner ready.

"Katie? You home?" He walked inside and saw her curled up in the living room on the couch with a tissue in her hand. He went to her. "Hey, honey, what is it? What's wrong?"

When she looked up at him, he could see her eyes were swollen and red. "Oh, Bob, why? Why did it have to happen?" she cried.

He sat down next to her, put his arms around her and said, "I don't know, honey, I don't know." He held her until she stopped crying, not knowing what else to do or say. After a while she sat up and reached for the box of tissues on the coffee table, pulled out a fresh one and blew her nose. He rubbed her back and sat on the couch next to her, wondering what had happened. "Did you go to the shop today?"

"Yeah," she answered, her eyes welling with tears.

"Did something happen there?"

She wiped her nose. "Yesterday it was good to get back, and I thought today would be good too. Martha was great, and it was nice to smell the flowers and just be busy again. You know, get my mind off of everything. It was all fine until this afternoon until I answered the phone this afternoon, and…." The tears began rolling again, and she looked away, wiping her eyes.

"What, honey, who was it?"

"It was a man calling in an order of flowers for his wife, who had just had a baby," she choked, as another wave of grief overtook her. Bob held her again while she sobbed. "I couldn't even talk to him, Bob. I handed the phone to Martha and I just left."

"Oh, honey." He didn't know what to say. What could he possibly say that would make it better? It just was what it was.

"I don't know if I should go back, Bob. I thought I was ready, but maybe I'm not."

"It's okay if you're not, Katie. Maybe you just need some more time."

"But it really did help to get out of the house and get busy again. I don't know."

"Just ease into it, Katie. When you're ready, you can go back. You don't have to jump back into it right away. Just do what you can."

"I know. That's what Martha says too. She's been great." She blew her nose again.

Bob stood up and said, "Katie, why don't you just stay there and rest a while. I'm making dinner tonight."

"Oh Bob, I can help." She started to get up.

"No, I insist. How about if I get you a cup of tea?"

Katie sat back on the couch, took a deep breath, wiped her nose, and thought once more how lucky she was to be married to a guy like Bob. "All right then. That sounds good. Thanks, hon."

As Carolyn prepared dinner Thursday night, she mentally reviewed the family activities for the next day. Andrew had a baseball game tomorrow night and Eric would be flying home tomorrow afternoon from his business trip, hopefully in time to make the game. Annie's science project was due tomorrow. Maybe she'd be able to get to the gym after dinner tonight if the kids didn't need her for anything. It sure would be nice to get in a workout before the weekend came and things got crazy again. Sometimes it seemed like her life consisted of work, keeping track of her family's activities, and running from one place to the next. She stirred the spaghetti sauce and checked the pasta to make sure it wasn't about to boil over.

She yelled upstairs, "Annie, can you help with the salad? Andrew, the table still needs to be set!" After a minute, Annie came down to help. "Where's Andrew?" she asked Annie.

"In his room."

"What's he doing?"

"How should I know? The door was shut."

"Great. He probably didn't even hear me. Annie, can you break up this lettuce in the bowl?" She handed Annie the head of lettuce and the salad bowl, and picked up the phone. She called Andrew's cell phone number and he answered, "Yeah?" "Andrew, please come down to set the table. We're about ready to eat." Sometimes the best way to get his attention was on his cell, even if he was just upstairs. "Be there in a minute," he said.

A few minutes later, as they were eating together, Carolyn asked, "Annie, is your science project ready to turn in tomorrow?"

"Yeah, I think so. I'll call Kendra after dinner and make sure her part is done."

Andrew helped himself to more salad and asked, "Science project? What's it on?"

"We're doing a polygraph," she answered.

"What, like a lie detector? How's it work?"

"We monitor a person's blood pressure and perspiration and observe breathing rates, then we ask them questions."

"Does it work? Can you tell if they're lying?"

"Yeah, it works pretty good."

"What kind of questions do you ask them?"

"Oh, first we ask easy ones, like what's your name, your favorite food, where you go to school, stuff like that."

"Yeah? Well, maybe you should ask some really juicy questions, like have you ever mooned someone, or taken illegal drugs."

"Andrew!" Carolyn tried to rein him in. "Annie, I think that's a great idea for a science project. Do you need me to help you with any of it tonight?"

"I could help you think up some questions," Andrew offered. Carolyn glared at him.

"No, I think we're good, Mom, but thanks."

They ate quietly for a while, then Carolyn said, "Andrew, where's your game tomorrow night, home or away?"

"It's a home game."

"Oh, good. Your dad should be flying home in time to make it, but that will make it easier."

"Cool. Coach says I'll be starting. I hope Dad can come."

After dinner they took their dishes to the sink, and Carolyn rinsed them and loaded the dishwasher. After she'd finished cleaning up, she went upstairs and knocked on Annie's door.

"Come in," Annie said.

She opened the door and saw that Annie was on her bed reading a book, and her backpack and papers were all over the floor. Annie looked up and saw that her mother was focused on the mess on the floor. "Mom, I'll pick it up later."

"Is your science project in here somewhere?"

"Yeah." Annie was annoyed and wished her mom would leave her stuff alone.

"Can I see it?"

"Mom," Annie rolled her eyes, drawing out the word. "It's fine. I did my part and we're ready to turn it in."

"Well, I'd like to see it, if you don't mind, you know, just check it over and see if I can help with anything." Carolyn still liked to review Annie's homework and projects, not that Annie wasn't capable of doing it correctly, but it just felt like that was her job as a mother. She started sorting through the papers on the floor trying to find something that looked like a science project, when some a paper caught her eye. The words written in Annie's handwriting said, "I am here, Annie. Come to me. Trust me." Her breath caught sharply. "Annie, what's this?" She asked, showing her the paper.

Annie jumped off the bed and grabbed it from her. "It's nothing! Would you just leave me alone! I said I did the science project, it's all done, just leave me alone!"

"But why did you write those words?" Carolyn tried again.

"I don't know. It's nothing!" Annie flopped back on the bed, crumpled the paper in her hand, and opened her book again.

Carolyn couldn't imagine why Annie had jotted down the very words she herself had heard that one night, but it was obvious Annie didn't want to talk about it. Teenage daughters were sure a lot harder to talk to than boys of the same age. It had never seemed as hard with Andrew. She just didn't know how to reach Annie any more. They used to be so close, and sometimes Annie still seemed like a little girl who needed her mother, but other times she seemed so far away and there was nothing she could say or do to bring her back, so she just had to let go and wait for another one of those close moments. She turned to leave, and on her way out she said, "Annie, I think I'll go to the gym if you don't need me for anything tonight. Andrew will be here."

"Fine, Mom." Annie's nose was in her book.

When her mother closed the door behind her, Annie exhaled and set down the book. She unfolded the crumpled piece of paper in her hand and looked at the words. How could she have just left it sitting out like that? She never wanted to forget what she'd heard that night, but she also didn't think she could ever talk about it with anyone either, especially not her mom. She loved her mom, but sometimes it seemed like she was so busy trying to be a "good mom" that it was hard to have a real conversation with her about anything.

She got up from her bed, found the science project on the floor and checked it against the teacher's assignment handout to make sure they'd covered everything. As long as Kendra brought the blood pressure monitor, perspiration pads and her part of the write-up, they should be set. She picked up all the papers on the floor, organized them, and put them back into her backpack. She re-folded the crumpled piece of paper and stuck it in the small zippered section.

CHAPTER FOURTEEN

Even though the weather had warmed up, Ralph decided to spend the night at the shelter so he could shower Friday morning and put on some clean clothes. The shelter had offered him a clean pair of gently used pants and shirt to wear to his job at the church on Friday. He woke early on Friday to shower and shave, and as he looked in the mirror, he realized he could probably use a haircut too. But at least he was clean and sober, and going to work for the first time in years. He ate breakfast at the shelter before heading out for his walk to the church. He figured it would take about an hour, and he was on his way before eight o'clock.

He was glad it was warm and that he didn't have to wear his shabby coat. It felt strange to be "going to work" again, and as he walked, he grew excited but also nervous. How would the others in the church treat him? Rick was a great guy, but how would the others feel about him being there? Would they know he was a homeless drunk? Okay, former drunk. What would he say if they asked him questions about himself? He didn't want to lie, but he didn't want to be completely honest either. Well, he'd just deal with that when the time came. If it was too weird, he'd just leave.

By the time he reached the block of the church, he'd almost talked himself out of the whole thing and he just wanted to turn around and forget it. But he didn't want to disappoint Rick, and heck, he was already here, so what did he have to lose? His self-respect? He'd lost that a long time ago anyway. He slowed his pace as he approached the church parking lot. There were a few parked cars near what looked to be a main entrance, so he headed in that direction, and opened the door to step inside. He was looking around, unsure where to go next, when a man walking by said, "Can I help you?"

"Uh, yeah, I'm supposed to meet Pastor Rick here to help stuff bulletins."

"Oh, sure! Well, come on over this way and I'll show you where they are." The man offered his hand as they walked and said, "I'm Fred."

"Hi Fred, I'm Ralph."

"Nice to meet you, Ralph. The bulletins are back in this room over here. Hey, Rick, there's someone here to help," he said, leaning his head into the room.

Rick looked up from the bulletins. "Thanks, Fred. Ralph! Good to see you!" Rick said, walking over to shake hands.

Maybe this was going to go okay after all. The man named Fred had seemed nice, and so far no one else had acted like he didn't belong there. "Come on in, and I'll show you how this works. Fred, do we have all the materials ready to go?"

"We're waiting for one more insert, Rick. It should be ready in just a few minutes. They're running the copies right now. I'll bring 'em over when they're done."

"Great, Fred. Thanks." He turned back to Ralph as Fred left to go back down the hall. "Looks like we're not quite ready. How's it goin' Ralph?"

"Just fine, Rick. I hope I'm not too early."

"No, not at all. Let's go get something to drink while we wait for the last insert." They walked over to the coffeemaker outside in the hallway, and Rick poured them each a cup. They went back to the room, and as they sipped, Rick showed him the stacks of papers that needed to be folded and inserted into the bulletins. As he was explaining, Fred returned with the final copies. Once Ralph felt like he understood the process, he jumped in to begin. Rick left him alone to work, saying, "I'll be right down the hall in my office over here, Ralph," pointing to another set of doors. "If you need anything, just stop over."

"Sure. Thanks." Ralph continued to fold. It felt good to be productive again, even in such a small way. 'Rome wasn't built in a day,' he thought.

Carolyn set cereal bowls out for breakfast on the table, and poured juice for the kids and coffee for herself as she heard an announcement on the radio. "This just in from the National Weather Service. Conditions are coming together for the possible formation of tornados later in the day. We'll be under a tornado watch all day, so be sure to stay tuned in throughout the day as we provide updates. If conditions change to cause a warning to be issued, we'll let you know as soon as possible."

She glanced out the kitchen window over the sink, seeing only a sunny sky. She walked over to the living room window to check a different direction and saw a few dark clouds on the horizon, and thought, 'I sure hope Andrew's game doesn't get cancelled.'

Annie came down for breakfast then, dropped her backpack on the floor, got a box of cereal out of the pantry, milk out of the refrigerator, and sat down at the table.

"Good morning," Carolyn said to her, walking back into the kitchen.

"Mornin'," Annie mumbled.

"Got your science project?"

"Yeah, Mom."

"Just wanted to make sure. Hey, they just said on the radio there might be bad storms later on." Annie looked up from her cereal and out the window. "We'll have to wait and see, I guess." Andrew came downstairs and headed for the door. "You eating breakfast?" Carolyn said as he passed by.

"Yeah, I'm just gonna put my stuff in the car. I'll be back."

Carolyn always urged them to eat breakfast at home in the morning, but she herself didn't like to eat until she'd been up a while. She knew they'd get hungry at school before lunchtime, and she could eat something after they'd left or at work later on. Andrew came back in, grabbed the box of cereal in front of Annie and poured some into his bowl.

"Andrew, I just heard on the radio there may be storms today."

"Oh?"

"Yeah, I hope your game doesn't get cancelled."

"Me, too. You think Dad'll make it tonight?"

"He should if his flight's on time. We're all planning to be there, right, Annie?"

"I guess." Annie didn't especially like going to his games, but she knew she probably wouldn't have a choice, unless she could make some other plans with a friend. Maybe Kendra would ask her to spend the night.

Andrew finished his cereal first, set his bowl in the sink and headed for the door. Carolyn stood up and said, "Hug?" He turned to hug her and left. She checked the clock and said to Annie, "Looks like you've got about ten minutes. Are you almost finished?"

Once Annie left on the bus, Carolyn tidied up the kitchen, finished getting ready for work and left the house about thirty minutes later. Most of the rush hour was over, and she liked her flexible hours at the library. She was able to see the kids off to school in the morning and usually be home within an hour or so after Annie got home. They were good about letting her take off early on days she wanted to attend an after-school activity.

She checked different radio stations in the car to see if there were any weather updates, but only heard the same message she'd heard at home. She hoped Eric's flight would be on time and that they could all go to Andrew's game tonight. She knew he'd be tired from traveling, but he always enjoyed going to the games. Even though all the kids' activities sometimes made their lives feel stressful, she couldn't imagine what they'd do if they didn't have all those things going on. What did they do together before kids? Was there ever a time when they weren't busy? Their lives were a constant whir of activity, and while it was often exhausting, she realized she kind of liked it that way. She didn't know what she'd do with herself if it weren't for all the busy-ness. Still, sometimes she wished she could slow down just a little.

CHAPTER FIFTEEN

Around noon on Friday, Rick stopped back by the office where Ralph was stuffing the bulletins. "Hey, Ralph, how ya doin' in here?"

Ralph looked up from the table where he was working. "Just fine." He was well more than halfway through the stack. "Shouldn't be too much longer. The finished ones are in these boxes over here," he said, pointing to the corner. "Is that okay?"

"That's great. Hey, I'm gonna go get some lunch. You want to join me? My treat."

Ralph paused, "Well, I don't know...I should probably get this finished." The free meal offer sounded good though.

"Oh, come on, you can finish after lunch. I have something I'd like to talk to you about."

"Well, all right, then." Ralph organized his stacks so he could pick up where he'd left off.

They walked out to the parking lot towards Rick's car. Ralph was accustomed to walking everywhere, and couldn't even remember the last time he'd been inside a car. He opened the door to get inside, thinking how odd such a simple act felt.

After Rick got in and started the car, he pushed a button to open the windows and said, "Wow, what a gorgeous day."

The sun was shining, the sky was clear, and a breeze was barely blowing. But Ralph noticed that something in the air seemed a little off, like a storm was beginning to brew. He leaned forward to check the sky, but saw no clouds. He'd lived with the elements long enough to know when the weather was turning, though, and it sure felt that way to him. But he responded, "Yeah, it sure is."

After they had ordered, Rick said, "You know, I mentioned there was something I wanted to talk to you about."

"Yes?" Ralph took a sip and set down his soft drink.

Rick cleared his throat and glanced around. He wasn't sure how to start this conversation. Finally he said, "Remember how you told me about the voice you heard that night?"

"Yes?"

"Well, you're not the only one who heard it."

"Yeah, I heard that there were some monks on TV that said they heard it too."

"Yeah, the monks...but someone else came to me and said she heard it too."

"You mean someone you know?"

"Yeah. She doesn't usually attend our church, but she came last Sunday and then she called to set up a meeting with me afterwards. She wanted to know what I thought about these people who said they heard God speak to them, so I told her I thought it was definitely possible, and then she told me that it had happened to her too."

"Oh? What'd she hear?"

"It's the strangest thing, Ralph. She heard the same words you said you heard, and on the same night. 'I am here. Come to me. Trust me.'"

"Really." Ralph took another sip of his drink.

"Yeah. She said she knew it was God and that it's changed her life."

"Huh." Ralph wondered why Rick was telling him this. He decided to confront it head-on. "So what do you make of all this? You think we're all telling the truth?"

"Yeah, I do, Ralph. I guess the thing I keep wondering about, is why did only some people hear it and not others?"

Ralph didn't answer.

"The thing is," Rick continued, "A lot of people are really skeptical about this whole thing, including many in my own congregation. Since God has never spoken to them, they assume it can't happen to anyone else. In fact someone called my office this morning and asked me if I was going to waste any more time in my next sermon talking about this 'blasphemous bunch of kooks' who say they're hearing God. It was all I could do to be civil to her and not make things worse by saying what I really wanted to say."

"So what did you say?"

"I told her I was sorry that she thought I was wasting time on this, but that I thought it was important to address it and not to discount the idea that God could actually speak out loud to people in this day and age. Then she said if I was going to continue with this 'nonsense,' as she put it, her family might just have to look for another place to worship."

Neither spoke as the waitress came with their food. They waited until she was gone and Rick continued. "I just don't know how to get across to people that just because this didn't happen to them, it doesn't mean it couldn't have happened to someone else."

They continued in silence while they ate. They both looked up as the song playing on the radio was interrupted with an announcement about a tornado watch. They glanced out the window.

"Well, it sure doesn't look bad out there, but you never know in the Midwest, do you?" Rick said.

"Nope," Ralph said, chewing.

They finished their meal with small talk and occasional looks out the window to check the weather. Ralph wondered why Rick had brought him here. Did he just want to tell him about the other person who heard God? But he liked Rick, and he appreciated a hot meal, so it was fine with him if Rick wanted to talk about it. But he also wanted to get back and finish those bulletins before the weather got worse. If he returned to the shelter early enough, he could get a bed for the night, but if not, he'd be weathering the storm under a bridge somewhere.

They arrived back at the church and Ralph continued where he'd left off, picking up the pace a little now that he knew what he was doing. When he had finished the job later in the afternoon, he placed the last stack of bulletins in a box, straightened the room, and walked over to the main office to find Rick. The secretary at the front desk was on the phone. She waved him back to Rick's office. He walked back and tapped lightly on the door, which was standing open.

"Hey, Pastor, I'm finished with the bulletins. Do you want me to put the boxes somewhere for you?"

"Great, Ralph. Thanks so much. No, you can just leave the boxes there in the room. But can you help me with something else before you leave? We just got a shipment of supplies in, and I need to get this stuff put away before the weekend."

"Well...." Ralph decided to be honest with Rick. "Actually, I kinda wanted to try to get into the shelter tonight, with the storm comin' and all."

"Oh!" Rick felt guilty that he hadn't even thought about where Ralph might spend the night, and was at a loss for words. "Well, sure."

Then it was Ralph's turn to feel bad for catching Rick off guard. So he said, "But it's okay, I can stay and help."

"Oh, no, if you need to go, that's fine."

"It's okay. Now where's that shipment?" Rick had been so generous, giving him this job today, it was the least he could do.

"Are you sure, Ralph?"

"I'm sure, where is it?" Ralph looked behind him, back into the office.

Rick led him down the hall where several boxes were stacked, and showed him the shelves where the supplies were stored.

"Here they are. How about I give you a ride over to the shelter when we're done here?"

"Well, if it's no trouble..."

"No trouble at all, I'm happy to. Thanks for staying to help me out with this."

Katie decided to go back to work Friday and try it again. Bob kept telling her to just take it easy and give it a little more time, but sitting at home feeling sorry for herself didn't sound like much fun either, so when his alarm went off Friday morning, she got up with him. The shop didn't open until ten, so she sipped coffee and read the newspaper while he showered. When she arrived at the shop later, Martha greeted her with a smile and a hug, "Good morning, Katie! How are you today, hon?"

"Okay. How are you, Martha?"

"I'm fine. I'm glad you came back, but are you sure you're ready to?"

"Yeah, I'm tired of sitting around the house by myself. I'm really sorry about leaving like that yesterday."

"Oh, for heaven's sake, no apologies necessary. I'm just sorry you had to take that call. I'll pick up the calls today, and you can just do the arranging."

Katie wanted to tell her it was all right, she could answer the phone if needed, but she went along with her. She knew Martha was trying to protect her, and she appreciated it. "Okay," she agreed.

The day passed quickly, since several orders had already come in, and more followed throughout the day. She threw herself into the work, and was thankful to be able to occupy her mind with other things for a change. Later in the afternoon, they were still waiting for Arnie, the delivery man, to come back to the shop for the last two orders.

"Martha, I'll go ahead and deliver these two on my way home. They're pretty close," Katie offered.

Martha checked the clock, and said, "Are you sure?"

Katie could tell she was worrying about her again. "Yes, I'm sure. They're right on my way."

Martha finally agreed and they were cleaning up to prepare to close for the day when an announcement interrupted the radio program. "Folks, we've just learned that a tornado has been spotted in the air, and several counties are now under a tornado warning." Martha reached over to turn it up and they heard their county listed in the watch area, but not under a warning. They walked to the front of the store together to look out the window and saw ominous clouds off in the distance. They stepped out the front door since no one was in the shop and looked around. It was strange how the sky was still mostly blue and sunny, yet the dark clouds were swirling a little further away.

"Gee, that doesn't look good, does it?" Martha said as they looked together.

"No, it doesn't."

"Honey, don't you worry about delivering those two arrangements. We'll just have Arnie do it when he gets back. I'll wait for him. You just scoot on home now." They turned around to go back into the store, and Martha locked the front door.

"Martha, it's no problem…those addresses are right on my way, and it won't take but an extra ten minutes at the most. The storm isn't going to get here that soon."

"Well, I'd just feel better if you got on home. Let's go ahead and close up early. I'll call Anie and see where he is."

Katie swept the floor while Martha called him. Arnie still had three orders to deliver and was about thirty minutes from the shop, so it would be awhile before he could make it back.

"Martha, I'll take them," Katie insisted, picking up the first arrangement and taking it out the back to her car. Martha could see it was useless to argue with her, and she figured if Katie was going to do it, then she better get going as soon as possible. She carried the second order out to Katie's car, and made sure Katie had the addresses and cards, and said, "Hurry then, and I want you to call me on my cell phone when you get home, okay? Thanks for doing this, Katie. I'll call Arnie and let him know he doesn't need to come back."

"Sure, Martha, you're heading home soon, too, I hope?"

"Yes, just as soon as I get everything shut down and locked up here. Now quit worrying about me and go!"

Martha waved as Katie pulled out of the back lot. She sniffed the air, noticing how different it smelled and how still it was. After another quick glance at the sky, she hurried back into the shop to finish closing.

Katie pulled onto the main road, and then glanced at the time on the dash clock. Five-thirty. She hoped Bob had been able to get out of the office already and could beat the storm home. This one looked like it could be a bad one. The radio station interrupted the song that was playing with a series of beeps and a weather update. "We interrupt this program with a special weather bulletin. Tornados have been spotted in some rural areas west of the metro area and are reported to be moving in this direction. If a tornado is spotted, act quickly and move to a place of safety inside a sturdy structure, such as a basement or small interior room. If you are in a car and see a tornado, take shelter in a nearby building, if one is available, or take cover in a low-lying area, such as a ditch. Do not, we repeat, do not try to outrun a tornado in your car."

Katie shivered and looked up at the still mostly sunny sky. She picked up her cell to see if she could reach Bob. He picked up on the second ring, "Hi hon, how ya doing?"

"I'm fine, how are you? Where are you?"

"I just left work, and I'm on the way home. Traffic is a mess. People are driving like maniacs trying to beat the storm."

"Then I guess you've heard the weather reports?"

"Yeah, it looks really weird out, doesn't it? Where are you?"

"I'm in the car headed home too. Actually I have a couple of deliveries to make first, but they're close to home."

"Katie, maybe you should just go straight home."

"It'll be okay, Bob. It's not that bad out yet. It's still mostly sunny here. I have time."

"Katie, are you crazy? Please, just get home!" Bob was further west where the clouds had already darkened the sky.

"Okay, okay," she said, but she still thought she'd have time to deliver the orders. She knew they'd wilt and be ruined if she didn't get them delivered soon. He didn't need to know. She'd still be home long before him, since she was already close to the first delivery address.

"Call me when you get home, hon?"

"Yeah, I will. Okay, talk to you soon."

"Okay. Love you."

"Love you, too."

She made the first delivery quickly and returned to the car to check the second address. As she drove, she noticed dark clouds moving in fast and the sky changing colors. The wind had picked up too, and seemed to be swirling in many directions. It wasn't too much further though, and she turned the corner, rolling down the street slowly to check the house numbers against the paper she held in her hand. She spotted the address, pulled along the curb in front of the house, and shut off the ignition.

She stepped out of the car with a quick look at the sky, and went to the hatchback to pick up the arrangement from its carrier, making sure the card was attached. She locked the car since she'd left her purse inside, and carried the flowers up the driveway. The fast-moving dark clouds now covered more than half the sky, and the air felt charged with energy. She shifted the flowers in her arms to free her hand to ring the doorbell and waited. A girl who appeared to be around twelve or thirteen opened the door.

"Yes?" the girl said, peeking around the partially opened door. Katie smiled.

"Hi. I have some flowers here for Carolyn Stockton. Is she here?"

"That's my mom. No, she's not home yet." A gust of wind whipped around the corner of the house, seemingly out of nowhere, almost sweeping the flowers out of Katie's hands. She gripped the vase more firmly.

"Well, would you like to take these for her?" She raised her voice to compete with the wind, as it picked up again, now combined with a low roar. The girl didn't answer, but stared at the sky behind her, so Katie turned to look, protecting the vase from the wind with her body. The sky was now a greenish-black, like the color of a bad bruise, and the wind was throwing dust around in circles out in the street around her car. Katie turned back to the girl, hoping to hand the flowers to her so she could make a dash for the car. But the girl was frozen in place, her eyes wide and her jaw open. As Katie pushed the flowers toward her, she screamed, and Katie turned around again to see a funnel cloud snaking its way through the sky. It wasn't on the ground, just weaving back and forth haphazardly in the sky. Katie pushed the girl into the house and followed her inside with the flowers, shutting the door behind them.

"Are your parents here?" she yelled over the wind.

"No, I'm by myself!"

"Do you have a basement?" The girl's eyes were huge, but she nodded. "Well, let's go! Show me where it is! Come on!" As the girl ran, she followed her across the living room, around the corner to the basement door, and down the stairs.

When Bob hung up with Katie, he glanced at the sky and switched the radio stations, trying to get an updated weather report. He was glad she was on her way home, and hopefully she'd be there before the storm got worse. He could see the edge of a storm almost directly overhead. To the east, the sky was still clear blue, but the dark, menacing clouds were quickly catching up and overtaking it. His cube in the office building wasn't close to any windows, so he'd had no idea of the impending storm until he walked out of the building. He finally found a station with a weather report, advising about the potential threat of tornados, and how some had been spotted in the air west of the city.

He turned on to the main boulevard and waited at a light before entering the interstate, noticing how impatient the other drivers seemed to be. People were cutting in front of each other just to get one car ahead--everyone trying to beat the storm home. 'Road rage waiting to happen,' he thought. He told himself to just relax and take it easy. Everything was going to be fine if everybody just relaxed. When the light turned green, he followed the stream of cars up the entrance ramp to the interstate. Traffic was crawling along, and there wasn't anything he could do to speed it up, so he switched the radio to one of his favorite CD's and sat back to wait it out.

CHAPTER SIXTEEN

Eric paced in front of the gate, checked his watch and looked over at the window, holding his cell phone to his ear. He walked over to check the flight chart again and sighed, noticing that more "delayed" and "cancelled" notices appeared next to flights. The good news was that his flight was still listed as on time, but that could change at any time. Out the window he saw the plane arriving at his gate then, and breathed a sigh of relief. At least they had a plane. The weather in the Midwest was wreaking havoc on flights throughout the rest of the country. He sure hoped he could get out of Seattle on time and make it home for Andrew's game tonight. It had been a long week (weren't they all?), and he would hate it if he couldn't even make it in time for the game. He tried Carolyn's cell again, and finally she picked up.

"Hi, Eric," she said brightly.

"Hey, how ya doin'?"

"I'm fine, where are you?"

"I'm at the airport, waiting to board my flight. So far they have us listed as leaving on time, but a lot of flights are delayed and cancelled, so I don't know. Where are you?" He watched people filing off the plane that had just arrived at his gate.

"At work. I sure hope you make it. Andrew's really hoping you can make it to his game tonight. He's going to start."

"I know, I know. I hope I make it too. But there's nothing I can do about it." Didn't she think he was doing the best he could?

"I know. I'm sorry, I just want you to be here."

"How's the weather at home?" He hoped there wouldn't be any delays on the other end.

"It's nice right now, but there've been talking about tornado watches all day, so I guess it could get bad."

"From the news reports I've seen here, it looks like there's a big storm front crossing the middle of the country. Hold on a minute, they're making an announcement." He listened to gate agent along with everyone else and they all groaned when they heard her say their flight would be delayed, that they needed to wait for clearance from air traffic because of the threatening weather conditions. "Sheesh," he said into the phone.

"What? What'd they say?"

He ran his hand through his hair, pacing. "There's a weather delay for our flight."

"How long?"

"An hour. Hopefully we'll get out of here then."

"Can you call me when you board, so I'll know? Maybe you can still make it to the game."

"Yeah, all right. Talk to you later." They disconnected and he found a seat in the gate area. He knew Carolyn would be disappointed if he didn't make it in time, but what could he do? He wished he could see more of Andrew's games, but his work always demanded so much of him. It wasn't like he chose to do all this travelling, it was just an expected part of the job. Somebody had to put food on the table, didn't she realize that? Sometimes he just felt like a meal ticket for the family. Work hard, pay the bills, and watch them have all the fun. They acted like his business trips were all fun and games, with golf rounds, luxury hotels, and fancy dinners. But sometimes he got tired of it all--sleeping in strange hotels, being politically correct every waking moment. Even the golf wasn't as much fun as it should have been. He had to be careful not to play too well. He couldn't upstage the client, and yet he couldn't let them know he wasn't trying hard either.

He drew in a deep breath and sat back in his seat, watching the monitor with the national weather report. The radar showed a huge vertical red line cutting through the mid-section of the country, just to the west of Kansas City. He wondered if Carolyn had received the flowers he'd ordered for her, since she hadn't mentioned them during their conversation. He hoped they were delivered before he got home tonight. He'd ordered them on a whim…just something to surprise her since he'd been traveling the last several weeks in a row. Couldn't something just work out okay for once?

Later that afternoon, Carolyn was sorting through a stack of donated books when Eric called again to say that his flight had been delayed another hour. It would be close, but if he drove directly from the airport to the sports complex, he might still catch some of Andrew's game--that is, if the game was even played. Tornado watches alone weren't enough to cancel baseball games in the Midwest, but the weather was worsening, and lightning or a tornado warning would postpone or cancel the game.

Her boss walked over. "Hey, Carolyn, do you want to leave early today to beat the storm?"

"Thanks, Kay, I think I will, if you don't mind. I'll just finish this stack and go."

"No problem. See you tomorrow then. Be careful. It's looking kind of bad out there," Kay said, as they both looked out the window at the darkening sky.

"Okay, thanks." Thank goodness she had an understanding boss, who would let her leave early for her kids' activities, and even encouraged her to leave early on days like today. She finished checking through the books in her stack and went to get her purse out of her locker in the break room. "You heading out?" Jane asked, also getting her purse.

"Yeah, are you?"

"Yeah."

They walked outside together. "I'm so glad it's finally Friday."

"Me too," Carolyn agreed.

"Do you have plans for the weekend?"

"Andrew has a baseball game tonight, so we're going to that. Eric is flying in from out of town right now, so I hope he makes it in time. I'm working tomorrow. How 'bout you?"

"No, I'm off tomorrow, so I'm taking my mom shopping and out to eat for her birthday."

As they walked to their cars, they both looked up at the sky. "That doesn't look good, does it?" Jane said.

"No, it sure doesn't. I'm glad we could leave early. Be careful," Carolyn said, as she opened her car door.

"Yeah, you too. Bye!"

As Carolyn started her car, she could see dark clouds quickly enveloping the sky. The air had been still when she and Jane first walked outside, but now a sudden gust of wind blew against the side of the car. She was anxious get home since she knew Annie was there by herself. She'd talked to her a little while ago and she was doing fine, but the storm seemed to be moving in fast. She pulled out of the parking lot, keeping one eye on the sky and another on the road. At the first stoplight, she got her cell out of her purse and was about to call Annie when the radio came on with an announcement. She turned up the volume.

"…very dangerous storm. We urge everyone to take cover immediately. Tornados have already been spotted in the sky in our area, though none have touched down. We repeat, we are now under a tornado warning…"

She looked up again. She didn't see any tornados, but the sky was now a peculiar shade of green and the wind was bending the tree leaves so that only the lighter color on the back sides showed. She wondered for a brief second if she should turn around and go back to the library, but it didn't have a basement and Annie was home by herself, hopefully in their basement. She called her home and got the machine.

"Annie, it's Mom. Are you there? Hello?" She waited for her to pick up, but heard nothing. "Are you okay, honey? Annie?" Still nothing. "Annie, if you can hear this, you need to get down in the basement, okay? I hope you're already down there. Call me back when you get this message, okay? I'm on my way home and I'll be there soon. I love you, honey."

She disconnected and swore. Damn Eric for not getting home when he was supposed to. Damn the airlines. Damn the weather. Then she turned her anger on herself, wondering how she'd let this situation happen. Why hadn't she been watching the weather closer while she'd been at work? She should have left earlier and been home by now.

Everyone else on the road seemed to be in just as much of a hurry to get home as she was. No one wanted to get caught out in the storm, especially if it started to hail. People were driving erratically, running red lights, cutting each other off to get a little further ahead. Carolyn tried not to get caught up in the frenzy. The last thing she needed was to have an accident. She muttered, more to herself than anything, "Oh God, just get me home in one piece. God, let Annie be safe."

She decided to try Andrew's cell. Maybe he'd pick up. The team would probably be practicing or reviewing strategy before their game tonight. She punched his speed dial number and waited.

"Hey Mom," he answered. What a relief.

"Andrew, are you okay?"

"Yeah, I'm fine."

"Where are you?"

"I'm in the locker room with the team. We were outside taking batting practice and it started thundering, so Coach made us come in. We still don't know yet if we're gonna get to play."

Thank God he was safe. "Andrew, have you heard we're under a tornado warning? Does the coach know about it?"

"I don't know. Maybe that's why we're in here."

"Well, see if you can all go to the lower level of the school." She knew the locker room was on the ground level.

"Oh, Mom, quit worrying. We'll be fine."

"Andrew! I'm serious. This is a bad storm. Tell him to get everyone to the lower level! Let me talk to him!"

"Yeah, okay, Mom. I'll tell him. Well, I gotta go. He's trying to talk to us now. Bye."

"Love you," she tried to say, but he'd already disconnected. She swore again, knowing he probably wouldn't say anything to the coach about moving to the lower level of the school. Hopefully the coach had enough sense to do it anyway. She thought about calling the school's main office, but she couldn't remember the number and she'd have to look it up in her address book, and she needed to keep her eyes on the road. People were still driving like maniacs, and she'd better concentrate on her driving.

She wasn't far from home, when she felt the gust of wind followed by a roar. It sounded like a train, but there was no train crossing nearby. The ferocity of it was horrifying, and she turned around to see where it was coming from. There it was, like a black monster, spinning in the sky, throwing debris around in circles. She screamed, "Oh my God!" as a huge piece of metal flew straight toward her car. She ducked and covered her head as she slammed on the brakes, and heard the screeching of metal on metal and glass breaking. Then everything went black.

CHAPTER SEVENTEEN

When Ralph and Rick finished unpacking and storing the last of the supplies at the church, Rick thanked him again and went to his office to lock up. Sandy, his secretary, had stopped by earlier to ask if she could leave early because of the storm, and Rick had assured her that would be fine. Rick locked the doors behind them, and they walked outside to his car. The air was heavy with humidity and the clouds were an odd assortment of colors, some puffy white, some dark, and some light blue, all mixing around together.

Living on the streets had turned Ralph into a pretty good weather forecaster, and he could tell a storm was imminent. He hoped there would be room for him at the shelter, because this looked like the kind of storm that brought in a lot of people from the streets. Only the hard-core would ride one of these babies out and refuse to take shelter somewhere.

They got in the car, and Rick was turning out of the church parking lot when his cell phone rang. He picked it up and saw that it was Sarah.

"Hi honey, how are you?"

"Hi, I'm fine, where are you?"

"Just leaving the church. I've got one quick errand to run, and then I'll be home."

"I guess you've seen the weather then? It's looking bad, Rick. There's a tornado warning. Can't you just skip the errand and come straight home?"

"No, I need to drop someone off first. But I'll be home right after that."

"Well, hurry. I'm in the basement, and I've got the TV on down here. They've already spotted some tornados in the sky."

"Okay, hon, I'll be home as soon as I can."

They disconnected, and both men looked up at the sky as they drove. It wasn't far to the shelter, but Rick was glad Ralph wasn't out walking in this. He felt bad for keeping him at the church so long, and that the weather had gotten so bad without him even noticing. The sky looked like it could open up at any minute and start pouring. A few large raindrops plopped on the windshield and the wind picked up.

"Here it...," but Rick was interrupted by the screaming of a tornado siren outside. He picked up the pace, and neither man spoke as they continued to the shelter. The rain came hard then, accompanied by a roaring wind. They approached an intersection and waited for a light to change so they could turn on to the street of the shelter. The car rocked with the wind as they waited, almost as if it might become airborne any second. Ralph pointed at something in the sky on his side, and yelled over the wind, "Look!"

Rick leaned over to see where he was pointing. "Oh, my God!"

A funnel cloud in the sky was bearing down. The light turned green and Rick gunned the accelerator, racing down the street and into the parking lot of the shelter. Ralph jumped out and ran for the shelter, but when he turned around, he saw that Rick wasn't following. He yelled, "Rick! Come on!" Rick was still in the car, staring at the tornado in the sky above them. Ralph ran back to the car, opened Rick's door and yelled, "Come on! Get out!" Finally Rick mobilized into action, turned off the car, grabbed the keys, and followed Ralph into the shelter.

They saw no one else inside and Ralph ran across the room, remembering the stairs that led to the shelter's basement. He yelled back at Rick, "This way!" As Rick followed him down the stairs, they heard the roar above them, which covered everything else, the screams of the people in the basement, the crashing and shattering of things above. They huddled on the floor next to the others already there, closed their eyes and covered the back of their heads with their hands. Rick couldn't help but think about Sarah and whether he should have gone home to her first. He prayed to God she was safe.

Eric crunched the last of the ice in his cup, as the flight attendant made her way down the aisle. He threw his cup into the sack she held out, and listened as the captain made an announcement.

"Folks, this is Captain Jim here and I have some good news and some bad news. The good news is we're gonna get you safely to Kansas City today." Several passengers groaned. If that was the good news, what was the bad news? "The bad news is we're looking at another delay. Kansas City ATC has informed us there's some heavy weather at their field, and they've put us in a holding pattern until the weather clears. We're anticipating holding for about thirty minutes. So, folks, as soon as that weather clears down there, we'll get you safely on the ground. You can just sit back and relax, and we'll keep you updated. Sorry for any inconvenience this is causing you." He clicked off.

Eric grimaced and heard other passengers muttering. They knew it wouldn't help matters to get upset, but there was a general sense of frustration. He pulled the airline magazine out of the seat-back pocket and thumbed through it to distract himself. An article caught his eye. "God is in the Small Stuff." He scanned through it, recalling how their family used to go to church regularly. When had they stopped going? Why had they stopped? Maybe it was when Andrew's team had games every weekend, often on Sunday mornings. On the Sundays when they were home, they just wanted to sleep in and not go anywhere. He didn't believe you had to go to church to have a spiritual life, and the article said the same thing, that God was all around, even in the small things, like nature, birds singing, grass growing, clouds in the sky, and in how we treat each other in our daily lives. He couldn't agree more. But it had been a long time since he'd really thought about anything spiritual, and an even longer time since he and Carolyn had talked about that kind of stuff.

He remembered how they used to have long, deep conversations back when they were dating and first married. Now their conversations revolved around kids' activities, homework, sports, calendars, paying bills, and getting the chores and errands done. When had they stopped talking about anything meaningful? It was hard to even think of a way to do it. Maybe it would help to try going back to church sometime. He'd heard that the church they used to attend now had a rock band. That might appeal to the kids, and heck, even he would enjoy it if they were any good. He decided to try the idea out on Carolyn when he got back home and see what she thought. Yes, when he got back, he'd talk to Carolyn about this idea of going back to church. Maybe it was just what their family needed.

CHAPTER EIGHTEEN

Katie ran to follow the girl down the stairs and into the basement, still carrying the flowers with her. It was a bold thing to do in a stranger's house, but when they'd seen the funnel cloud in the air, she didn't think twice. She just ran. Now they were in a corner of the basement, furthest from the stairs, when Katie realized she was still holding the flowers, so she set them down on the floor next to her. The noise was almost unbearable. Katie looked over and saw that the girl was sobbing, and she yelled at her over the noise, "Get down! Put your hands over your head!" She crouched on the floor herself and the girl followed suit, both covering their heads with their hands.

The storm raged above them, and they could hear glass shattering above them. When it seemed like the noise couldn't possibly get any louder, it did. A loud rush, like a giant vacuum cleaner, passed overhead, and Katie put her hands over her ears. It felt like the air was being sucked out of her body. She realized the girl next to her was screaming, and though she felt like screaming too, she reached over to put her arm around her, pulling her close and then put her own hands over the girls' ears. How long could this go on? How much longer could they bear it? She closed her eyes, half praying, half crying, just hoping to survive. Then something even louder came through the noise of the storm. It sounded like a voice, yet how could anyone be heard over all this?

The words boomed, piercing through the storm. "Peace! Be still and know that I am God!" They seemed to come from within the room, yet there was no one there, and no normal voice could have been heard over the din anyway. Katie opened her eyes and saw nothing but the dark room around them. The girl stopped screaming. The storm began to diminish, and over the next few minutes, the noise slowly ebbed until it was completely quiet.

They looked at each other and around the room without speaking, still breathing heavily, waiting to see what would happen next. They looked up at the stairs. There were no windows in the basement, and it was dark except for a small amount of light coming from under the door at the top of the stairs. It was eerily quiet, and after their breathing had slowed and nothing else happened, Katie finally stood and whispered to the girl, "Are you okay?"

Her eyes were huge as she nodded. Katie felt as scared as the girl looked, but she tried not to show it. "Good." She looked up at the door above them, then back to the girl, realizing she didn't even know her name. "I'm Katie. What's your name?"

The girl started to speak, then choked and coughed. Finally she squeaked, "It's Annie."

"I think we're okay now, Annie. Are you sure you're all right?" She studied her more closely. Annie nodded again, still hunched down on the floor. "All right then. I'm gonna go up the stairs and see what's going on." There had been no more noise as they'd talked and it sounded like the storm had finally passed.

"No! Don't go!" Annie flung her arms around Katie's legs to keep her from leaving.

"It's okay," she said, bending down to hug her. She didn't want the girl to be scared, but she wanted to see what had happened above them. She didn't even have her purse or her cell phone, since she'd left them in the car. "Come on, why don't we go together then," she said, pulling Annie up to stand next to her.

They held their arms around each other as they walked to the bottom of the stairs. They ascended slowly, wondering with each step if the staircase would hold them. When they reached the top, Katie opened the door and peeked into the house first. Nothing was obviously out of place, as far as she could tell, so she opened the door more fully and they walked into the room together.

Katie still didn't see any signs of damage, but when she heard Annie's sharp intake of breath behind her, she turned to see what she was looking at. A large window in the living room had shattered and everything in that room was in disarray--the pictures on the wall were crooked and a few things were broken on the floor. They walked over to the room together, then through the other rooms, but didn't see any more damage. Katie looked through the open living room window and saw that her car was still on the street where she'd left it. It didn't appear to be damaged from what she could see. She turned back to Annie, who was staring at the broken glass on the floor, as if in a trance.

"Annie, it doesn't look too bad. Just a broken window. It'll be easy to fix. Don't worry." Annie still stared. "Why don't we try to get a hold of your parents? Do you know where to reach them?" Katie really wanted to just get in her car and go home, but she couldn't leave this girl alone.

Annie continued to stare, then finally she processed Katie's words and said, "I think my mom's at work. My dad was out of town. He was supposed to be back by now."

"Okay, let's try calling them. I'm sure they're worried and will want to know that you're okay." Katie walked into the kitchen, with Annie following, and found the phone on the kitchen wall. She picked it up and said, "What's your mom's number, hon?"

But when she held the phone to her ear, there was no dial tone. She clicked the receiver but still heard nothing. Annie's chin quivered, so Katie hung up the phone and walked over to hug her. "It's gonna be okay, we'll get a hold of her. Everything's gonna be okay." She pulled her away to look at her, setting both hands on her shoulders. "Listen, I'm gonna go out to my car and get my purse and my cell phone. Then we'll try calling your mother from my cell, okay?"

She waited for Annie to nod, then opened the front door and walked down the driveway. The sky was still cloudy, but cast a different light than before, a brighter shade of blue. The clouds still looked unsettled, but the wind had died down. Her car appeared to be undamaged, and she beeped the remote to unlock it, and opened the door to see her purse still sitting on the passenger seat where she'd left it. She picked it up, reached into the outside pocket for her phone, then closed the door and headed back to the house.

She wanted to call Bob, but first she'd try to reach this girl's mother, who must be frantic with worry. She took a quick glance around the neighborhood as she walked back up the driveway. There were tree limbs and trash in the street and yards, and she noticed a few other homes had broken windows too. But all in all, it didn't seem too bad. The roofs were still intact as far as she could see, and most of the damage looked fairly minor, considering what they'd just gone through.

Annie was standing on the front porch, looking around at the neighborhood. Katie checked her phone as she walked toward her. The screen looked normal and showed three bars, indicating good reception. She handed the phone to Annie and said, "Here, try calling your mom with this."

Annie took it from her and dialed her mom's work number. She waited but no one answered. "They must have closed. No one's answering," she said, handing the phone back to Katie.

"Does she have a cell?"

"Yeah, I'll try her on that." Annie dialed that number and waited. She heard her mom's voice mail message. She spoke into the phone, "Hi Mom, it's Annie. Just wanted to tell you I'm okay. Come home soon, okay? Bye." She handed the phone to Katie.

Katie felt a wave of protection for the girl sweep over her. "You said your dad was out of town?"

"Yeah, but he was supposed to be back today."

"Well, does he have a cell number you can try?"

"Okay," and Annie took the phone again and tried her dad's number. She got his voice mail and hung up without leaving a message. "I guess I could try my brother," she said. "He's probably at school, but he has a cell too." Katie nodded to her, so Annie dialed again.

"Hello?"

"Hey Andrew, it's me, Annie."

"Annie! Where are you? Are you all right?"

"Yeah, I'm fine. I'm at home. A big storm just came through here."

"Yeah, I know. It came through here too. We're all in the basement at school right now. Is Mom home with you?"

"No, I'm here alone. Well, actually there's someone here with me."

"Someone's there? Who?"

"A lady who was delivering flowers." She couldn't remember her name. What was it? Kathy?

"Some lady who delivers flowers is there with you? Where's Mom?"

"I don't know. Maybe she's still at work. I tried calling her there, but no one picked up."

"She called me a while ago and she was on her way home. She should have been there by now." Andrew was worried now.

"Well, she's not here."

"But some lady is there?"

"Yeah, but it's all right." Annie looked over at her. "She's nice. She went down in the basement with me when we saw the tornado."

"You saw a tornado? Oh my God! Did it hit our house?"

"I don't know. The living room window is broken, but I think that's all." Annie started to tear up. "It was so scary, Andrew."

"My God! Are you sure you're okay, Annie?"

"Yeah, I'm okay," she sniffed. "But can you come home?"

"Sure. You just stay put and hopefully Mom will be there soon. I'll get out of here as soon as I can and come home, okay?"

Annie sniffed again. "Okay."

"Annie, is that flower lady still there?"

"Yeah."

"Well, put her on the phone and let me talk to her."

"Okay." She handed the phone to Katie. "My brother wants to talk to you." Katie took the phone from her and said, "Hello, this is Katie Griffin."

"Uh, hello, this is Andrew. I'm Annie's brother. What are you doing there?"

Katie bristled, but realized he was just looking out for his little sister, so she said, "I was delivering flowers to Carolyn Stockton at this address, and when I was at the door, we saw a tornado in the sky, so your sister and I ran into her basement together. It was really nice of her to let me in the house. She's fine and it looks like your house is mostly okay too."

Andrew listened. The lady seemed nice, but he still felt funny about a stranger being at the house with his sister, without his parents there. "Are you sure Annie's okay?"

"Yes, she's fine. Just a little shaken."

"I'll be there as soon as I can. Tell her I'm on my way."

"Okay, I'll tell her." They hung up and Katie said, "Your brother says he's on his way home. I'm going to call my husband now and let him know where I am," and she dialed his number and waited.

She heard the phone ring a few times, and then it stopped and went dead. She looked at the screen which said, "Call failed." She tried again with the same result. Her phone still had three bars, so she wasn't sure why this was happening, but maybe the cell receptions weren't working everywhere. She tried his cell number and their home phone, with repeated failures. She knew he'd be worried if he got home and she wasn't there, and he couldn't reach her.

She looked back at Annie, whose eyes welled with tears as she stared at the broken glass in the front yard. Her heart went out to her, and she knew she couldn't leave her alone, no matter how much she wanted to get home herself. She'd wait until her brother arrived, which would hopefully be very soon.

"Hey, Annie, why don't we go wait inside and wait for your brother. I'm sure he'll be here soon," Katie said, putting an arm around her and guiding her back inside. Annie wiped her tears with her sleeve and followed her into the house. "I can stay here with you until your brother gets here, if you want me to."

Annie's eyes showed relief. "Yeah, okay, if you don't mind."

"I don't mind. Come on, let's just sit down and wait. We've been through a lot, haven't we?" She tried to smile at Annie. They sat down at the kitchen table, and then noticed how quiet it was in the house and that the power was out. None of the usual noises were there--clocks ticking, air conditioner running, refrigerator whirring.

"It's so still," Annie said, looking around.

"Yeah, I guess it is." They sat quietly.

Annie broke the silence. She looked over at Katie and whispered, "Did you hear it?"

Katie looked around. "Hear what?"

"That voice. In the storm. Did you hear it?"

Katie looked back at her. She wondered if she'd imagined it, or maybe it had just been the wind. But now she knew it wasn't in her head, it had been more than that. She nodded at Annie. "Yeah. You heard it too?"

Annie had been holding her breath and finally exhaled. "So it wasn't just me..."

"No, it wasn't just you."

"What did you hear it say?" Annie still wondered if they were talking about the same thing.

"I heard it say, 'Peace.' And then, 'Be still and know...'"

"...that I am God," Annie finished with her. "Is that what you heard too?" Katie nodded and neither spoke as they thought about it. "It's so weird," Annie finally said.

"Yeah..."

"I heard that voice once before." Annie couldn't believe she'd said it out loud, and to a perfect stranger no less.

Katie looked shocked. "You did?"

Annie was embarrassed. Maybe she shouldn't have told her. She looked away.

"No, really? You did? When did you hear it before?"

Annie decided to just tell her the truth. She'd probably never see this lady again, and it felt good to finally tell someone. "I heard it a couple weeks ago, on a Sunday night."

"Sunday night?" Katie repeated, sitting back in the chair.

Annie thought she didn't believe her, so she got up to walk away. Katie said quickly, "No, wait. I believe you. I really do."

"You do?" Something in Katie's voice made Annie stop and turn back to look at Katie. Was Katie just being a grown-up who said what she thought a kid wanted to hear, or was she being sincere?

Katie looked back at her and said quietly, "Yeah, I do." Then after a long pause, she added, "Because I heard it then, too."

CHAPTER NINETEEN

Ralph and Rick ran to the basement of the shelter, and when their eyes had adjusted to the darkness, they could see that about thirty other people were crouched on the floor too. The people made room for them to crouch alongside them, and they all listened to the roar overhead. It sounded and felt like a freight train passing right above them. A few people screamed, but they could barely be heard over the storm.

Rick was afraid, but instinct and habit took over and he began to pray. "God, help us. Keep us safe. Let this storm pass, God, please let it pass us by." He continued praying, even though he couldn't hear the sound of his own words. The storm grew even louder, though it seemed unimaginable that could be possible. Rick's head felt like it was about to explode from the pressure and the noise. He closed his eyes and cried out, "God help us!"

An even louder roar seemed to suck all the oxygen out of the air, and was immediately followed by a clearly audible word: "Peace!" Everyone gasped, just as the storm also began to ebb. Rick looked around the room and saw others doing the same, beginning to take their hands away from their heads and faces. No one seemed to know what to do, so they just waited, almost frozen in place.

Where had the word come from? Had someone spoken it? It hadn't sounded like a human voice, since no human voice could have been heard over the storm's ferocity. The storm continued to ebb and more words boomed into the room: "Be still and know that I am God." Rick whipped around, looking for the source of the voice, wanting to believe it was God but wondering if it could be true. A woman fainted on the floor across the room, and those around her tried to resuscitate her. Others mumbled prayers, not knowing what else to do. Except for a few movements and the mumblings, there was no other noise. The storm had come to an abrupt halt.

Rick saw Ryan and Shauna, shelter employees, not far from him, so he stood up to walk over to them. When they saw him coming, they stood up and looked around without speaking. The basement appeared to be undamaged, but it was hard to imagine what might have happened to the building above them. Was it even there?

Shauna started up the stairs, but Ryan stopped her. "Wait," he said, holding her arm. "Let's make sure the storm has completely passed." She stopped on the first stair, and looked back at Rick and Ryan.

"Did you hear that?" she whispered.

They nodded, looking at each other.

"Where'd it come from?"

The three continued to look at each other, but no one said anything. They each had an answer in their mind, but no one wanted to speak it out loud. Finally Rick turned to the others in the basement with them and called out, "Is everyone all right?" People answered affirmatively. He saw that the woman who had fainted earlier had regained consciousness, her head resting in another woman's lap who was fanning her. He didn't recognize either of them, but he asked, "Is she going to be okay?"

The woman replied, "Yeah, I think so." Shauna walked over to check on her and helped her sit up. She appeared a little dazed, but was able to respond to questions.

They waited a few minutes, making sure there the storm had passed, and finally Shauna said, "I'm going up to take a look." She started up the stairs, this time followed by Ryan and Rick. She opened the door at the top and cautiously looked out. "Oh, my God," she whispered, stepping into what was left of the room. They followed her and took in the horror in front of them. It was hard to tell there had even been a room above them. The roof was gone, along with most of the building's walls, stuff was everywhere, furniture upside down and splintered, barely recognizable. It was amazing there was even a floor left.

Others from the basement began to follow them up the stairs, and as Rick noticed them coming, he urged them to be careful. He wanted to make sure the stairs and floor would hold them, but if so, they should probably get out of the basement as soon as possible, in case it caved in at some point.

"Folks, come up carefully, and then step over away from the building as quickly as possible." One by one they ascended the stairs and gaped at the scene in front of them, carefully stepping around the debris to get out of the building, or whatever there was left of it. Rick, Shauna and Ryan led them several yards away, to any clear space of ground they found. Rick looked up at the sky and saw only a few clouds left, blue sky opening up behind them. It was hard to believe the horror of what had just happened by the look of this seemingly peaceful sky.

Ralph was one of the last to emerge from the basement, staying to see that each person made their way safely up. When he finally came up himself, he found Rick and said, "There are still a couple ladies down there that can't get up the stairs by themselves. Can you help me with them?"

They went down the stairs together and walked over to where the two women were sitting on the floor together.

"Hello ladies. You need some help?" Rick asked.

"I use a walker and I don't know where it is," one told him.

"All right, we'll try to find it, but right now we need to get you upstairs. Ralph and I are going to help you, okay?"

Each woman nodded. The two women were large, and it would take both men to help them up the stairs. They positioned themselves on each side of the first woman and helped her stand, supporting most of her weight for her. They walked her to the stairs, and then stood beside her so they could lift her one step at a time. Rick didn't recognize her as one of the "regulars," but he spoke to her as they walked. "We've got you, honey. Almost there."

Once they reached the top, they helped her outside. As they walked, she looked around and said, "My Lord." They helped her sit down away from the biggest debris piles and, after wiping the sweat from their brows and taking a deep breath, they headed back for the other woman. She was able to stand on her own, so Rick put an arm around her and Ralph helped support her from behind as they climbed the stairs. After helping her find a place to sit, they looked around, trying to find the first woman's walker, but they didn't see it anywhere. Rick pulled out his cell phone and dialed 911, but the call failed. He tried again, unsuccessfully, and then yelled out to the group, "Has anyone called 911? I can't get through."

Shauna shouted from a few yards away, "I've been trying and I can't get through either." A few others said they hadn't had any luck either.

"Well, keep trying," Rick said. "Everyone, keep trying. We have some people here who need help as soon as possible." An older man had fainted after walking up the stairs, and others were having trouble breathing. Rick scanned the area around the shelter and almost choked. Many buildings were damaged, cars were upside down and lying on lawns, debris was everywhere. But of all the buildings, it looked like the shelter had suffered the most. Only one outer wall was left, and it was hard to tell where the building had even been before.

Rick and Ralph stood side by side, looking around together in all directions. Where did one start? Everything was such a mess and there must be people all over who needed help.

The pilot clicked the mike on to update the passengers and everyone leaned forward to listen. "Good afternoon, folks, Captain Jim here again with an update for you. Well, uh..." A pause from the captain is seldom a good sign. "It looks like things down in Kansas City didn't progress as we were hoping, and we're gonna have to land in Wichita." A collective groan rose from the passengers. He continued, "Once we get fueled back up, we'll check on that weather

again and see if we can head on back to Kansas City. We'll be landing in about ten minutes, so the seat belt sign is back on, and I'm
gonna ask the flight attendants to prepare the cabin for landing."

Eric exhaled loudly and checked his watch again. There was no
way now he was going to make Andrew's game. Just his luck. Well,
he just hoped everyone back at home was safe. He'd try to call Carolyn from his cell as soon as they landed.

Bob watched the storm clouds roll in and get darker on his drive
home from work. When he couldn't reach Katie on her cell, he'd
called the shop and talked to Martha, who told him that Katie had
taken a couple of arrangements with her to deliver on her way home.
He'd thanked her for letting him know, but cursed when he hung
up, wondering why Katie couldn't have just gone straight home. He
tried her cell and their home phone again, unsuccessfully. He left
messages at both and waited for her to call back as the traffic plod-
ded along. Everyone was in a hurry to get home and out of the
storm before it hit, but no one was getting anywhere very fast. He
slammed his hand on the steering wheel. "Dammit, people, get a
move-on!" He knew he needed to calm down, so he turned on the
radio, hoping to distract himself.

The station was giving a traffic update. "Traffic is moving very
slowly throughout the metro this afternoon." Duh, no kidding.
"But there have been no accidents reported, so this is just due to the
increased volume of rush hour traffic. We are under a tornado warning, so please be careful out there if you're on the road. If you do
see a tornado while driving, try to stop and take shelter in a nearby
building, or leave your car and go to a low-lying area, such as a ditch.
We want you all to make it home safely, so please just take your time
and drive carefully. We sure don't need any accidents at this point,
which would just make things a lot worse."

A guy in the lane next to him honked at the car in front of him,
which he apparently thought was going too slow, and the guy in the
other car responded with an obscene gesture, which made the other
guy in turn, honk again. Tempers were flaring on the road, and Bob
breathed deeply to try to keep his own in check. "Just calm down,"

he said more to himself than anyone else. He turned to another station playing music, to take his mind off the commute.

When he finally rolled into his driveway, big fat raindrops had started to plop on the windshield. He pulled his car into the garage, got out and walked back out to the edge of the garage. He was disappointed to see that Katie's car wasn't there yet. He looked down the street, hoping to see her coming, and pulled his cell out of his pocket again to try her, just as the rain began to pelt down. The sky had grown very dark with a greenish cast, and he listened into the phone at her voice mail message again. He closed the phone to disconnect and was walking toward the door to the house when he heard the alarm. The tornado siren was on a pole at the end of their block and it screamed its warning through the neighborhood. He looked back out the garage at the sky and saw the wall cloud, with black clouds at the bottom trying to organize into a funnel cloud.

"Dammit!" he yelled, looking down the street again for her car. "Where are you, Katie?" Then he heard a loud humming that quickly built into a roar, louder even than the siren that was still screaming. When he looked up again, he saw it, the roping black clouds reaching down out of the sky, throwing things around in circles as it came closer to the ground and moved toward his street. He froze, unable to tear his eyes away from the thing that seemed to have a life force of its own. His reverie was broken by a tree limb that splintered and crashed into his yard, finally jolting him into action. He ran to the door and pushed the button to put the garage door down, slammed the door behind him, and ran to the basement.

CHAPTER TWENTY

"Ma'am, can you hear me? Ma'am?" Carolyn heard a far-away voice and she thought she was responding, but even though she tried to move her mouth, she didn't hear anything coming out. She hoped she wasn't dead. This felt like some kind of out-of-body experience. She couldn't feel or see anything and then she thought maybe her eyes were closed. She tried to open them, but for some strange reason it was requiring a lot of conscious effort. After trying for a while, she was finally able to focus, and she tried to figure out where she was. She saw a woman with dark hair looking back at her.

"Oh! You opened your eyes! That's good. Just stay with me, okay? I've called for an ambulance and it shouldn't be long," the woman was saying. An ambulance? What had happened? Who needed an ambulance? She tried to look around, but when she moved her head she felt a stabbing pain and she groaned. "Don't move. Don't move anything," the dark-headed woman said.

Carolyn closed her eyes against the pain throbbing in her head, and now she felt it in her leg too. She managed to ask, "Wha-at happened?"

The woman's hands closed over hers and she said, "There was a storm and you've had an accident, but you're gonna be fine. You just hang in there with me, okay?" Carolyn opened her eyes again as the woman spoke. Who was she? Was she an angel? She almost didn't seem real, but right now nothing seemed real except the pain which was getting worse. The woman continued to hold her hands and soothe her, telling her everything was going to be okay. She heard a siren and wondered if it was the ambulance the woman had mentioned.

The siren got louder then abruptly stopped, and Carolyn heard voices all around her. She heard the angel woman talking to someone else. Someone put something around her neck. She felt herself being lifted onto a hard board and now the pain was excruciating. They kept asking if she could hear them, but it just seemed like too much effort to respond, and she finally succumbed to the strong urge for sleep.

Robin stood on the street outside Jackie's and watched the ambulance drive away, hoping the woman would make it. She'd met some friends after work there for happy hour. They'd already had a few drinks when the storm hit. When the warning siren sounded, they'd crowded against a wall in the back, away from the front windows. The noise was horrendous as the storm passed through, but amazingly, the windows in the bar stayed intact.

When the storm finally relented and the alarm stopped, most people resumed their seats or pool games. But Robin was no longer in a partying mood. She'd picked up her purse, said good-bye to her friends, and stepped outside to leave. That's when she'd seen the car crashed into a parked car right across the street, and there was some sort of metal debris through its front windshield.

Then she'd seen someone slumped over the steering wheel. She didn't usually think of herself as the Good Samaritan type, but she was the only one outside and somebody needed to do something, so she ran over to the car. Was the person even alive? Robin had talked to the woman, who did seem alive, then called an ambulance, and now they'd taken her away, and she was left standing there, trying to decide what to do next.

She went back into Jackie's and saw her friends toasting each other with drinks to celebrate the fact that they'd survived the storm. Why hadn't any of them come outside and offered to help? Surely they'd seen the ambulance and tow truck outside. She walked back to the bathroom to rinse off the blood she'd gotten on her hands, and then went back outside, wondering if anyone else might be hurt, but she didn't see anyone. Drivers were navigating the street carefully, avoiding the glass left from the accident and the debris from the storm. She could see that a few windows were shattered in nearby buildings.

She walked to the lot where she'd parked her car. None of the cars looked damaged from the storm. She beeped hers, got in and sat down. She realized then that her knees were shaking, and it felt good to sit down. She still couldn't believe none of her friends had come outside to help. It annoyed her that sometimes all they seemed to care about was partying. It didn't even matter to them that someone had gotten hurt right outside of Jackie's.

Up until a couple of weeks ago, her life had been all about partying too. Everything else was just filling in the time between party-time. But there had to be more to life than this. She couldn't imagine spending the rest of her life working, sleeping, and partying in between. She knew that what she'd heard that Sunday night on the bathroom floor hadn't been her imagination. It had been real. Then there it was again, just a few minutes ago, the same voice, in the middle of the storm, this time with different words: "Peace...be still, and know that I am God." She had looked around at the others there, but their faces registered no acknowledgement of hearing it. How could they not have heard it? The noise had been deafening, but the words had boomed right through it.

When the storm ended, she even dared to ask a few of her friends if they'd heard it. They answered with blank stares. 'Hear what,' they'd asked. They looked at her like she was crazy. Was she just drunk? Delusional? Had she been the only one that heard it?

She wrapped her arms around the steering wheel of her car as the sat in the parking lot and rested her head on top of them. She prayed, "Oh God, what's going on? Was that really you? Are you real?" She waited a while and heard nothing. But she felt oddly comforted again, embraced by peace, the same kind of peace she'd felt that time on the bathroom floor. She wanted a different life, but she wasn't quite sure how to go about it getting it. She leaned back in her seat, closed her eyes and immersed herself in the serenity of the moment.

CHAPTER TWENTY-ONE

Andrew's coach wouldn't allow anyone to leave until he'd received word from school administration that the game was officially cancelled because of the storm. Once the worst of the storm had passed, he was finally notified, so he called the team together in the basement and said, "Listen up, gentlemen! I've just gotten official word that our game today has been cancelled, but it will be rescheduled for a later date." The boys grumbled and began packing up their bags. The coach raised his voice to get their attention again, "Before you leave, I want to remind you to be careful driving, for those of you who drove. I understand that the storm has done some major damage out there. You should plan to drive straight home and re-connect with your families there. Am I clear? Do not go out to the field, do not go out to eat, do not hang around the parking lot. Go directly home." He looked slowly at every boy in front of him to make sure he was perfectly clear, and then dismissed them. "All right. Go."

Andrew picked up his sports bag and backpack, and followed the other guys up the stairs, down the hall and into the school parking lot. He looked for his car, and it looked okay. He saw debris blowing around in the parking lot, but the clouds in the sky were dissipating.

"Hey Andrew, where ya headed?" his friend John yelled as he headed to his own car in the next row.

"Home. Why, where are you going?" He threw his bags in the back seat.

"Some of us are going to Pizza Boys. Wanna come?"

"No, I gotta get home and check on my sister. She's home by herself."

"Oh. Well, come on by later if you want."

"Yeah, okay," Andrew said as he got in the car.

Even though the coach was a control freak, most of the guys did what they wanted anyway, just to prove they could. It was a challenge to see what they could get away with. Most days, Andrew would have joined them at Pizza Boys, but today he wanted to check on Annie and make sure she was all right, especially since he still hadn't been able to reach their mom. He tried her cell again as he pulled out of the school parking lot. Still went to straight to voice mail. Some of the other guys weren't able to get cell signals in the school basement, so maybe her phone wasn't getting a signal either. It was weird, because she always had it with her and always picked up or called him right back when he called. Maybe her battery had gone dead.

He drove home, dodging stuff in the road, not even sure what most of it was or where it had come from. A lot of it looked like building materials. The cars in front of him were driving slowly, and he followed them around the bigger pieces of debris. Some traffic lights worked, but others blinked red and yellow, and others were out completely.

It took him longer than usual to get home, and when he pulled into the driveway, he saw a blue car parked in front of their house. The flower delivery lady? Thank God it was a woman, and not some strange man in the house inside with Annie. He jumped out of the car, leaving his bags, and walked quickly to the front door, which was standing open. He noticed the glass in the front yard from the shattered front window. He took the stairs in one leap and opened the screen door.

"Annie?" he called out, looking around for her.

"Yeah, Andrew, I'm back here," she answered, coming out from the kitchen in the back of the house, followed by a woman.

Andrew wasn't usually a hugger kind of guy, but he wrapped his arms around Annie without even thinking about it. Then he held her away from him, looking her over, and said, "Are you okay?"

"Yeah, I'm fine. Are you okay? I'm glad you're home."

"I'm fine. Is Mom here yet?" He asked, letting her go and looking around.

"No. I still don't know where she is. I haven't been able to reach her."

"Me either." He looked at the woman standing behind Annie.

Annie said, "This is Katie. She's been here with me."

Andrew offered his hand, which Katie shook. "Hi Katie, nice to meet you. I'm Andrew."

"Hi Andrew, nice to meet you, too."

"Thanks for being here with Annie. So you were delivering some flowers?"

"Yeah," Katie said, remembering that the flowers were still in the basement. "Oh! I think I left them downstairs. I took them with me when we ran down there to get away from the storm." She turned to get them.

"That's okay, we'll get 'em later," Andrew said. Even though the lady seemed nice enough, he just wanted her to leave.

"Katie's been really nice, Andrew. I'm so glad she was here with me," Annie said, smiling back at Katie.

"Yeah, well, that's nice," Andrew said. It was awkward, having this stranger in the house that Annie was suddenly chummy with. He turned to look into the living room and saw the glass from the shattered window. "What a mess. Are you sure you're okay?" He looked at Annie again.

She nodded, but Katie spoke up. "We went to the basement when we saw the tornado coming. We were fine down there, but when we came back upstairs, we saw that this window had blown out. So far, that looks like the worst of the damage to your house, but the power and phone lines are out."

"Did you guys check around upstairs yet?" he asked.

They looked up the stairs together. "No, we didn't think about it," Annie said.

"I'll go look." Andrew headed up the stairs.

Katie stayed downstairs with Annie while Andrew things upstairs. She thought she'd wait until he came back down and make sure everything was okay and then she'd leave. She really wanted to get home to Bob. She knew he'd be worried crazy if he got home and didn't find her there. They heard Andrew walking around upstairs.

Annie called up, "Is everything okay up there?" She started up the stairs herself, and was halfway up when he headed back down.

"Your room looks fine and mine looks fine, but a window shattered in Mom and Dad's room."

"Oh, no," Annie said, putting her hand over her mouth.

"It's not too bad," he tried to reassure her. "There's just some glass on the floor and a few things got blown around in there, but nothing we can't fix."

"Well, that's good," she said, looking up the stairs.

"I'm gonna try Mom again," Andrew said, pulling out his phone. They waited, but he closed the phone to hang up. "Still can't get her."

"What about your father?" Katie asked.

"Yeah, I'll try him," Andrew said, pushing buttons again. "He's supposed to be flying in from out of town today." They waited while he listened to the phone. He closed it. "Nope, he's not answering either."

Katie decided to speak up. "Look, if you guys are okay here until you get in touch with your parents, I think I'll go ahead and go. Unless you want me to stay, which I'd be happy to do..."

Andrew cut her off. "No, we're fine. You can go." Then he realized he didn't sound very grateful, so he added, "Hey, thanks again for being here with Annie and all."

"No problem. I'm glad I could help." She smiled at Annie, who walked over to hug her before she left.

"Thanks, Katie."

"Sure, honey, you take care of yourself now, okay?" Katie hugged her back, and turned to both of them before she left. "Just call me if you need anything, or if you want me to come back. I wrote my name and number on a piece of paper on the kitchen table."

"I'm sure we'll be fine, but thanks," Andrew said.

"Bye, then." Katie walked out with a last wave to Annie and got in her car, anxious to get back home. Andrew and Annie closed the front door and looked at the mess in the living room.

"I'll get a broom and dustpan and start cleaning up this glass," Andrew said. He handed her his cell phone. "Why don't you keep trying to get a hold of Mom."

"Okay," Annie said, dialing her number again.

Katie's drive home was tricky, with power outages and things strewn all over the roads, but it wasn't far, and when she drove up the street to her house, she saw Bob out in the front yard watching for her. Her eyes welled up with tears of gratitude that he was safe. She waved and he walked behind her as she pulled into the garage. She jumped out and embraced him. "Oh, Bob, thank God you're safe." He pulled her to him hard.

"Katie, I'm so glad you're home. Where have you been? I've been so worried about you. Are you okay?" He pulled her back to get a better look at her.

"I'm so sorry. I'm fine, really. I thought I could get those deliveries made before the storm."

"I'm just glad you're okay," he said, hugging her again with a kiss. "It was a bad storm," he said, as they walked together to the driveway to have a look around. For the first time, she noticed the damage in their neighborhood. A few houses had lost shingles from their roofs and she saw some broken windows, but all the houses were still standing. She looked up at her own house and didn't see any damage.

"Is the house okay?" she asked.

"As far as I can tell, but I haven't checked it over real well yet. God, it was awful."

"I know," she said.

"Where were you?" Bob asked.

"I was gonna leave early and come home, but we still had two deliveries left and they were both close to home, so I offered to take them since Arnie was running behind. I delivered the first one down on Lakeland Street, and was at the next house on Cherry when the storm hit."

"Oh my gosh, what did you do?"

"I was on the front porch waiting for someone to answer the door, and a girl came to the door, and while I was talking to her, she pointed to the sky and we both saw a tornado. She let me in and we ran down to their basement. Did you see it too?"

"Yeah, I did, right here in the driveway when I got home. I ran for the basement too. It was unbelievable."

"I know. It was so loud. I've never heard anything like it in my life. I mean, you'd think living in the Midwest, we've grown up with tornado warnings and all…but when you see one up close, it's just a whole different thing."

"Were you and the girl okay in the basement?" Bob asked.

"Yeah, she was pretty scared. I was scared too, but we just stayed down there until it was all over."

"Was anyone else there with you?"

"No, just the two of us. She was in the house alone. Bob, I felt so bad for her, that's why I couldn't just leave, even after it was over. She couldn't get in touch with either one of her parents. Finally her brother came home from the high school and he's there with her now."

"How old is she?"

"About twelve or thirteen, I'd guess. Her name is Annie. Really sweet girl."

"Was their house damaged?"

"There were a couple of broken windows, but I think that was all."

Bob hugged her to him again and they walked inside the house through the garage. They walked through each room of the house together, looking for signs of any damage but they didn't find any. It was beginning to get hot inside, since the power was off and the air conditioning wasn't running, so Katie opened some windows.

"I'm gonna walk around the outside of the house and check things out," Bob said. Katie went with him. They saw some minor damage--limbs down in the yard, patio chairs turned over, the table was on its side and a broken umbrella. They righted the chairs and table, and the two flower pots that had dumped over. As they picked up around their yard, they noticed others doing the same thing. They walked over to Dan, their next-door-neighbor.

"Are you guys okay?" Bob asked him.

"Yeah, we're okay, how about you?" Dan answered.

"We're fine. Katie was gone during the storm, but she just got home and was fine, thank goodness. Were you home when it hit?"

"Yeah, we all went to the basement. Unreal, wasn't it?" Dan said, running his hand through his hair.

"It sure was. Never seen anything like it in my life."

"The kids were all screaming in the basement, but the noise outside was even louder than they were."

"That must have been pretty scary for them." Dan and his wife Sue had two children, a two-year-old and a four-year-old.

"Yeah. Sue's still inside trying to calm 'em down. I thought I'd have a look around out here. Is your power on?"

"No, yours?" Bob asked.

"Nope. Phone's out too. I hope we get it back soon. You got any damage to your house?"

"Nothing that I've seen so far. You?"

"We've got one blown-out window in a room upstairs, but that's it as far as I can tell. The stuff out here may be messed up a little, but no biggie," Dan pointed to his patio furniture, which was also toppled.

"Well, I guess we got off lucky this time," Bob said, turning to go back into his yard.

"Yeah, you can say that again," Dan agreed.

Katie walked back into the house. She just wanted to sit down. Now that the adrenaline was wearing off, she began to shake. It was sinking in just how lucky they'd been. What if she hadn't been standing at Annie's front door when the tornado hit, and had been driving in her car instead? What if Bob hadn't made it home in time? The debris flying everywhere could have caused an accident or even killed one of them. Then she thought of poor Annie in the house all by herself. What would have happened if Katie hadn't been there with her? Would she have gone to the basement? She could have been hit by glass from the front window and been badly hurt. Katie sat in the chair holding her head in her hands, and thought about all these things and about how much worse it could have been.

When Bob came back inside, he saw her and walked over to her. "Katie, what's wrong? Are you okay?" She looked up at him and began to cry. He bent over next to the chair and put his arms around her. "What is it, honey?"

She looked at him through her tears. "It's just so scary to think what could have happened, Bob. It could have been so much worse. What if I had lost you?"

"Well, you didn't. I'm here and I'm fine," he soothed her, stroking her hair. He held her for a while, and then got up to get her a tissue.

She had to know something. She looked at him and he could tell she wanted to say something, so he said, "What? What is it?"

"Bob, did you hear anything in the storm?"

He stared back at her. "I thought maybe I'd imagined it," he said quietly. "Did you hear it too?"

"Yeah."

"The voice?"

"Yeah."

"What did you hear it say?" he asked her.

"The storm was so loud and scary, and then I heard it say, 'Peace. Be still...'"

"'...and know that I am God,'" he finished for her.

She nodded. "Yeah, that's what we heard too."

"We?"

"Annie and me, down in her basement."

"She heard it too?"

"Yeah, we talked about it afterwards."

"Wow."

"I know. I mean, the storm was terrible, and then when that happened, I could hardly believe it. And for her to hear it too."

"It was almost like God calmed the storm," Bob said. "You know, like in the Bible story when Jesus calmed the storm?"

"Yeah, that's just what I thought. But here's the other thing, Bob. When Annie and I were talking about it, she said she'd heard it once before."

"Are you kidding me?" he said, hardly believing this. "When did she hear it before?"

"The same night we did." They stared at each other. "And she heard the very same thing we did."

CHAPTER TWENTY-TWO

After Eric's plane had circled the skies over Kansas City for thirty minutes, they were finally diverted to Wichita, and now they were sitting on the tarmac waiting for the storm to pass. The captain told them they'd either be instructed to take off again, or they would de-plane at the gate at Wichita and be put on a later flight. While the plane was on the tarmac, cell phone use was permitted, so Eric had tried Carolyn several times but hadn't been able to reach her anywhere—work, cell or home. Based on the captain's updates, it sounded like the storm that had passed through Kansas City might have been a bad one. Other passengers around him had reached friends and family on their cell phones and he'd overheard people talking about a tornado touching down. He hoped his family was safe. He felt helpless not knowing anything.

He tried Andrew's cell.

Andrew answered quickly. "Hey, Dad!"

"Andrew! Are you okay? Where are you?"

"I'm home, and yeah, we're fine."

"Thank God. Mom and Annie are okay too?"

"Well, Annie is, but Mom's not home yet."

"Where is she?"

"I don't know. I haven't been able to reach her."

"That's weird, I haven't either." His concern grew. "But you guys are okay? I heard there might have been a tornado there."

"Yeah, Dad, we're fine. I think there was a tornado, maybe more than one. I was at school in the basement when the storm hit. Then the coach said our game was cancelled and I came straight home."

He realized that if Carolyn wasn't home, Annie must have been home alone. "Was Annie there by herself during the storm?"

"Yeah." Then he corrected himself. "Actually no, there was a lady here with her."

"A lady? What lady?"

"Some lady who was delivering flowers to the house." Ah, the flowers he'd ordered for Carolyn. He'd almost forgotten about that. "She came into the house with Annie when they saw the tornado and the sirens went off, and they went to the basement together."

"My gosh. Is Annie there? Can I talk to her?"

"Sure. I'll get her." He yelled away from the phone. "Annie! Dad's on the phone and he wants to talk to you!"

He heard him hand her the phone. What a relief to hear her voice. "Hi, Dad."

"Hi, honey. Andrew says you saw a tornado. Are you okay?"

"Yeah, I'm okay. It was kinda scary." She sniffed and he could tell she was trying to be brave in front of her brother.

"I'm sure it was, honey. I'm so glad you're okay though."

"Where are you, Daddy? When will you be home?"

When was the last time she'd called him Daddy? "Well, I'm sitting at the airport, but not at our airport. They diverted our flight to Wichita because of the weather, and now we have to wait and see what they're going to do next. Hopefully they'll get this flight back in the air once they see the storm has passed. But it may be a while yet before I can get home."

"Okay," she sniffed.

"Do you know where Mom is, Annie?"

"No. She should have been home by now."

Eric's stomach dropped. Where was Carolyn? She usually got off work early on Fridays when Andrew had a game. He couldn't imagine what had gone wrong and why she hadn't gotten in touch with any of them. His sense of unease and helplessness grew, but he didn't want to alarm Annie.

"I'm sure she's fine, honey, and she'll be home soon. Don't worry. Everything's gonna be fine."

"Okay, Daddy."

It killed him not to be there for his little girl. "Honey, you just sit tight now and I'll be there as soon as I can. Now, put Andrew back on the phone, okay? I love you, Annie."

"Okay, love you too, Daddy." His stomach flipped again. He heard her hand the phone back to Andrew.

"Yeah, Dad?" Andrew said.

Eric didn't want to scare him, but he also had a bad feeling about Carolyn not being home yet. "Andrew, is everything okay at the house?"

"Mostly. We've got a couple broken windows and the power's out."

"What about the phone? Is it working?"

"I don't know, let me check." He waited, then Andrew said, "No, it's dead."

Eric thought for a minute and realized that if Carolyn had been hurt, it would be difficult for anyone to notify them. He checked his watch. It was after six, well past the time Carolyn should have been home. He weighed in his mind whether to risk alarming Andrew or having him make some phone calls.

"Andrew, I need you to do something for me. I need you to look up some hospital phone numbers and call them to see if your mom might have been admitted."

"How am I supposed to do that, Dad? The internet's out since the power is out."

"The old-fashioned way, Andrew, use the phone book." Did kids these days even know how to use one?

"Where is it?"

He tried to be patient. "In the kitchen drawer, Andrew."

"Aw, Dad, I'm sure she's fine. She'll be home, don't worry."

He felt himself getting hot under the collar. Why couldn't Andrew just do what he was told? He took a deep breath and tried to steady his voice. "Andrew, I hope you're right, but we both know that she should have been home hours ago and I'm worried. Now will you just do this? I'd do it myself, but I don't know how much longer I'll be able to make calls on the plane here. If she's hurt in a hospital somewhere, they may not be able to reach anyone since the home phone is out."

"Okay, okay," Andrew gave in. "Which hospital do you want me to call?"

He gave him the names of the three Reyport hospitals, and said, "Now don't scare Annie when you make these calls, okay? Try not to get her upset, but we need to find your mom. After you make the calls, call me back on my cell and let me know what you find out."

"Okay, Dad," and Andrew hung up.

Eric sat back and inhaled deeply, followed by a long exhale. Thank God the kids were safe, but he wouldn't be able to rest easy until he knew where Carolyn was. He held his cell phone ready, knowing that Andrew wouldn't call back so soon, but anxious to hear what he learned. He looked at the screen and stared at the low battery indicator. Geez, why hadn't he charged his phone in the hotel room last night? He hoped it had enough juice for at least one more phone call.

CHAPTER TWENTY-THREE

Ralph helped the shelter employees pick up around the grounds, sorting through things that looked salvageable, and trying to clear a pathway to walk.

Rick wiped his brow as he walked over to him. "Hey, Ralph, let's just leave the rest. We can do more tomorrow. It's starting to get dark."

Ralph stood up and stretched his back. "Okay." He looked around, wondering where he'd go to spend the night. There was certainly no room in the inn, so to speak.

"Ralph, would you wanna help me with something? We've decided to open the church as a temporary shelter, and we need some volunteers to help set up beds and prepare food. You'd be welcome to stay there too if you wanted."

Ralph took off his hat and scratched his head with his other hand, wiping the sweat from his brow with his arm. He thought for a few seconds, and figured why not. It wasn't like he had a lot of options. Rick had gone out of his way to help him with the job at the church today. Had that really been today? It seemed like ages ago. But the people at the church had seemed nice enough. It was the least he could do to offer to help Rick in return for all he'd done for him.

"Yeah, sure, I guess I can do that," he answered Rick.

"Great," Rick said with a thankful smile. "We've only got a few volunteers lined up and we need more, so I appreciate your help. Let's finish up here and I'll take you over to the church with me."

Ralph admired Rick's uncanny ability to help other people, while at the same time making you feel that you were the one helping him out. How did he do that, exactly?

After getting in touch with Sarah and making sure she was okay, Rick had been on the phone with some of his staff. They'd been hesitant at first, not knowing whether the congregation would approve, but they'd finally agreed to use the church as a temporary shelter for anyone affected by the storm, including the homeless people whose regular shelter had been destroyed. They decided it was the kind of thing God called the church to do, to help those in need. On an impulse, Rick had asked Ralph to help him. It felt like the right thing to do at the time, and since Ralph knew a lot of the people from the streets, maybe he'd help them feel more comfortable about coming in.

Rick extended the offer to the "regulars" still hanging around the demolished shelter, though most had wandered off. Two men accepted his offer, and the four of them got into Rick's car and drove across town to the church.

Staff members had already determined that the church hadn't sustained any obvious damage, and that it could be used for shelter. As Rick drove through the neighborhood, they could see that other structures weren't so lucky. It almost seemed like the storm had selectively chosen specific buildings to destroy. One sat completely untouched while the one right next to it was practically demolished. Rick drove carefully around the stuff still littering the roads.

When they reached the church, they got out of the car and followed Rick toward the fellowship hall entrance. The hall had its own entrance on one side of the building, which would be convenient for people coming in to seek help. Someone had already put a sign in the parking lot, with an arrow pointing people to that entrance. Rick saw two men in the parking lot unloading cots from the back of a truck.

"Hey, you found some beds!" he said.

"Yeah, the Salvation Army is loaning them to us," one of the men replied.

"That's great! Go ahead and set them up in the fellowship hall." He turned to Ralph and the other men. "Come on, and we'll see what we can do to help."

They went inside and he saw Sarah with three other women in the church kitchen, and the aroma of their good cooking wafted through the room. About a dozen people were already seated at tables in the hall, some visiting with each other, and others staring straight ahead with glazed-over eyes.

He walked over to the kitchen and embraced Sarah. He kissed her and said, "Hi honey, I'm so glad you're okay. Thanks for coming over here to help out."

"Sure," she said with a smile. "I'm glad you were okay too. It was awful."

After hugging Sarah again, she returned to her work in the kitchen and he walked back to Ralph. He was standing by the two men who'd ridden with them, who had taken seats at the table.

"We need to move some of these tables so we can clear a place for the beds coming in. We'll put the beds on one side of the room and the tables and chairs on the other." The room was fairly large, about a hundred feet by eighty feet, but they'd need to use it for both sleeping and eating. The people seated at the tables got up to help move them to one side of the room.

Over the next hour, more people came in looking for a place to spend the night, and by the time the meal was ready, there were about twenty-five hungry people ready to eat. Rick was heartened by the church members' reactions—many had responded by volunteering themselves, other had brought in towels, bedding, toiletries, drinks, food and other supplies. Maybe these people weren't as wrapped up in themselves as he'd initially thought. He tried to forget those who'd resisted the idea of setting up the shelter in the church, saying it was too big of a liability risk. He was just glad that most hadn't agreed with them, and that they'd gone ahead and done this thing to help their community.

When the meal was ready, he made an announcement. "Friends, can I have your attention for a minute?" He waited for everyone to get quiet, looking around, amazed at all that had been accomplished in such a short time. Everyone looked at him expectantly.

"What a blessing it is to have you all here with us tonight. It fills my heart, and I want to thank everyone who came to help, and all of you who have joined us in your time of need. We are truly one in the spirit, and it's amazing what God's love can do in our community when we work together." He cleared his throat to keep his emotions in check. "Let's thank the Lord together before we eat." He bowed his head and others followed.

"Oh merciful and loving Father, we come to you tonight with hearts that are heavy but hearts that are also blessed. We thank you for the safety of these people tonight, God, and we ask you to extend your mercy on those who are struggling and suffering from the effects of the storm today. We know that only you are the one who can make things right and work something good through the devastation we've seen, and we're just gonna trust you to do that, God. We know that you are God..." Rick choked on these last words, thinking about what he'd heard during the storm. "God, bless this food that we're about to eat, and give us strength and patience for the days to come, and most of all, help us to keep loving each other through your spirit."

When he finished, they all said, "Amen," and he asked the people seated at the tables to remain there, and that the church members would serve them there. He decided that after all they'd been through, the last thing they should have to do was wait in line to eat. Rick didn't know if they'd have enough for everyone, or where they were going to get the next meal, or how long they could keep this shelter going, but he would leave it in God's hands and just take things one step at a time.

CHAPTER TWENTY-FOUR

"Mom?" Annie peeked into the hospital room before entering. She saw her dad standing next to the bed, so this must be the right room. He waved her in, and Andrew followed her inside. "Is she awake?" she whispered to her dad when she saw that her mother's eyes were closed.

He walked over to hug her and then Andrew. "Yes, she's just resting."

Carolyn's eyes fluttered and then opened as she tried to focus. Eric touched her lightly on the head and said, "Hey honey, the kids are here." Her eyes darted back and forth trying to find them. They walked closer to the bed.

"Hi, Mom," Annie said. Andrew walked around to the opposite side of the bed. Andrew said hi to her too, and her eyes registered both of them and she tried to respond.

"An..."

"Take it easy, honey, don't try to talk," Eric said. He turned to his children. "She just got out of surgery a little while ago, so she's still groggy. They aren't going to let us stay very long, but we'll come back later."

Annie's eyes began to fill as she saw her mother's leg in traction and the bandage around her head. "Are you okay, Mom?" she asked.

Carolyn could hear Annie speaking from a long way off, and she wanted to say yes, she was going to be fine, but for some reason, the words just weren't coming out of her mouth. She could see the fear and concern on the faces of her family and she didn't want them to worry.

"She's gonna be fine, Annie," Eric said. "The doctors say the surgery went well, and it's just going to take some time for her to recover now. Your mom's a fighter. She'll be okay."

"When will she get to come home, Dad?" Andrew finally said.

"They said in a few days, if her recovery goes well."

Annie couldn't contain her emotions any longer and she burst into tears. "Oh, Mom, I love you so much!" She wanted to hug her mother, but was afraid to disturb the tubing and wires all around her. Carolyn's eyes moistened and she wanted more than anything to comfort her daughter.

"She's gonna be okay, Annie, come on now, don't cry," Eric said to her, pulling her to him to hug her. He knew it was going to be hard for the kids to see her, and he'd tried to prepare them for how she would look, but it was still startling to see her face so swollen and bruised.

A nurse walked in. "Okay folks, visiting time is over, she needs her rest. Say good-bye and let your mom get some sleep now." Eric was thankful for the nurse's take-charge attitude. He wasn't sure how long they should stay and he wanted to be there for Carolyn, but he could tell she was trying to stay awake for them when she really needed to sleep. They said good-bye, and he followed his children out of the room. As they stepped into the hallway, Annie fell into her father's arms sobbing.

"There, there, she's gonna be okay, I promise. Come on now, there's no need for these tears." He hated to see her cry. Andrew stood off to the side, looking away from them down the hall, fighting his own emotions.

"But, Dad, she looks so bad!" Annie said, wiping her eyes. "Is she in pain?" Her chin quivered.

"No, honey, they've given her lots of pain medicine. She's in no pain."

A nurse walked by and offered her some tissues which she used to blow her nose. The three of them walked down the hall together. "How about we go home for a while and let her rest, and we'll come back later this afternoon?" Eric suggested.

"Are you sure it's okay to leave her?" Andrew asked. "What if she wakes up and wants to see us?"

"They want her to sleep for awhile, but we'll come back and see her again this afternoon and evening."

They continued down the hall to the elevator, and then walked outside.

When Andrew had called around to the hospitals the day before, he'd found the one that had admitted Carolyn, and called his dad back to let him know. Eric had spoken to a nurse at the hospital who said Carolyn was in ICU and was stable, and that they were going to keep her sedated until the next morning, when she would undergo surgery for her leg. Eric had called Andrew back with this news, and he'd insisted on driving over to the hospital to be with her. Andrew and Annie had stayed at the hospital until their dad's plan finally landed late that night, and then he told them to go home and get some sleep.

When Carolyn came out of surgery the next morning, he called them again and said they could come back to the hospital if they wanted to see her, which is what they'd done.

Eric and Andrew split up to go to their cars in the parking lot, Annie riding with her dad. As Eric drove home, he looked around the city and realized for the first time how bad the storm must have been. It had been dark when he'd arrived at the hospital, and though some traffic lights hadn't been working and some signs had blown over, he couldn't absorb the full impact of the aftermath until the light of day. Complete buildings stood in piles of rubble, great piles of debris stacked up on sides of the road, branches and trash strewn everywhere.

'*Good God,*' he thought, '*it looks like a war zone, and my wife was out driving in it.*' He was thankful that neither of his children had been hurt. When they turned onto Cherry, he gasped to see the damage to neighboring houses, some missing sections of their roofs, many with windows blown out. Andrew hadn't told him how bad the damage was when they'd talked on the phone. They'd only talked about Carolyn and their own house.

He followed Andrew's car into the driveway, both parking in the garage, since Carolyn's car wasn't there. He remembered that he needed to call the police department and find out about her car. But for now, he got his bag out of the trunk and carried his things inside the house, set them down, and then went into the living room where he saw a sheet hanging over the living room window.

"We hung that sheet up until we could get the window replaced," Andrew said.

"Good idea," he told them.

"I tried to sweep up the glass in the living room, but I might have missed some," Andrew said. "Now that the power's back on, I can get out the vacuum cleaner and sweep better."

"Okay, well, let's not go running around barefoot until then," he said with a smile. It looked like Andrew had done a pretty good job taking care of things.

"Dad, a window blew out of your room too, but that's the only other thing we saw," Annie told him.

"Well, I better go take a look then, huh." He walked up the stairs to their bedroom, followed by the kids. Andrew had told him about both of the broken windows on the phone. He saw a small blanket hanging over the gaping hole and some glass shards still in their bedroom. Some pictures had blown off the wall and there was glass on the floor from their broken panes. He could tell that the kids had tried to set things back in place, like the plant that had apparently dumped over, and some books, but he could tell it had been quite a mess. He turned to them. "So your rooms were okay, no other windows broke?"

"No, none that we've seen," Andrew answered.

"Hmm. Well, I guess I'll get a dustpan and work on some of this glass."

"Do you want me to help?" Annie offered.

"Sure, if you want. Why don't you get the dustpan and broom and a box out of the garage to sweep the glass into. I'll pick up in here a little." Annie went to find the things he'd asked for, and as he began picking up some of the books on the floor, he saw Carolyn's Bible lying open. He picked it up to see that she'd underlined a verse in the book of Psalms. "Be still and know that I am God." He was still looking at the page when Annie came back into the room with the dustpan, broom and a box.

"Got it, Dad." He turned to look at her. "What's that?" she asked.

"Mom's Bible," he said. "I was just reading something she underlined."

"Oh? What?"

He read the verse to her, and watched her drop the things in her hands--the dustpan, broom and box--all clattering on to the hardwood floor.

CHAPTER TWENTY-FIVE

Robin woke up on Saturday morning feeling strange, not with her usual headache, but with more of a heart-ache instead. She rolled over to check the clock next to her bed. It wasn't yet eight so she rolled back over to see if she could go back to sleep. There was nowhere she needed to be today, and she was exhausted from the events of the day before.

As she rested in bed with her eyes closed, it all came back. She'd left work early for two reasons, because of the storm and because it was Friday, and she'd met up with her friends at Jackie's. She had planned to wait out the storm there, and then head on home. When the tornado sirens had sounded, they'd all huddled in the back of the bar, away from the front windows. Then there was the voice again in the storm. Why hadn't the others heard it? It had been so surreal. The storm was howling like crazy and then the voice spoke and calmed the storm. She could still hear the words, *'Be still. Know that I am God.'* They seemed vaguely familiar; where had she heard them before?

Then there'd been the woman in the car, and her call to 911 for help. Had the woman survived? She didn't even know her name. She wished there was some way to find out about her, but she couldn't think of any. Her heart ached for the woman; she'd been in so much pain. She realized she wasn't going back to sleep, so she finally kicked off the covers, went into the kitchen, made coffee and sat down to watch TV. Maybe there would be a news report about the storm, and maybe even something about that woman.

She channel surfed until she found a local news station giving an update on the storm. It was worse than she'd thought. There was video footage of homes and businesses that had been completely leveled, cars and trucks flipped over, ambulances taking people to the hospital. She sat in shock, and felt thankful she'd been so lucky. The news station listed some locations that had been set up as temporary shelters for people who had been displaced from their homes, and she was surprised to see the name of Pastor Rick's church on the list. They were asking for volunteers to help at these shelters, and would welcome anyone that could come and help for any amount of time.

Robin recalled her conversation with Rick. He'd been a good listener, not at all patronizing, and he'd seemed to believe her about what she'd heard. She thought about what she'd planned to do today-- housework, errands, meet up with the gang again that night. Maybe she'd skip the housework and drop by the church and offer to help for a little while, before running her errands. Maybe it would settle the uneasy feeling she'd had since waking. She might even get an opportunity to talk to Rick about what she'd heard in the storm.

She showered, dressed and left the apartment about an hour later. She noticed a lot of downed trees and branches as she drove toward the church, but not a lot of structural damage. The more severe damage must have happened across town.

She drove into the church parking lot and saw a lot of cars on the opposite side of the main entrance she'd used before, so she parked near them. There were two pickup trucks backed up to the doors with men unloading them. She walked toward them and said she was there to volunteer.

"Good. We can use the help. Go on inside and find Rick or Cheryl." She nodded and entered the building, looking for Rick because she had no idea who Cheryl was. Someone inside saw her looking around and asked if she was there to help. She nodded and was directed toward the kitchen, where they needed help preparing the lunch meal.

She walked into the kitchen and said, "Hi, I'm here to help," to the two women working inside.

"Great! Come on in, we can sure use you. I'm Ann, and this is Cheryl. She's in charge of the volunteers."

"Hi," she said, extending her hand to Ann, then to Cheryl. "I'm Robin."

"Nice to meet you, Robin," Cheryl said. "Come on over here. We'll put you in charge of making the drinks. We need to mix up a batch of lemonade and make some iced tea." She showed her where everything was, and went to work with another volunteer.

Robin measured the lemonade mix into the stainless steel container and took it over to the sink to fill it with water. She was working on the iced tea when Pastor Rick popped into the kitchen.

"Ladies, what time do you think we'll be ready to serve lunch?" he asked them.

Ann checked her watch and said, "I think we can be ready in another half hour or so."

"Okay, I'll let everyone know." He noticed Robin by the sink and said, "We met recently, didn't we?"

"Yeah, I'm Robin," she said.

"Robin! That's right. I remember now," he said, pointing in the air. She wondered if he remembered the topic of their conversation. She could see the wheels turning in his head, but he gave nothing away. He turned to leave the kitchen, saying, "Okay, I'll let them know lunch will be ready in about a half hour."

About twenty-five people had spent the night in the church hall, and the few things they'd brought with them were scattered all around. Some of the children chased each other around the hall, their parents looking on, tired and emotionally spent. Everyone was happy to hear that lunch was coming soon, even though it was just sandwiches, salad and brownies. It was one less thing they had to worry about. Many had spent the morning on the phone with insurance adjusters and family members, trying to figure out what they were going to do next.

Cheryl asked Robin to take the drink containers to a table outside the kitchen, where people could serve themselves. Robin was carrying the iced tea container over to the table, and was so startled by someone she saw walking through the door that she almost dropped it on the floor. She almost didn't recognize him. It had been at least four years since she'd last seen him, and he'd aged a lot since then.

She jostled the tea, but managed to set it down, with her face turned away so he wouldn't see her. She kept her back to him as she walked back into the kitchen. So far it didn't seem like he'd seen her. She waited and watched from around the door to see where he was before venturing back out. He was looking around, and finally asked someone where Rick was. Someone pointed him in the direction of a side room.

She heard Rick say, "Hey, Ralph." It was him, then. The two men talked for a minute, but she couldn't hear what they were saying. Then Ralph went back outside, seeming to follow some instruction Rick had just given him. Was he here to help too? Or was he using the church as a shelter? How did he know Rick? She wouldn't put it past him to look for a free meal and lodging. She tried to find a way to slip out of the church unnoticed. Why had she come here anyway? It had seemed like a good idea at the time, but now she just wanted to get away as soon as possible.

"Robin, can you get the lemonade and the cups?" she heard Cheryl asking her. "Then we'll make another batch in these containers here. We may not have enough out there." Geez, the woman was a regular drill sergeant. Fine, she'd stay and make up the extra batches, then find a way to slip out.

She glanced around the corner to make sure Ralph was still gone, then took the lemonade out to the table and came back for the cups. While she mixed the next drink batch, another woman pointed to some baking pans and asked her to bring them over to the counter. She needed help pouring the brownie batter into them and getting them into the oven. Then someone asked her to put the plastic silver-ware out on the serving counter, and this continued until lunch was finally served.

She was finally about to slip out when she saw Ralph come back in through the door and sit down at a table. He looked like he'd been working hard, his shirt stained with perspiration and dirt. He took off his hat and wiped the sweat from his forehead with the sleeve of his shirt. She'd have to hide out in the kitchen where he couldn't see her until he left again.

Rick came back in to check with the women in the kitchen to find out if they were ready, which they were. The aroma of brownies baking drifted through the room, making everyone even hungrier.

"Okay, everyone, as we prepare to eat, why don't we all gather here and say a word of thanks together?"

Rick waited while parents rounded up children and the commotion calmed down. The women in the kitchen were still bustling around. "Ladies, will you come on out and join us for the blessing, then I promise you can get back to work, okay?" They took a break from their preparations, wiped their hands on towels and aprons, and walked out of the kitchen.

'*Crap,*' Robin thought, '*he's going to see me if I go out there.*' But she had no choice, since Rick was waiting on all of them to join the group. '*Fine then, if he sees me, he sees me. I'm not the one who has anything to hide.*'

As she stepped out with the other ladies, he seemed not to notice her. But then she saw the look of surprise on his face when it registered. She stared back at him across the room as Rick asked them to bow their heads and take the hand next to theirs. She bowed her head and held the hands on each side of her.

"Gracious Father, I thank you for all my brothers and sisters here, those who are taking shelter with us, those whose hands have helped provide this food today, and all those who are serving in other ways. God, I ask that you bless this meal and bless all of us as we try to do your will. Amen."

Everyone began to talk and the women returned to the kitchen, children ran to the front of the line, and Robin and Ralph stared at each other across the room. Finally Robin turned to go back into the kitchen to see what she could do to help. There was no reason to hide from him any more, he'd already seen her, so what difference did it make now? She would continue to help in whatever way she could.

CHAPTER TWENTY-SIX

Katie hadn't planned to work Saturday, but then Martha called to tell her that Arnie couldn't make it in because his house had been damaged from the storm. Bob wasn't keen on her leaving again, since he was still shaken by what had happened on Friday, but Katie didn't want to leave Martha in a lurch. She was thankful that she and Bob had gotten home safely, and that their house had withstood the storm. The least she could do was to help Martha with the deliveries since Arnie hadn't been so fortunate. Bob suggested that he go along with her and they could make the deliveries together. Katie figured if he'd feel better coming along, that was fine with her, and it really would be nice to have his company.

They walked into the shop together around noon, and Martha greeted them.

"Hey, you two, how nice to see you both!"

"Hi Martha. Bob said he'd ride along and help me with the deliveries today. So your house was okay from the storm yesterday?" Katie asked. Martha had told her on the phone that she hadn't had any damage.

"We were fortunate too, nothing major to deal with. Boy, it's sure a wreck around town though, isn't it?"

"Yeah, I couldn't believe it when I drove in this morning. Some people sure have it a lot rougher than we do," Martha said.

"How many orders do we have today?" Katie asked, walking behind the counter to sort through the paperwork.

"Six for delivery, and then I have that wedding for this afternoon."

"Oh my gosh, I forgot all about the wedding! Can you imagine trying to have a wedding after all that's happened?"

"I know. But the church was fine, so they're going ahead with it. I'm so glad we got the wedding flowers done yesterday. They're all in the cooler ready to go, and I can take care of those, but I need your help with the other deliveries. Thank you so much for coming in today to help me. I really appreciate it."

"Oh, it was no problem," Katie said. "Did Arnie have a lot of damage at his house?"

Martha nodded. "It sounded like it, from what he said on the phone this morning. A lot of missing shingles from the roof, some guttering that tore off, several broken windows—it sounded like a real mess."

"Was anyone home when it happened?"

"I think his wife and daughter were in the basement, from what he said. He was making a delivery on the other side of town when the storm came through, and he pulled into a parking lot and was okay. But he felt bad that he wasn't home with them. I'm sure it was scary."

Katie shuddered, imagining what Arnie's family was going through, and she was glad she'd come in so he could be at home today. She pulled out the six order forms and began checking the addresses and plotting her course on the city map. As she reviewed the route with Bob, a name caught her eye. Carolyn Stockton. But then Martha started talking to her and she forgot about it.

They put the finishing touches on the six arrangements, and Bob helped her load them into the racks in the back of the car. They waved good-bye to Martha, and drove to the first address. Their mood was somber as they drove, seeing the aftermath of the storm everywhere. Many buildings had lost all or parts of roofs, road signs were twisted and mangled, and the power was still out in many intersections. Most of the larger debris in the streets had been cleared, but it still took extra time to make the deliveries because so many intersections had become four-way stops, due to the power outages. They saw two different news crews along the way, filming some of the worst of the damage.

When they had finished the first four home deliveries, they stopped for a quick lunch and then headed to Reyport Community Hospital for the last two. They pulled into the parking lot a little after two and each carried a vase into the hospital.

Katie spoke with a woman at the reception desk, who looked up the names on her computer. She wrote down the two room numbers and tucked them next to the cards in each arrangement. She said she'd have someone deliver them up to the rooms.

Katie and Bob had turned to leave and were walking through the doors when something clicked in Katie's head. Carolyn Stockton. That was the name on the delivery she'd made yesterday in the storm. Annie's mom. She stopped abruptly and Bob ran into her from behind.

"Whoa," he said, "What's goin' on?"

"I just remembered. Carolyn Stockton is the lady I was delivering flowers to yesterday when the storm hit. But why would she be here?"

Bob didn't say anything.

"Oh my gosh, maybe she was hurt in the storm. Bob, why don't we take those flowers up to her room ourselves."

She turned around and he followed her back through the doors to the reception desk. Bob wondered if this was a good idea, but when Katie made up her mind, he usually just went along with her. "We'd like to go ahead and deliver those flowers to Carolyn Stockton, if that's all right with you," Katie said to the receptionist.

The woman checked the room number she'd written down. She's in ICU, so she can't have flowers in her room. But you can leave them at the nurse's station up there if you want to."

Katie nodded.

"She's in room 504. You can take those elevators right over there," pointing behind her.

Katie thanked her, picked up the arrangement and walked toward the elevator. When the doors opened, they stepped in and Bob pushed 5. Katie felt a little awkward about going to see this woman she'd never met, but she felt compelled to do it. She hoped the woman was going to be all right.

When the elevator opened at the fifth floor, they stepped out and checked the directions on the wall to room 504. As they walked down the hall, Katie saw a familiar face in the waiting room.

"Annie!" she said to a girl watching TV.

The girl looked up, at first not recognizing her. Then she said, "Oh, Katie! Hi!" Katie noticed Annie's brother sitting in a chair on the other side of the room. He gave a little wave.

"Andrew, right?" He nodded. She looked back at Bob. "This is Annie and Andrew, the two kids I told you about." Bob shook hands with Andrew and said hello to Annie. "This is my husband, Bob. We have flowers here for your mother, from her friends at the library."

"Oh, that's where she works," Annie said.

"She can't have them in her room, but we can leave them over here at the nurse's station."

Annie nodded and walked with Katie over to the counter, where Katie set them down and told the nurse. Then Katie turned back to ask Annie, "Is your mom okay?"

"Yeah, she had a wreck in her car yesterday during the storm, and she had to have surgery today. But they think she'll get to come home in a few days," Annie said.

"Oh, my gosh. Was it a bad accident?"

"Yeah, something flew through the air and busted her window when she was driving home. It knocked her out, but somebody called an ambulance. She's got a concussion and a broken leg."

"Oh my gosh, I'm so sorry," was all Katie could think to say.

They stood in the hall for a minute, and then Annie said, "Would you like to see her?"

"Oh, no, that's okay," Katie said.

"It's okay, come on," Annie said, walking toward her room.

Katie wasn't sure this was a good idea, but Annie kept heading in that direction, so she followed her. Bob stayed behind, talking with Andrew.

The lights were out and the blinds were closed, and Carolyn appeared to be asleep. The poor woman's face was swollen and bruised, her head was bandaged, and her leg was extended in a cast in front of her. She wished there was something she could do to help.

Katie had turned to leave, when a small sound came from Carolyn's direction. When she looked back at her, she saw her eyes fluttering. Annie walked closer to her.

"Mom?" Annie said, putting her hand on her mother's arm.

"An--," Carolyn tried to speak as she met Annie's eyes. Katie was standing near the door.

"You're gonna be fine, Mom."

"You…okay?" Carolyn squeaked.

She nodded. "I'm fine, Mom," Annie said.

"Storm…"

"Don't try to talk. We're all fine. Yes, there was a storm, but we're all okay."

"Andrew…Dad…." Carolyn couldn't seem to speak more than one word at a time.

"They're fine," Annie said. "Dad got home last night. He's right outside making some phone calls." Carolyn relaxed and closed her eyes. "You just rest, Mom. We'll be right here." Carolyn opened her eyes and saw Katie. She looked questioningly back at Annie.

Annie spoke up. "Mom, this is Katie, she was at our house yesterday delivering flowers when the storm came."

Carolyn tried to lift her hand to wave, but couldn't. Katie walked closer to her and said, "Hello, Mrs. Stockton. I'm so glad to see that you're going to be all right."

"House?" Carolyn eked.

"Yeah, she was with me yesterday, Mom, during the storm. She went to the basement with me," Annie explained.

"House…?"

"The house is fine, Mom. Just a couple broken windows, and Dad's getting those fixed today."

Carolyn relaxed again, and turned her eyes back to Katie. "Thank…," she said.

"Oh, it's okay, I'm just glad your daughter let me come to the basement with her so I could be safe. You've got a very special daughter here, Mrs. Stockton."

Carolyn tried to smile and closed her eyes. They knew she needed to rest, so they turned to go. As they walked into the hallway, Katie saw that Annie's eyes were filling with tears. Katie put an arm around her.

"Your mom's gonna be just fine," she said, squeezing her shoulder. She didn't know that for sure, but she wanted to comfort Annie. They walked back down the hall to the waiting room to find Andrew and Bob. As Annie wiped the tears from her eyes and Katie still had her arm around her, Eric came around the corner. He looked puzzled to see a stranger with his daughter.

Annie hugged him, and he looked at Katie, still trying to figure out if he knew her from somewhere. Katie could tell he was confused, so she introduced herself.

"Hello, I'm Katie Griffin, and this is my husband, Bob. We were here delivering flowers to your wife."

Eric shook their hands, introduced himself and thanked them, but he still wondered why she'd had her arm around his daughter. Annie cleared it up for him. "Dad, Katie's the one who was at the house with me yesterday."

"You mean during the storm?" Annie had told him about some flower delivery lady who had run into the basement with her when she'd seen the tornado.

"Yeah, she stayed with me."

"Oh. Well, I'm sure thankful to you, then," he turned back to Katie, smiling.

"It was no problem, I'm just glad Annie let me in to get out of the storm. It hit so fast, I couldn't believe it."

"Katie was great, Dad," Annie spoke up again.

"Well, thanks again," Eric said.

Katie said to Bob, "Well, we'd better be going. It was very nice to meet you, Mr. Stockton."

"Please. Call me Eric," he said.

"Okay, Eric, it was nice to meet you, and I sure hope your wife's recovery goes well. You have two very special kids here," she smiled at Annie and Andrew.

"Thank you. I agree," he smiled back.

CHAPTER TWENTY-SEVEN

Ralph finished his lunch, wiped his mouth with a napkin and deposited his trash in the container. He stepped outside to be alone and felt his eyes welling. When he'd first seen Robin, he couldn't help but stare. She'd changed so much since he'd last seen her. He could tell she wanted nothing to do with him, and he couldn't much blame her. When Michelle had kicked him out of the house four years ago, he hardly cared--even when she told him to stay completely out of their lives. The only thing he seemed to care about came from a bottle. He told himself he was just respecting her wishes when he didn't try to contact them, even missing Robin's high school graduation.

He knew he deserved everything that had happened; he only had himself to blame. But he never imagined how bad things could become. When Michelle had first told him to leave, he hoped it was just a temporary separation, so he took a short-term lease on an apartment. He'd planned to prove to her he could get his drinking under control. And he'd really believed that he could. But that wasn't how it happened.

Six months later he was drinking more than ever, and when Michelle filed for divorce, he just went along with it, giving her the house and most everything else. He'd secretly hoped this would make things easier later when they reconciled. What a fool he'd

been, thinking they might actually get back together. But when he got laid off from his job, the money disappeared quickly. He still couldn't believe he'd actually stooped to living on the streets, but he hadn't had much of a choice.

Rick came up behind him then, giving him a pat on the shoulder and Ralph quickly wiped his eyes on his sleeves. "Hey buddy, you okay?"

Ralph looked away. "Yeah," he said, clearing his throat and trying to suppress his emotions.

Rick stood beside him at the edge of the parking lot. "This has been quite a day, hasn't it? I think we got everyone fed for lunch, now we've just gotta get something planned for dinner."

"Yep," Ralph agreed.

Rick glanced over at him. "You sure you're okay?"

Ralph looked away and then back at Rick. "It's just…well, I saw someone today I hadn't seen in a long time."

"Oh? Who was that?" Rick asked.

"My daughter."

"Oh…"

"I haven't seen her in over four years. Not since her mother kicked me out."

"And you saw her here today?"

"Yeah, I think she was helping in the kitchen." Rick looked back toward the kitchen. "She's gone now. She made a pretty quick exit after she saw me."

"Oh."

"Yeah, I can't blame her for not wanting anything to do with me."

They stood in silence.

Finally Rick spoke. "Well, maybe that's not why she left. You never know."

"Oh, I know."

Rick wasn't sure what to say. "Ralph, I don't know what might be going on with her, but I do know this. I've seen an amazing change in you over the last week or so. I can tell God has been touching you…even speaking to you." He said the last part a little quieter, so no one could overhear. "I know that God still works miracles. So don't give up on yourself, and don't give up on your daughter. I know God hasn't."

Ralph turned away, not wanting Rick to see the tears welling up again. He cleared his throat. "Yeah, well, I better get back to work."

Rick patted him on the back, and thought to ask, "What's her name, Ralph?"

"Who, my daughter?"

"Yeah."

"Her name's Robin," he said, putting his hat on and heading back inside to help with the clean-up. As Rick watched him, he thought about the young lady he'd met recently named Robin, and all that she had shared with him.

When Robin left the church, she tried to focus on her errands. She drove back across town to her regular grocery store and sat for a minute in her car, not quite ready to go inside. Her heart was still beating fast and she wanted to calm down. She thought about the man she'd just seen for the first time in four years. How could he have just exited their lives for four years, without once ever trying to get in touch?

Even though he'd looked dirty and unkempt, his eyes had looked clear, he was steady on his feet, and he didn't seem like he'd been drinking. What was he doing there, though? It looked like he might have been a volunteer, but she wasn't sure. Her mother had written him off after the divorce, telling her he was just a deadbeat dad who wouldn't pay child support, but she'd always secretly hoped he'd try to contact her somehow. She couldn't believe he hadn't even come to her high school graduation. She'd lost all contact with him when he'd moved out of his apartment, like he'd disappeared off the face of the earth. She'd wondered if he'd left town or maybe even died. Had he been here all along? If so, why had she never seen him? Why hadn't he even once tried to find her?

She took several deep breaths and finally went inside to do her weekly grocery shopping, picking up a few bottles of her favorite wine. She drove back to her apartment and put the groceries away. She picked up her mail, flipping through it on the way back inside- -electric bill, a couple catalogs and some junk mail. She opened the bill, hoping it wouldn't be too much and was relieved to see it wasn't.

Her job paid pretty well, considering she didn't have a college degree, and she usually had enough money to keep up with her bills, but sometimes she forgot to save for things like car insurance or un- expected repairs. The cash she got from the ATM every Friday went pretty fast when she partied with her friends, which usually meant she brought her lunch to work the next week instead of eating out. Still, she was making it and she hardly ever had to ask her mother for money.

She should probably call her mother this weekend, since it had been a while since they'd last talked. It was always an exercise on Robin's patience, though. When her dad left, it seemed like she and her mother had turned all their anger on each other. Robin blamed her mother for kicking him out. She'd always nagged her dad about something, for drinking too much, for not making more money, not being home enough. Geez, her nagging would have driven anyone to drink.

It wasn't like her mother didn't drink too—she did. She just didn't drink as much as her dad. But she could go on some pret- ty good benders herself, and she was a mean drunk when she did. Robin learned to get out of her way when that happened, spending the night with friends, or once, even spending the night in her car. Sometimes she'd wished she could just go live with her dad. When she was growing up, she'd always felt a special bond with him. But then when he left and didn't bother to stay in touch with her, she began to believe what her mother said about him, that he didn't love either one of them and never had.

The phone rang, interrupting her thoughts. She answered.

"Hey Robin, wanna go out with us tonight?" It was her friend, Lisa.

"I dunno...where are you thinking about?"

"Well, we were gonna go dancing at Club Cher. You know how they have those good ladies' night deals on drinks? But they're not open tonight because of the storm."

"Really? What happened?"

"I guess they got some roof damage or something. So we thought we'd go back to Jackie's instead."

"That was some storm, wasn't it? Have you seen all the damage?"

"Yeah, pretty freaky, huh. I'm just glad my place was okay." Lisa lived in an apartment complex a few miles away from Robin. "So, you comin' tonight?"

Robin didn't feel like it. After what had happened yesterday and then today seeing all those people at the shelter trying to figure out how to pick up the pieces of their lives—it almost seemed disrespectful to be out partying when there were so many people who had lost homes and even loved ones. "You know, I think I'll pass tonight, Lisa. But, thanks anyway."

"Aw, come on Robin. Why not?"

"I just don't feel like it, you know…the storm and everything…"

"Well, it's not like you were affected," Lisa said. "Let's go out and celebrate that we all got through it in one piece."

Robin bristled. "Look, it did affect me, okay? Just because I wasn't hurt or none of my stuff was destroyed doesn't mean it didn't affect me."

"Okay, okay, I'm sorry," Lisa said. "Suit yourself. You want to sit there by yourself and get all depressed about it, fine with me."

"I'm not depressed about it! I just don't want to go out tonight." She tried to calm her voice. "Look, I'll catch up with you next time."

She hung up, irritated with Lisa's attitude. How could she even be friends with someone like that? Was she that way, too? She decided to clean up her apartment and go rent a movie for the evening. It would be nice to stay home for a change.

When she returned from the video store, Robin turned on the TV and watched the local news reporting on the storm and listing shelters where people could get help. She saw the church's name where she had helped earlier in the day. She was glad she'd gone and helped, even if it had resulted in her seeing her father there. Heck, maybe she'd even go to the service there again tomorrow, and offer to help again at the shelter. And if her father was there, fine. She'd just deal with it. There was a part of her that was tired of being angry at him. Maybe it was time to hear the other side of the story.

CHAPTER TWENTY-EIGHT

Bob and Katie walked out of the hospital Saturday afternoon, after delivering the flowers, and decided to go out to eat. It was early enough that they wouldn't have a long wait, and maybe after dinner they'd have time to catch a movie too. They agreed on a steakhouse and went inside to be seated. When they'd placed their orders, Bob said, "I sure hope she'll be okay."

Katie knew who he was referring to, and agreed, "Yeah, me too. She looked pretty bad, but hopefully she'll recover quickly and be able to go home in a few days." Neither spoke, each thinking about Carolyn and her family.

"Those poor kids. Especially Annie. Can you imagine going through all that, without either one of your parents being home?"

Bob reached across the table to squeeze her hand. "I know. I'm glad you were both all right. Maybe it was good that you were there with her. Even though you about scared me to death!" He smiled. "Next time there's a tornado, could you make more of an effort to get home?" he kidded.

"Well, if you say so. But seriously, it was a good thing someone was there with Annie. I just hate to think what might have happened to her if I hadn't been there."

"What? You don't think she would've gone to the basement?"

"I don't know. She seemed pretty stunned. Maybe she would have."

"Well, I hate to think what might have happened if you hadn't been able to get to a basement." Bob shuddered and reached for his iced tea.

"Yeah, I think somebody up there was looking out for all of us."

"Thank God," Bob said.

Katie murmured, "Yeah."

The waitress came with their food and set their plates down in front of them. As they ate, they sampled some of the food on each other's plates like they usually did.

"So what movie do you want to see tonight?" Katie asked. He suggested a couple and then checked his phone to get the movie times. "What do you want to do tomorrow?" Katie asked, taking a bite of her steak.

He thought as he chewed. "I dunno. I guess I'll mow the grass." Then he added, "You wanna try a different church somewhere?"

She looked down at her food without answering.

"It's no big deal. We don't have to go," he said, taking that as a no.

"It's just that that guy last week really ticked me off."

Bob recalled how the pastor had pointedly made fun of people who claimed to have heard God speak out loud. "Well, let's try somewhere else."

She looked up at him, "Where, then?"

"We could try the one over on Cherry. A friend of mine at work said she went there last week and the guy there spoke about it too, people hearing God, but he was a lot more open-minded about it. She really liked him."

Katie picked up another bite from her plate and thought as she chewed. "So he wasn't condescending about it? Cause I can't take that again. I swear I'll get up and walk out."

"Well, let's sit in the back, just in case," Bob said with a smile.

CHAPTER TWENTY-NINE

Ralph scrambled eggs in the fellowship hall kitchen on Sunday morning so that other volunteers could attend to their regular Sunday morning activities at the church. He'd also bedded down at the shelter himself the past two nights, and Rick had given him some odd jobs around the church, mowing grass, planting flowers, along with helping out in the shelter.

There were now about fifteen people using the shelter. Some had moved into motels after confirming reimbursements with their insurance companies. Others had gone to stay with family. He wondered how long the shelter would stay open. He was now the only homeless person staying there. The others had stayed Friday night, but had left yesterday after the last meal was served, preferring their independence on the streets. But Ralph was thankful to have a place to stay, and the work gave him a sense of accomplishment he hadn't felt in a long time. He would do whatever he could to help Rick, after all Rick had done for him. It also kept his mind off the booze.

It was still early, a couple hours before the first church service started, and Rick stopped by to check on everyone.

"Good morning! How's everybody doing?" He looked around the room. A couple people were still asleep on their cots. The others greeted him.

"Well, it's a fine morning and we have a lot to be thankful for, in spite of everything that's happened," he said brightly. Heads nodded in agreement.

"Amen to that, brother," one man said.

"I just wanted to invite you all to join us in the worship service this morning, if you'd like. There's absolutely no pressure, so don't feel like you have to if you don't want to. But we're a real casual bunch here, no one has to dress up or anything, and I would feel honored if you came up and joined us. There are two services, at nine-thirty and eleven, so feel free to come to either one." Then he offered a quick blessing for the food, and went into the kitchen to see how he could help.

He greeted Ralph and the two others, Sam and Meredith, who were preparing the food.

"Eggs are done," Ralph said, removing the pan from the stove, and scraping the eggs into the large serving tray.

"The biscuits and sausage are finished too, and I think we're almost ready," said Meredith. "Sam, can you make sure the coffee and juice are out, and the silverware?"

"Got it," Sam said, making the final preparations.

"Ralph, how ya doing this morning?" Rick said, squeezing his shoulder.

"Real good," Ralph said, turning around to Rick.

"Have things been okay here?"

"Yeah, just fine."

Rick was curious about his daughter, but he didn't want to pry. Better to let Ralph bring it up first. The Lord had taught him a few things about people and he'd learned that no one liked to be pushed into anything. "Anything I can do to help here?" he asked.

Ralph shrugged, but Meredith was quick to snap up his offer. "Can you move that trash can over here?" she asked. "We need it over here by the serving area."

He moved it, and Meredith came out of the kitchen to let everyone know breakfast was ready. Rick stayed and ate breakfast with the group. He sat with a family he hadn't met yet and chatted with them while they ate. When he finished, he got up to leave, and on his way out, he passed Ralph. "Hey, I hope I'll see you in church this morning."

"Yeah, maybe." Ralph didn't want to say no outright, but he didn't have any clean clothes, and the thought of people stares made him uncomfortable.

When everyone finished eating, they cleaned up the kitchen and Ralph sat down at one of the tables. Several had decided to go to the church service, but others were still sitting around, either trying to decide or just plain ignoring the idea.

As he saw some of them getting ready to go, he realized he didn't look any worse than they did, and Rick would probably appreciate it, so why not. He went into the restroom to wash up and comb his hair, taking a deep breath as he looked in the mirror. '*It's been a long time*,' he thought. '*But maybe it's time for a change.*'

Everything else had changed in his life over the past week, and for whatever reason, he felt open to changes, and more alive than he'd felt in years. It was still a little scary and uncomfortable, but he thought, '*What have I got to lose? What I've been doing hasn't been working, maybe it's time to try something else.*'

As Ralph walked up the stairs to the hallway leading to the sanctuary, he began to lose his resolve. He could still turn around and go back downstairs, and he almost did until he saw one of the families staying downstairs, the Birches. They were waiting in the hallway upstairs outside the restroom for Megan, their youngest. They said hello and asked him if he was going to the service. Too late now. He said he was. They asked if he wanted to sit with them, and he agreed. At least he'd know someone. That would make it a little easier.

Megan emerged from the restroom and they walked down the hall together, Ralph leading the way. Since he'd been helping out in the church over the past few days, he knew his way around the building and grounds, but he'd never seen it full of people. The church bustled with activity, and he wondered what kind of people attended there.

He saw people moving through the halls, everyone trying to get somewhere, herding children, standing and chatting, but for the most part, not paying any attention to him or the Birches. A few people smiled at them as they walked past, and that seemed encouraging. He didn't want to stand out in any way.

They made their way down the busy hall, finally reaching the sanctuary entrance. Ushers stood at the open doorways and offered bulletins to those walking in. They each took one, walked inside and stood in the back trying to figure out where to sit. Ralph saw Pastor Rick shaking people's hands, and when Rick saw their group, his eyes lit up and he walked over to them.

"Here, let's find you all a place to sit!" He led their group toward the middle of the sanctuary where there was a mostly empty pew. Ralph would have preferred to sit somewhere in back, but it was too late now. "I'm so glad you all decided to come today." He smiled and shook each of their hands.

They arranged themselves in the pew while Rick continued greeting others around them. Ralph glanced around but didn't see anyone he knew. Why would he? The kind of people he knew weren't likely to be here. He opened the bulletin in his hands and read through it while they waited for the service to start.

For the second Sunday in a row, Robin surprised herself by going to church. She couldn't remember the last time she'd gone to church two Sundays in a row. Her family had been an Easter-and-Christmas-only family when it came to church. She'd liked the music in the church last week when she came, and especially the preacher's sermon.

She felt something shifting inside her, some change that had begun that night on her bathroom floor when she'd heard those words, and she wondered if her life would ever be the same. She didn't enjoy doing the things she used to, she didn't even enjoy hanging out with her old gang much any more. It just seemed so pointless. It was almost like the storm this week had blown out the last bit of debris in her life, and when she'd heard the words again during the storm, there was no mistaking it. God was trying to get her attention. So here she was, at church, for the second week in a row. Would miracles never cease?

She wondered if she'd see any of the people she'd worked with in the church kitchen yesterday. As she walked into the building, she wondered what the sermon would be about this week. She headed toward the sanctuary doors, took a bulletin from an usher, and looked around for a place to sit.

Her eyes froze when she saw him, sitting there right in the middle. What was he doing here? What if he saw her? She almost turned around and left, but then she decided she wasn't going to give him that power. So what if he was here? She'd just sit in the back and slip out when it was over, and hopefully he'd never even see her. She had as much right to be here as he did, so she sat down and waited for the service to begin.

Katie and Bob were running late. Katie had forgotten her cell phone and since she hated to go anywhere without it, she made Bob turn around to go back home for it. They hadn't gotten far from home, so she figured it wouldn't take long. But once home, Bob decided to go in and change his shoes, which he'd decided were too uncomfortable, and by the time they left home the second time, they had little time to spare before the church service was scheduled to begin. When they arrived, the parking lot was full, so they had to park a good distance away. They hurried toward the main entrance of the building. It had seemed like a good idea last night, to try out this church, but now Katie felt stressed and she wondered if all the hassle would be worth it. Oh well, they were here, might as well give it a shot.

They walked inside and saw the sanctuary to the left. The ushers were closing the doors as the service began, but one held a door open when she saw them coming, and they hurried inside. They each received a bulletin and they stood in back, orienting themselves and looking for a place to sit. The usher pointed out some empty space in a pew toward the back, so they headed there. As they sat, Bob saw a woman he knew from work, sitting on the same pew. She looked over at him, nodded and smiled.

A man in front was welcoming everyone and making announcements, and then he led the congregation in a prayer. "Gracious heavenly Father, we thank you for this beautiful day. We know that even though many in our community have suffered and struggled this week, you are the one who will lead us through it all. God, we come here today to worship you and rest in your Holy presence. I ask you to touch each and every life here today and help them know that you are here with us. In Jesus' name, Amen." Then he asked them to all stand and greet one another, so Katie and Bob stood along with everyone else.

Bob introduced his friend to Katie. "Katie, this is Robin from work. She's the one I told you about that had come to this church."

"Oh, hi, Robin. It's nice to meet you," Katie said, shaking her hand.

"Hi Katie, you too."

"This is our first time here. Do you come here often?" Katie asked her.

"No, it's only my second time."

Then they realized they should be greeting others around them too, so they turned and shook some hands. The band began to play and the music leader led the singing. Robin had never seen guitars or drums in a church before coming here last week. It sure was a lot different than the church she'd attended as a child, almost like a big party.

Katie was drawn into the music. She'd never heard songs like these before. She was accustomed to traditional hymns at church. As she listened to the words, she was surprised to find tears welling up in her eyes and her heart felt moved in a way she'd never felt in church before.

When she brushed a tear away, she saw Bob glancing over at her. She wondered if he felt it too. The singers and musicians on the stage looked joyful, and it seemed clear that this was more than just a ritual to them. She wanted to wrap herself up in the music and never leave. There was joy and peace in this place, and it surprised her that she could feel that the first time here.

She'd always associated church with rituals, guilt, and belief systems that she couldn't quite go along with, a place you were supposed to go if you wanted to be in "good standing," whatever that was. But this place was different, like the people genuinely wanted to be here. She glanced around, noticing all ages of both men and women, which also surprised her. The churches she'd attended in the past were made up primarily of women, most of them older. They were nice and all, but she just never felt like she fit in.

When the music finished, they sat down and Katie reached for her purse to get a tissue. She dabbed her eyes and wiped her nose.

The speaker said, "As we go to the Lord in prayer this morning, let's remember those who were affected by the storm this week. We are blessed to have some of those people worshiping with us this morning. Let's also remember the following people who are struggling…" and he mentioned some by name and what they were struggling with, cancer, deaths in their family, and other illnesses.

They bowed their heads. As he prayed, Katie felt goose bumps all over. He talked to God like he was talking to a friend standing right there. No thee's, thy's or thou's. None of the flowery language she was used to hearing in church. His prayer came from the heart, and his voice broke a couple times as he prayed for the storm victims.

She wiped at her eyes and nose as he continued. The way he talked to God made him seem like the kind of God she'd heard at the hospital and in the storm--one who cared and was right there with them, one who was bigger than the world and could even calm storms. But then if that was true, why did he let some things happen? Why did she have to lose her baby? Why did the storm have to do so much damage, even killing some people? Couldn't he have stopped it sooner? If he could let these terrible things happen, did he really care? She'd wondered about these questions many times, never with a good answer. The words of his prayer caught her ear.

"God, sometimes we just don't understand why some things happen on this earth. We know that you are all-powerful, but we can't help but wonder why you let some bad things happen to good people. Sometimes, God, it can almost seem like you've forgotten us or that you don't care." He paused, and when he spoke again, his voice was full of emotion.

"God, we know we have to trust in you, we know this, but sometimes it's hard. But thank you for being with us, and for reminding us of this in all the ways you do. Through the beauty of nature, through the love we share with others, through the grace shown to those in need. And sometimes even speaking to us, God."

This got Katie's attention. She even opened her eyes and looked up as he continued to pray. She noticed Bob looking up and then at her. Had he just meant what he said, or was it a figure of speech?

"So God, we just ask you for strength now. We know we can't understand all these things right now, so we need your help with faith and strength. We're gonna trust you to supply it, God, because sometimes life is just too much to cope with on our own, and there's no way we can do it in our own power. So thank you in advance, God, for the strength I know you'll provide. Thank you for all those times you've provided it, and for the strength you're providing right now, this very minute, to those who are desperately needing it."

As he closed the prayer, Katie heard many sniffles around the room, and saw several others dabbing at their eyes. She'd already gotten more out of this church service than all her previous times in church put together, and they hadn't even gotten to the sermon yet.

They sang another song, one she'd heard on the radio. Once more she was struck by the sincerity in their voices and on their faces. Nothing about it seemed forced. They did a good job with the song, too. It sounded a lot like the original recording. In some ways, it was even better because their faces reflected the feeling behind the song.

When they finished, the musicians sat down and the man who had prayed stood up, not behind a pulpit, but down on the floor, at their level. He was dressed casually, in a polo shirt and khaki pants, and he looked fairly young, maybe in his early to mid thirties. Katie wondered if he was the pastor but she wasn't sure, since he didn't introduce himself. He began to speak.

"As we all know, these last few days have been difficult ones for our community. The storm on Friday devastated many buildings and many lives. We don't have to look far to see the devastation, and most of us were either affected personally or we know someone who was. We've been busy trying to clean up and help people who are worse off than we are, and in the middle of it all, maybe some of us are wondering 'why.' I know I've wondered it myself over the past few days. Why did it all have to happen?

"I'm not going to try to answer that question here today. I don't think it's even possible to know the answer yet, and maybe we never will. Does it even help to try to figure it all out or assign blame? I've heard some religious leaders say that devastating storms are God's punishment for the immoral society we live in. I don't happen to believe this myself. I think storms happen. It's not for us to figure out why they happen, but to figure out what we're gonna do during them and afterwards.

"Many of you have helped in our effort to provide shelter to people who were left without homes after the storm. I think this is a good way for us to show the love of Christ to others in need. I am so thankful for all you've done to help these people, and for all that you're able to do in the coming days to help get them back on their feet.

"But is this enough? Are we doing enough when we reach out to help those we see in need? Well, certainly this is an honorable thing to do and we should do it. But what about the storms of our daily lives? What do we do about those?

"The tornados this week were one kind of storm, but there are many kinds of storms that can hit our lives. Storms of divorce, storms of addiction, storms of illness, storms of grief over the passing of loved ones. What do we do when these storms hit? Do we get angry at God? Do we get bitter? Figure out how to assign blame? Maybe ask 'why me?' These are natural human reactions, and I'll admit I've had them all too. And you know what? I don't even think God gets upset with us for having them. But then what? Where do we go from there? Do these storms draw us closer to God or do we push him away and hold on to our bitterness? That's the choice we make every time we face one of the storms of life."

Rick glanced at his notes, and took a deep breath. When he looked up, he focused on no one in particular. "I know Friday's storm is still on all our minds. But I want to take you back to a week or so before that. Do you remember what everyone was talking about before the storm?" He paused.

"Remember, people were talking about how God supposedly spoke out loud to some people, and there was all this debate about it? Did God really speak to people out loud? It was in the news, even on the Hailey show?" Katie turned to Bob, but he looked straight ahead, waiting for what was next. She stiffened and wondered if he was going to condemn it like the preacher last week had. Everything about the church service had been so good up until now, and she was feeling so touched. She hoped he didn't ruin what had, up to now, been a moving spiritual experience.

"Well, I'm not here to participate in that debate or to say yes, God spoke to those people or no, he didn't. Only those people know the answer to that question. But my question for you today is this: if God spoke to you, would you be ready to listen?" He was quiet while he looked around the room.

"I think this is what matters. Not whether God did or didn't speak to people recently, but would you be able to hear him if he spoke to you?" Katie and Bob traded glances and she leaned a bit forward to hear what was next.

"I believe that God speaks to us in many ways. He speaks to us in nature, through beautiful sunsets and sunrises. He speaks to us through other people, and through his word in the Bible. In the Old Testament, he spoke to Moses in a burning bush, and to the prophets in dreams. How has he tried to speak to you? Were you ready to listen? Sometimes we can get so caught up in our lives and activities, that we're not still enough to hear, are we? And when a storm like the one a few days ago comes, we're forced out of our routine. Maybe then we pause. Perhaps it is in stillness that God can best speak to us--when we're ready to be quiet and listen. But how often do we really do this?"

Rick walked slowly to the other side of the room. He opened his mouth to speak and then stopped himself. He seemed to be struggling with what to say next, or how to say it.

"You know...several people have come to me over the past two weeks and told me their stories of how God spoke to them, out loud.

I'm not going to share any of their names. That's for them to do if they wish. But I've been thinking a lot about what they told me, and one thing they all had in common was this--they were in a place spiritually where they were ready to hear God speak.

"The other thing they had in common was that they all knew without a doubt that it was God. He spoke, and they listened, and they were changed by the experience. They told me that a peace had come over them, and that they felt strong desire to draw closer to God. There are many places in the Bible where God says, 'Draw close to me and I will dwell in you.' And this is exactly what these people experienced, the desire to draw close to God and to have him be part of their life.

"Now I know some of you may be skeptical about all this and think this is just not the way God speaks to people in this day and age. Not out loud anyway. But I'm asking you to defer your judgment and accept that maybe God speaks in all sorts of ways. I understand how you might feel this way, because at one time, I'll admit, I thought the same thing. But, I've changed my mind about it." He paused, and again seemed to be undergoing an internal battle.

"I'm just gonna be honest with you," he said haltingly. "I wasn't planning to tell you this, but God is putting it on my heart to share it." Everyone seemed to be holding their breath.

"Here's the thing. It happened to me, too. God spoke to me, out loud." A few people gasped, but he continued.

"It had never happened to me before, but when it did, there was no doubt in my mind that it was God. My experience was much the same as what other people described. I was in my study, being quiet, struggling with my sermon, asking God for help, and he spoke. Out loud. Never in my life did I expect something like this to happen. But there's no doubt that I heard words and I knew they were from God."

Katie caught Bob's eye and they raised their eyebrows. She glanced around, noticing that Robin was completely focused on Rick, but she could pick out the skeptics in the audience, with their lips pursed and brows furrowed.

"Some of you may already know this, but when the tornado hit on Friday, I was on my way to the homeless shelter with a friend, and we got there just in time to run into the basement." He glanced at Ralph. "The tornado demolished the building. I don't have to tell those of you who experienced it how utterly horrifying it was. Even though I grew up here in the Midwest, I had never experienced anything like it.

"We were all in the basement praying, crying, just holding on to each other for dear life, and in the middle of the storm, we heard something. We heard the voice of God, and then the storm stopped." Up to this point he hadn't looked much at the audience, because he didn't think he could deal with the suspicion on their faces, but now he looked straight at them. What he saw was a mixture of reactions, some leaning forward listening to every word, some arms folded and mouths held tight, some just looking away or down. He continued.

"I know some of you may find this hard to believe, and I'm not here to try to convince you one way or another. But those of us who were there know what we heard." He looked at Ralph again and Ralph nodded almost imperceptibly.

"I'm sharing this with you today for two reasons. The first is to say that yes, God does speak to people even today, in many different ways. The second is to ask you again... are you ready to hear him? Because if you're ready, he'll find a way to get through. Then it's up to you as to what happens next. You can refuse to listen, or you can pretend it didn't happen and go about your business, life as usual. Or you can use it as an opportunity to draw closer to him. I'll guarantee you this...if you choose the latter, to draw closer to God, he will work with you in ways you can't even imagine."

Rick took out his handkerchief and dabbed at his forehead and eyes. It had taken a lot out of him, this sermon, and he felt completely spent. When he put his handkerchief back into his pocket, he looked out at their faces again.

"As we go about our lives this next week, many of us will have a lot on our minds, a lot to deal with. I know many of you are repairing extensive damages to your homes. A few have lost everything you had. I know some were hurt and are in hospitals, and a few even lost their lives from the storm. All over our community, people are hurting and struggling. Where do we even begin to help?

"I'm challenging you today. In the middle of all the commotion, find some quiet time. Find some stillness and spend it with God. I'm not guaranteeing that you're gonna hear him speak in an audible voice, though I wouldn't rule it out either. But if you're quiet, and you learn to bring stillness into your life, God will reach you and help you. If you can keep your spirit open, you'll begin to know what it is he's trying to tell you. Maybe he wants you to help someone clean up their home, or to help in a shelter like the one we have downstairs, or maybe he just wants to give you strength to deal with your own problems. But unless you purposely take time to be still and listen, you may never know.

"Before we close today, I want to thank all who trusted me with their stories of how God spoke to them. I know many of you probably felt like you were going out on a limb to talk with me about it, and it means a lot to me that you shared your experience with me. It has filled my soul to listen to you and to learn from you.

"During this next week, if any of you would like to talk with me, I am available to talk with you too. In fact I'd love to hear what happens when you take the time to be still and see what God wants to communicate." Rick then asked everyone to bow their heads and he led them in a closing prayer.

When he finished and they all stood to leave, Bob and Katie looked at each other without a word. Bob could hardly wait to hear what Katie thought of the sermon, but he'd wait to ask her in the car. Robin followed them into the aisle, and he turned to her.

"Hey, it was good to see you here today," he said.

"You too," she said. "I don't really know anyone else here." They made their way out of the sanctuary and paused to chat again outside.

Katie asked Robin, "So what do you do at work?" Robin explained a little about her job and Katie listened. Robin knew about their recent loss and wasn't sure if she should say anything about it, but decided to go ahead.

"I just want to tell you how sorry I am about your baby."

Katie's eyes filled. "Thank you," she said, unable to say any more. Robin felt awkward then, so she turned to leave. "Well, see you later," she said as she walked away.

"Yeah, see ya," Bob waved. Katie looked around at the others milling around. She wondered what they'd thought of the sermon, but she didn't hear anyone talking about it. She was surprised to see someone she recognized.

"Bob, look!" She hurried ahead, with Bob following. "Hey, Annie!" she called when they got a little closer.

Annie turned around, and Katie noticed that her brother Andrew was with her too. Annie's face lit up in recognition and she waited for Katie to catch up to her.

"Hi, Annie!" she said, giving the girl a hug. "How's your mom?"

"Pretty good. They say she might get to come home tomorrow."

"Oh, that's great!" Katie looked over at Andrew. "Hi, how are you?"

"Fine."

Katie could tell he was just trying to be polite. "Well, it was good to see you guys." She and Bob had turned toward their car when Annie spoke up and walked closer, outside of Andrew's hearing range.

"Hey, Katie," then with her voice lowered, "What did you think about what that preacher said?" Andrew was heading toward his car.

"Come on Annie, let's go!" he called to her.

"Just a minute!" she waved, and turned back to Katie.

"You mean what he said about hearing God?" Annie nodded. "I thought it was pretty amazing, what did you think?"

"Yeah, me too," Annie said. She leaned closer to Katie, not sure what Katie's husband thought and not wanting him to hear, "Isn't it weird that we heard it too in the storm?"

"It was weird," Katie agreed. "It's kinda cool, don't you think? Maybe there were others who heard it in the storm too."

"Yeah…" Annie thought about that.

"Annie, come on!" Andrew yelled from across the parking lot.

"I better go, I just wondered what you thought," Annie gave Katie a last hug.

"I'm so glad we were together in that storm, Annie." She pulled away to look at her. "Call me any time and we can talk about this or anything else. I would really like for us to stay friends."

"You would?" Annie had never had an older person for a friend.

"Yeah, I would." Katie smiled at her.

"Okay, well, gotta go. See ya Katie. I'll call ya." Annie hurried to Andrew's car before he started honking at her. Katie waved, and turned back to Bob.

"What a neat girl. I really like her. I hope she'll call me." They walked together toward their own car. "I wonder if she comes here often. It was kind of strange that she and her brother were here together, but their dad wasn't here with them."

"He probably wanted to stay with his wife at the hospital," Bob said.

"Yeah, you're probably right."

They reached the car and got inside.

CHAPTER THIRTY

Rick was a little anxious as he stood in the back of the church after the service to shake hands with people as they left. He wondered what their reactions would be to the sermon today. He hadn't planned to tell them about hearing God's voice himself, but something had compelled him to say it.

As the congregation filed out of the church, he noticed that some people avoided him altogether, exiting through other doors. He tried not to take it personally, but he couldn't help but wonder if it was because they didn't like what he'd said. Of those that shook his hand as they left, most made no direct reference to the sermon, and quite a few wouldn't look him in the eye as they hurried to exit as quickly as possible. He met the eyes of some who had shared their stories with him this past week, and they smiled at him and thanked him for his message without saying more.

Ralph came through and shook his hand.

"Ralph, I'm sure glad you came today."

"Yeah, me too. It was a good sermon, Rick." The Birch family followed behind Ralph and also shook Rick's hand on their way out. They walked together toward the stairs leading back down to the fellowship hall and the makeshift shelter.

Annie climbed into the car and Andrew backed out impatiently. He was obviously in a bad mood, so Annie didn't say anything. She was the one that had suggested coming to church today. But when her dad had asked Andrew to take her, since he needed to be at the hospital with her mom, he'd been mad at her ever since.

She looked out the window on her side, thinking about what she'd just heard. She couldn't believe the preacher had said he'd heard God too. Then, to see Katie there. It was all so freaky. She wondered how many other people might have heard what she and Katie heard. Was everyone hearing God now? But she was pretty sure Andrew hadn't, and there was no way she was going to ask him. Maybe when her mom got better, she could talk to her about it.

Andrew raced the car up the street toward their neighborhood. Annie wished he'd slow down but she knew better than to say anything. He turned the corner onto their street, and pulled to a stop in front of their house.

"Hey thanks for taking me," she said, getting out. "I know you didn't want to."

"Yeah, whatever," he said. "I shouldn't have to go back now for a while."

"So I guess you didn't like it?"

He looked at her like she was crazy. "You're kidding me, right? You did?"

She looked away, said nothing, and walked up the driveway toward the house.

"Oh come on, don't tell me you believed any of that crap," he called after her.

She didn't want to argue with him, so she walked a little faster.

"You do, don't you?" he said, incredulously. "You believe it. God, Annie, you are so gullible."

"Shut up!" She yelled back, storming into the house.

"*Shut up,*" he mocked. "I should have never gone," he said, shaking his head. He followed her into the house. "Annie, if you really believe all this stuff about God talking to people, you should have your head examined. God doesn't talk to people any more."

"How do you know?" She didn't mean to keep yelling, but couldn't seem to help it. Her brother could really set her off.

"Because that's not the way it works. If there even is a God, which I'm not so sure of, he doesn't go around talking to people, and anyone who says he does is seriously psycho, if you ask me."

"Well, no one asked you." She ran up the stairs to her room and slammed the door. He was so aggravating. Just because he was older and a great athlete, he thought he knew everything. It made her sick. She almost wished she hadn't even gone to church, or at least not with him. But when she thought again about what the preacher had said, she was glad she'd been there. Even if it meant dealing with her idiot brother. She wasn't going to let his bad attitude ruin it for her. But she'd make sure to never go there with him again. In fact, the next time she wanted to go, maybe she'd call up Katie and go with her. That is, if her parents would let her. She'd have to think of a way to convince them.

When everyone had left, Rick took a look around and breathed deeply. '*Well*,' he thought, '*I've done it now*.' He'd told what he'd heard. But it felt more like a burden lifted from his shoulders than anything else. He wasn't sure how long it would feel this way-- maybe only until the complaints started coming in. But right now it felt pretty good.

He knew he'd connected with at least a few people, judging by the looks on their faces, and from some comments made on the way out. But what mattered most to him right now was that he'd shared his experience, even if not everyone believed it. He knew there would always be skeptics, and it wasn't his job to try to convince them of something they didn't want to believe. But he did hope he'd encouraged everyone to be respectful enough not to condemn others for what they may have experienced.

He decided to go down to the fellowship hall and see if he could help out with the lunch preparations. He wondered how long they'd be able to keep the shelter operating, but then he decided he'd leave it in God's hands. As long as people needed a place to stay, he hoped they could provide it to them, but he also knew that the volunteers and money wouldn't continue forever.

A few people were visiting in the hallway as he walked by, and most looked up to greet him. Two ladies noticed him, and returned to their conversation without saying anything to him. He told himself not to worry about it, but he couldn't help but wonder if they were talking about him. He could go nuts second-guessing himself if he let himself.

He saw a lot of activity in the hall—children playing with a ball, other children running in from outside, women in the kitchen preparing the next meal, men bringing in more supplies from a truck outside. His heart warmed and he thought, '*We're doing a good thing here.*'

Ralph greeted him as he carried in some supplies. "Hey preacher, how's it goin?"

"Not bad, Ralph, not bad."

Ralph set down the supplies and said, "That was a good sermon today."

"Thanks."

"You gettin' any bad rap for it?"

Rick looked away. "Oh, maybe a little. I'm not too worried about it though."

"Good. You know there's always gonna be doubting Thomases."

"Yeah, I know."

"I'm glad you did it," Ralph said, a little quieter.

Rick didn't respond for a minute. "I wasn't planning to. I guess it just kinda came out. Just seemed like the right thing to do."

"Well, good for you," Ralph said. "I'm gonna go get some more stuff out of this truck. Wanna help?"

CHAPTER THIRTY-ONE

"Mom, can I get you a cup of tea or something?" Annie asked as she came downstairs.

"No, that's okay, I'm fine," Carolyn said. She was sitting on the couch with her leg propped up on pillows.

"Are you sure? It's no trouble, I don't mind."

Carolyn smiled at her daughter, who had been very helpful since she'd come home from the hospital yesterday.

"Well, all right, that would actually be very nice," Carolyn said.

Annie went to the kitchen, filled the kettle and placed it on the stove. "Do you want black tea, green tea or chamomile tea?"

"How about green tea with honey? Are you gonna have some too?" Carolyn asked.

"Sure, green tea sounds good to me, too." Annie got the teapot and cups ready.

"Annie, I'm so proud of everything you've been doing to help out around the house." Carolyn was amazed at all that Annie had done. During the days she'd spent in the hospital, Annie had fixed dinner, vacuumed, and even done some laundry.

"It was no problem, Mom. I'm glad I could help." Annie bustled around the kitchen, emptying the dishwasher. Carolyn thought about the strange role reversal that had taken place in their home.

"I know Dad and Andrew have really appreciated all your help, too."

Annie didn't respond, but she smiled to herself as she put the dishes away.

"Why don't you come in here and sit down while we wait for the water to boil?" She saw Annie hesitate as the looked at the remaining dishes in the dishwasher. "Just leave those for now. Come and sit down."

Annie stopped what she was doing and walked into the room with her mother.

"How do you feel, Mom? Does it still hurt a lot?"

"I'm fine, Annie, just relax."

"Well, just let me know if you want something. Aren't you supposed to be lying down?"

"I'm tired of lying down. It feels good to be up and around a little bit," Carolyn looked out the window. "I missed being at home and just looking out at our yard. Look how green everything is out there."

Annie turned to look outside.

"There's so much beauty all around."

They sat quietly for a while, until the kettle whistled. Annie jumped up to remove it from the burner. She poured the water into the pot with the teabags. She waited for them to steep, and poured them each a cup. As they sipped, they looked out the window at the trees that had started to leaf out for the spring, and watched some robins hopping around in the yard.

"It's so nice just to sit here with you, Annie. I missed you so much while I was in the hospital. I had a lot of time to think."

"Yeah? What'd you think about?"

Carolyn looked away from the window at Annie, and set her tea on the table next to her. "I thought about a lot of things. I thought about our family, and how busy we all are. When I was lying there and couldn't do a thing, I wondered how in the world we've all gotten too busy to even have dinner together. How did our lives get that way?"

Annie shrugged, looking at her tea. "I guess they just did."

"Yeah, but is it a good thing? We've all gotten so caught up in being busy all the time, but why? What if we were to cut back on some of the things that are keeping us so busy?"

"Like what?" Annie was a little worried about what she might be asked to give up.

"I don't know…I guess we'll have to do some thinking about it. But I decided something when I spent all those hours lying in that hospital bed. I decided that I don't want to come back to the same life as before."

"What's wrong with that life?" Annie was really worried now.

"It's not that it was a bad life, 'cause it wasn't. But I think our family needs to make some different choices." Carolyn could see the anxiety in Annie's face, so she tried to put her fears to rest. "I want us to all sit down and talk about it when the guys are here too, and we'll get everyone's ideas. I think it's something we need to have a family meeting about."

Annie sipped her tea. Maybe it wouldn't be so bad, as long as they could all decide on the changes together.

"Annie, don't you ever feel stressed out, like your life is too busy?"

Annie looked over at her mother. "Yeah, sometimes, I guess…"

"Why do you think that is?" Carolyn sipped her tea and waited.

Annie looked at her to see if she really wanted to hear the answer. Carolyn waited.

"I guess it's mostly schoolwork. There are so many projects and homework. I worry about my grades or if I can get it all done on time."

Carolyn waited to see if she'd say more.

"There just never seems to be enough time. Or maybe I just wait 'til the last minute too much," Annie looked down.

Carolyn remembered the project Annie had been working before the storm came and had turned their lives upside down. "Did you get that science project finished?" she asked.

Annie nodded. "Yeah, I turned it in the day of the storm, last Friday."

Carolyn relaxed. "Oh good, I'd almost forgotten about it."

"I already got my grade on it," Annie smiled.

"Really? What'd you get?"

"I got an A!"

"Oh, Annie, that's great! I'm so proud of you!" Carolyn saw that Annie was beaming.

"And guess what, Mom? We get to enter our project in the State Science Fair."

"Aaagh!" Carolyn screamed with pleasure, throwing her arms into the air. "Come here and give me a hug!" Annie set her teacup down and hugged her, careful not to bump her leg. "Way to go, Annie!"

Annie returned to her chair, smiling broadly.

"When is the State Science Fair?"

"It's in two weeks."

"Now tell me again about your project. Wasn't it a lie detector test or something?"

Some of Carolyn's memories of things right before the storm still felt fuzzy. Sometimes she wasn't sure what was real or what she'd dreamed while on the medication in the hospital.

"Yeah, it's a lie detector test." Annie described how they measured blood pressure, perspiration and breathing rates to determine whether a person was telling the truth, and how they asked questions and recorded their answers along with the measurements.

As she was explaining, Andrew threw open the garage door and came inside, yelling, "Hey!" He slammed the door shut behind him, dropped his bags on the kitchen floor and walked through the kitchen to where they were sitting.

"Hi Andrew! How are you?"

"Good, Mom. How are you? How's the leg?"

"I'm fine, thanks. How was practice?"

"Okay, I guess. We have a game tomorrow night. What are you guys doing?" He walked back to the kitchen, got a glass out of the cabinet and poured some milk.

"We're just having tea and catching up. Annie just told me she got an A on her science project and it's getting entered into the State Fair."

"Oh yeah?" he said, glancing back at Annie. "Well, good for you."

Annie hadn't told him or her father about it yet, since they'd all been so focused on her mother and on getting the house back in order. They'd replaced the windows and cleaned up the mess in the bedroom and living room.

Andrew sipped his milk while he leaned against the counter and said, "So what'd you do your project on?"

"It's a lie detector test," she answered.

"Oh yeah," he said, remembering that they'd talked about it before. "So does it work?"

"Well, it's not a hundred percent accurate, but it works pretty well. Even the fancy ones aren't a hundred percent."

"So what kinda stuff do you ask people? Like 'Do you want Johnny to kiss you?'"

She knew he'd make fun of it sooner or later. "No, dummy."

"Well, what do you ask then?"

"We have a list of questions." She wished she could end this conversation.

"Well, let me know if you need any ideas for questions. I bet I could come up with some good ones. Like, you could ask people how old they were when they had their first drink, or if they've ever done drugs or stolen anything."

"Andrew!" Carolyn scolded. She wished her kids got along better. It seemed like whenever something good happened to Annie, Andrew was quick with a put-down or smart-aleck remark.

"Just tryin' to be helpful, Mom," he said in his most sincere voice.

Annie rolled her eyes.

"I'm sure Annie has plenty of good questions already."

"Oh, here's another one. How about you could ask that idiot preacher if he really heard God speak? Ha! I wonder what your lie detector would say about that!"

"Andrew!" Carolyn intervened. "That's enough. Why don't you go upstairs and get your shower. We'll start working on dinner. Your dad will be home in about forty-five minutes and we'll eat then."

"Fine," he said, setting his empty glass on the counter and holding his hands up in surrender. "I'm going." He picked up his bags and bounded up the stairs.

"He's such a jerk sometimes," Annie muttered.

"I don't know why he has to act that way," Carolyn said, much to Annie's surprise. "I guess he's just being a teen-ager."

They talked about what to fix for dinner. Annie would do the cooking while Carolyn instructed her from the couch. As Annie put the rest of the dishes away in the kitchen, Carolyn thought about something Andrew had said.

"Annie, what preacher was Andrew talking about?"

Annie continued without turning around. "Oh, just the guy we heard last Sunday when we went to church."

"You went to church last Sunday?" Carolyn thought this remarkable, considering they rarely attended church, and then only when she insisted.

"Yeah," Annie said, over the clattering of the dishes.

"Did you all go?"

"No, just me and Andrew. Dad was at the hospital with you."

"Which church did you go to?"

"That one down on Cherry."

"Did you like it?"

"Yeah," Annie said.

Carolyn sensed Annie's reluctance to talk about it, so she didn't press. But she'd like to hear more about the preacher who said he heard God speak. Had she dreamed something about that? About hearing God herself? Had the medication given her crazy thoughts and dreams?

She set her thoughts aside and focused on helping Annie get dinner ready. It seemed like years since they'd last sat down together for a family dinner, and she was looking forward to it. This was exactly the kind of thing she hoped they could do more of in the future.

CHAPTER THIRTY-TWO

Ralph helped load the last of the cots onto the truck. "That's the last one." Bill closed the doors, latched them, and turned to shake Ralph's hand before he left.

"Thanks, Ralph. Take care now." Bill climbed into the truck and gave Ralph a wave as he pulled out of the church parking lot. Ralph went back inside the church and looked around. Now that the cots were gone, he could clean the floor and leave. It had been almost two weeks since the storm, and the last family using the church shelter had left the day before.

Ralph got a broom from the storage closet and swept the floor. He was filling a bucket of water in the utility sink and preparing to mop when Rick came down the stairs.

"Ralph! There you are."

Ralph shut the water off. "Hey, Pastor."

"Looks like everything's almost back to normal around here, huh."

"Yeah, almost."

"Ralph, I sure appreciate everything you've done to help out around here, with the shelter and all."

"I was glad to do it," Ralph looked away, not wanting any praise for what he'd done. "It was actually nice to have a place to stay myself," he admitted.

"I know we had a lot of volunteers, but I don't know what we would have done without you here all the time."

Ralph shrugged and picked up the bucket from the sink. "Well, I'll just finish mopping this floor and then be on my way."

"Before you go, there's something I want to talk to you about. When you're finished here, can I treat you to lunch?"

"Sure." Ralph set the bucket on the floor and put the mop inside it.

"Come on up to my office when you're ready," he said, and turned to go back upstairs.

When Ralph had finished with the floor, he went into the restroom to wash up and run a comb through his hair. He retrieved his small bag of personal items, since he probably wouldn't be returning to the church after lunch. He wasn't sure where he was going next, but he might ask Rick to drop him off near his old stomping grounds after lunch.

It had been nice sleeping indoors, but he'd lived on the street before and he knew he could do it again. Still, it had been nice to be in a whole different situation these past two weeks-- with a place in the regular world, working at something that made a difference. His head felt clear, and even though he still felt a little shaky sometimes, he was amazed at how much energy he had now that he'd stopped drinking. He would always be thankful to Rick for helping him. He'd forgotten what it was like to have someone believe in you, someone who believed you could be a better man. It felt good.

It also felt good to pray again. He'd never been much of a praying man, but over these past two weeks, he'd learned what it felt like to talk to God. Rick had shown him that talking to God could be just like talking to a friend, and even though it felt awkward at first, the more he did it, the more he liked it. He felt the same peace he'd felt that first night when God spoke to him. Even though he hadn't heard him again since the day of the storm, he could feel God's presence with him, and he still felt the peace. It was like a new gift he'd been given, and he knew that even when he returned to the streets, he wouldn't be the same man as before. As he walked upstairs to find Rick, he realized he had a lot to be thankful for.

He greeted Sandy in the office. The people in the office now felt like his friends.

"Hi Ralph. Rick's in his office. You can go on back," Sandy said, waving him back.

"Thanks, Sandy." He walked down to Rick's office. The door was standing open and Rick looked up when he saw him.

"Hey there, you ready to go?" Rick placed a bookmark in his book and stood up. They walked outside and Rick suggested a near-by Mexican restaurant, which sounded fine to Ralph.

As they made the short drive, Ralph looked around. He hadn't been out much, since he'd been helping at the church the past two weeks. He noted that the streets had been cleared from the storm debris and that most of the broken trees and limbs had been cut and removed. The effects of the storm were still apparent though--some roofs were covered with tarps, misshaped trees that had lost big chunks of themselves, a few street lights sat at odd angles. But the worst signs of the storm were gone and for the most part, it appeared that life had returned to normal.

When they'd settled into a booth at the restaurant and ordered lunch, Rick turned to his business. "So Ralph, I'm wondering...what are your plans now?"

Ralph looked out the window behind Rick. "Oh, I dunno. I guess hit the streets again. See if I can find a job somewhere."

Rick paused before continuing. "Ralph, I have an idea for you. Now this is just an idea, and if you don't like it, that's fine. But I want to tell you about it."

Ralph looked back at him. "Okay..."

"You know how we lost the community shelter building in the storm..."

"Yeah..."

"Well, the shelter committee has been meeting to discuss plans for re-building. At first they just wanted to replace the building as it was, as inexpensively as possible. Then someone brought forth another idea, which was to make it a different kind of facility."

Ralph waited for him to continue.

"To make it even bigger and better than before. The idea is to make it a combination shelter. Part of it would still be a place for people to spend the night. But another part would be transitional housing--a place where people could stay longer and get help getting back on their feet. We all know it's important to provide warm beds for a night, but maybe there's an even bigger opportunity to help people who want to change their lives, who want to return to society with a job and a home. We want to help them do this. Provide them a place to stay, even with children, and give them counseling on finances, budgeting, job-hunting, and helping them get into a home of their own."

"Hmm," Ralph nodded. It sounded interesting, but he wasn't sure why Rick was telling him about it. It would be months, at least, before he could make use of such a place.

The waitress brought their food, and Rick waited while she set down the plates.

"So here's the thing, Ralph. We need a lot of help to build and create this place. I'm on the steering committee, and we've already gotten financial commitments from several corporations, which will allow us to get started. We think even more will follow suit when they see more of the plans. But we're gonna need some help, Ralph, and I think you're just the person we need."

Ralph stopped chewing. "Me? How could I help?"

"Ralph, you've been a huge help these last two weeks. You were there every day, making sure people had what they needed, helping with the cooking, the cleaning, the maintenance, whatever we needed. You have a real heart for people in need, and you understand more than most of us because you've been there yourself. You're a hard worker with a lot of compassion."

Ralph reddened and looked away.

"It's true, Ralph."

Rick took a bite, giving Ralph a minute to absorb what he'd just said. Then he set his fork down and leaned closer, choosing his words carefully.

"So here's what we need, Ralph. We need someone like you, someone who knows what people need, someone who can help in the planning of this new facility. I want you to be my right-hand-man, and to eventually help with the daily operations of the facility. Or you could do another job there, if something else sounded more appealing. I just know we need your help and I know you're the right man for the job."

Ralph chewed slowly, thinking about what Rick was asking. He wasn't sure Rick knew enough about him and he didn't want to disappoint him.

"I don't know..."

"Come on. Say you'll help me, Ralph."

"I'm just not sure. There are things you don't know about me."

"There are things you don't know about me too, Ralph. None of us are perfect, we're all..."

Ralph interrupted, "But I mean there are really bad things. I'm not a role model, if that's what you're looking for. I left my wife and daughter for Pete's sake. I've been on the streets for four years. I'm an alcoholic. I've done things you can't even imagine."

Rick sat back in his chair and waited for him to finish.

"Ralph, I guess what I'm trying to say is, we're all a work in progress. Maybe you've done things in your life you're not proud of. We all have. But is that the man you want to be now? That person you described? Is that still you?"

Ralph looked down. "I don't know. I don't think so, but I don't know."

"Well, that's not the person I've come to know these last two weeks. Our past doesn't have to dictate our future, Ralph. Jesus said we can all have a new life if we just believe. It's there for us any time we're ready to believe and trust him and turn our backs on our old life."

Neither spoke as they turned their attention to their plates. Then Rick spoke quietly, "I've already seen a huge change in you, Ralph. When God speaks to us, things change, don't they? And God did speak to us. We both know what we heard, in the storm and before. I'm so glad you came into my life when you did, Ralph. You'll never know how much you've helped me."

"Helped you?"

"Yeah, you helped me have the courage to tell people what I'd heard."

"I did?"

"Yeah, you did. I'm not sure I would've done it if you hadn't told me your story too. You've inspired me, Ralph, because I've seen the power of God at work in you. I have no doubt that he can change other people's lives, because I've seen him change yours and mine, and now I think we have a great opportunity in front of us. I'm not saying it's gonna be easy, Ralph, I know it's not. But why not give it a try? Don't you think it's the least we can do?"

Ralph wiped his mouth and set his napkin on his lap.

"I'm just not sure I'm the right person for you. I don't want to let you down. I mean, what if I start drinking again?" He might as well get his worst fear out in the open. "I've only been sober two weeks, Rick. What if I can't stay sober? I gotta be honest, there are times I really want a drink again." He glanced at a nearby table, where some people were enjoying margaritas.

"We'll deal with that if it happens, Ralph. But why live your life in the what-if's? I took a risk by telling people about how God spoke to me, and you're part of the reason I did it. Now maybe you can take a risk too, Ralph. I believe in you, Ralph, and I think you can do it."

Ralph's eyes moistened and he looked away. He couldn't imagine why Rick would have so much faith in him. He sure didn't deserve it. But even though he still worried about letting Rick down, maybe he ought to at least give this a try. It wasn't like he had a lot of other options, and the worst thing that could happen was it wouldn't work out and he'd just be on the streets again. So what did he have to lose?

He looked back at Rick. "All right, preacher. As long as you know what you're getting yourself into, then I guess you got yourself a deal."

Rick beamed and reached his hand across the table. When he shook it, Ralph noticed that Rick's eyes were also moist.

"This is great, Ralph. Just great. You'll see. God's gonna do some amazing things with us."

CHAPTER THIRTY-THREE

One year later

"Katie, over here!" Annie spotted her in the crowd and waved to get her attention. She was so glad Katie could make it tonight. She saw Katie and Bob winding their way through the people to reach Annie, where they hugged each other.

"You came!"

"We sure did," Katie said, her arm still around Annie. She looked around. "Is your family here, too?"

"My mom and dad are here, but not Andrew. He had a baseball game. You guys wanna sit with us? Our seats are up there," she said, pointing to the front of the room.

"Sure," Katie said, and they followed Annie to the row where her parents were seated.

Carolyn stood and waved as she saw them walking over. "Hi, you two! I'm so glad you could make it tonight." She hugged them both, and Eric shook Bob's hand. "I know it means a lot to Annie that you're here."

"We're glad we could make it, too. When Bob's grandmother got worse, we weren't sure if we were going to be able to. But she's doing better now, so we were able to get back."

Bob's grandmother lived out of town, and they'd spent the last week helping her move out of her home into a retirement facility, something she'd resisted for a long time. But when she got sick, she realized she just couldn't do it all any more, the cooking, cleaning, yard-work, grocery shopping. They were thankful that she'd actually looked forward to the move, once she'd agreed to it. They'd helped Bob's mother get her settled in, and were able to make it back home in time for this event.

They sat in the chairs Carolyn and Eric were saving, with Annie seated between her mother and Katie. Annie was excited and nervous, but having Katie here lessened her nervousness some. They chatted as the room filled with people. Almost every chair was filled and there were still many people filing in.

Rick greeted people around the room, and when he came to their row, he smiled.

"Here's some special folks," he said, shaking each of their hands. "I'm glad you all could be here tonight. I'm sure Annie's glad too, right, Annie?" Annie nodded and smiled back at him.

Carolyn put an arm around Annie and hugged her to her. "We are very proud of her, and we know she's going to do a great job."

"I'm sure she will," Rick agreed, then to Annie, "Thanks again for agreeing to speak tonight, Annie."

She blushed a little. "Sure."

Rick glanced at the clock in the back of the room and said, "It's about time to get this show on the road. Talk to you all later." He checked with a few others to make sure they were ready and made his way to the microphone up front.

Every seat was filled and extra chairs were being set up wherever they could fit them in. He waited a couple more minutes while everyone settled in. Some stood across the back of the room.

He tested the microphone. The din quieted, and he began.

"Good evening, everyone." His eyes scanned the room. "Wow, what a great turnout! I'm so glad you could all be here. It's an honor to be here tonight with all of you. A year ago today, our community experienced what was, for many of us, a life-changing experience. A tornado hit our town, killed seven people, destroyed many homes and buildings, and created a big mess for many of us. But it didn't destroy our spirit, did it? In fact, we've become an even stronger community in many ways. New friendships were created, and bonds were strengthened as we all came together to help each other."

Annie smiled at Katie, who returned her smile and squeezed Annie's hand.

"So tonight, we're gathered here to remember what happened a year ago, but more importantly, to celebrate the things that have happened since then. One of the most exciting things we have to celebrate is this building right here.

"We are on the site of the former community shelter, a place used by many needy people over the years to get a meal or to spend the night. As you know, it was almost completely leveled by the tornado. But today it's back, even better than before, because of all your support, contributions, and prayers. Now we still have a place for the needy to get a hot meal and a warm bed, but we're also giving them hope for the future—a place to get a new start, a second chance. You should all feel proud that your support and commitment to this place has already helped many families get that new start that they so desperately wanted.

"So without further ado, let's get on with our program. First, we have some people who will share their stories with you, and then we're going to open the mike up for anyone else that would like to speak. I encourage you to share your own story about something good that has come from the disaster of a year ago. Tonight is a time for us to gather, to celebrate and to be thankful for all the good that has happened in the past year."

Rick looked across to the first row of chairs. "Our first speaker tonight is someone who has become a good friend of mine over the past year, and I owe him a great deal of thanks for his efforts in getting this center built. If it weren't for him, this might never have been more than a dream. He's come a long way himself in the past year, but I'll let him share his own story with you. Folks, please welcome Mr. Ralph Parks."

The applause was hearty, accompanied by a few raucous cheers, and Ralph seemed a little embarrassed as he stood to go to the microphone. Rick shook his hand and patted his shoulder for encouragement before taking his seat.

Ralph cleared his throat and took a deep breath before he began.

"Good evening. It's an honor to be here tonight. Sometimes I can't believe a whole year has passed since the storm. But when I think about the man I was before the storm, it almost seems like a lifetime ago. Some of you may know that I was...homeless then. I was one of those people you see on the streets, dirty, begging for money, carrying a cardboard sign, sleeping under bridges or wherever I could find. And yes, drinking away most of the money I managed to beg for."

He cleared his throat again.

"But I wasn't always homeless. And I never wanted to be homeless. But through a series of stupid choices I made, that's what I was."

Ralph had been staring at the wall in the back of the room as he spoke, trying to forget about all the people in front of him, so he'd have the courage to tell his story. He paused now to blot his forehead with his handkerchief. He looked at some of their faces.

"See, there was a time when I had a family, a good job, a home, a nice car...and a bit of a drinking problem. I didn't really see it as a problem then. In fact, it seemed more like the solution to my problems, because the only time I felt good was when I was drinking. I didn't know how to feel good without it and after a while, I was even drinking at work just to get through the day.

"Well, it finally caught up with me and I lost my job. I won't say I was fired because I wasn't. I was given a choice, actually a very generous choice. My employer was willing to send me to rehab and let me keep my job, but I refused to go. See, I didn't have a problem, or so I told myself, and I sure didn't want to give up the one thing that made me feel good. So I quit. I told them what they could do with their job and I walked out. Real smart, huh."

He scanned the room, hoping he wasn't boring anyone.

"So I went home that day and decided not to tell my wife what had happened. I figured I'd just go find another job somewhere, and then I'd tell her. No sense in her worrying about it, right? And I sure didn't want to hear her nagging me about it.

"So every morning, I left the house, pretended to be going to work, and I really did plan to look for another job, but that never happened. What happened was I bought booze every day, and spent the rest of the day drinking it. Well, she finally caught on the first time I didn't bring home a paycheck. So, to make a long story short, she kicked me out and I didn't even care. All I cared about was drinking and escaping my pain.

"I had two kids that I didn't see any more. I kept telling myself I'd see her tomorrow. Every day it was tomorrow, and the tomorrows turned into four years of living on the streets, and not seeing her or anyone else I knew. When I got evicted from my apartment, I lived in my car. When my car was repo'd, it was just me and the shirt on my back. I begged people for money, and I'm ashamed to say I took it straight to the liquor store.

"Then one night, a little over a year ago, something happened to change my life. I was lying in an alley under a piece of cardboard, just wanting to die. I hated the man I'd become. I cried out to God that night. With everything I had left in me, I asked God to help me. And he did."

He stopped a minute to take a deep breath. He exhaled and continued.

"I know some of you may not believe it, but that night, God spoke to me. Out loud. When I cried out, God answered, and there was no doubt in my mind that it was God. He said, 'I'm right here, Ralph. Come to me. Trust me.' Not very many words, but they changed my life.

"I laid there, and felt a complete and total peace come over me, something I hadn't felt in years, or maybe ever. I was so used to numbing myself with alcohol, I had no idea what real peace even was any more, but that's what it was…real peace, like I'd never known.

"Well, I just laid there most of that night, soaking it up, thinking about what I'd heard, and when I got up the next morning, I felt like a new man. I walked around for a while and then sat on a bench in the park, wondering what to do next. I didn't even want a drink, which was strange, because that had been the first thought on my mind as soon as I woke up, for a long time. I just sat there, listening to the birds, watching the sun come up, noticing how the dew on the grass sparkled in the light. And for the first time in my life, I felt like God was real, and that maybe he really did care about me."

Ralph sniffed, and he took out his handkerchief to wipe his nose. He looked out at the audience and saw a blur of faces through his watery eyes.

"That morning I walked over to the community shelter, the place that was right here where we are tonight, to get one of the free lunches they hand out on Mondays. And then I talked with this guy over here." He motioned over to Rick. "I figured if anybody knew anything about God, it would be a preacher. So I told him what I'd heard and asked him if he thought I was crazy."

A corner of Ralph's mouth turned up.

"Well, if he thought I was crazy, he didn't say so. He listened, and said he thought it was entirely possible that what I'd heard was God. Well, there was no doubt in my mind that it was God, but it sure felt good to hear someone else say I wasn't crazy. So anyway, I left and as the week went by, I still didn't drink. But I didn't really know what to do with myself, so once more, Pastor Rick here helped me out. He gave me a small job at his church that week, and it was a little weird, but it felt good to be doing something productive again. I was still living on the streets, but at least I was working again.

"Then the storm came. It was a Friday, and Rick and I were on our way from the church to the shelter here when we saw the black monster in the sky. We ran into the shelter and got into the basement just in time. All of us down there in that basement felt lucky to have survived. But what you may not know is this...we heard God speak during the storm. All of us down in that basement...we heard God speak and then quiet the storm. Well, if the first time wasn't enough for me, the second time definitely got my attention."

Ralph smiled a little, pausing again.

"So, I've got a lot to be thankful for now. God gave me a second chance at life. He even gave me a second chance to hear him, and it was up to me to decide what I was gonna do. By the grace of God

I stand here today, and by the grace of a lot of you, who were willing to give me a chance," he said, glancing at Rick. "I'll always be thankful to God, and to all of you who gave me that second chance. I'm also thankful to my daughter here," and his eyes met Robin's, "who was willing to let her old man back into her life and give him another chance. I know I didn't deserve it, after all I'd put her and her mother through. But I thank you for it," he said, looking at her, "and I'll do my best to be the kind of father you deserve to have." He wiped at his eyes, and his chin quivered.

"Well, that's all. Thanks for letting me share my story."

He walked toward his chair, and the room erupted in applause. Robin hugged him when he sat down next to her. Rick made his way back to the microphone, and waited for the applause to die down before speaking.

"Ralph, thank you for sharing with us tonight. I know it wasn't easy for you. But you have to know that your story gives us all hope. Hope, that we can help create a better future for so many others out there who also need a second chance." The crowd applauded in agreement.

"Our next speaker is another special person. You may have even seen her on the news recently. Please help me welcome our local star, Miss Annie Stockton."

The crowd cheered Annie as she walked to the microphone. Rick lowered it a little, and she took a deep breath when she saw everyone looking at her. She wished now that she hadn't agreed to do this, but when she glanced over at her parents, and Katie and Bob, their smiles encouraged her, so she forged ahead, using some note cards for help.

"Hello. My name is Annie Stockton, and I am in the eighth grade at Bridgeton Middle School." She looked down at the note cards in her hands. "One year ago, the storm here in Reyport changed our lives, and it changed my life too. I was at home waiting for my mom to get home from work when the storm came. My brother was at school and my dad was flying home from a business trip that day. I was trying not to think about the storm, so I wouldn't get scared. I knew my mom would be home soon because she had just called me from her cell.

"Then the doorbell rang and I went to see who it was. I usually don't answer the door when I'm home by myself, but when I looked out the window, I saw a lady with some flowers. She looked nice," Annie said, looking up from her cards to smile at Katie, "so I decided to open the door. The lady was handing me the flowers when I saw the tornado coming, and I screamed. It was crazy windy, and then she turned around and saw it too, and she yelled that we needed to get to the basement."

Annie inhaled deeply before continuing.

"The lady at the door was Katie Griffin, who's sitting right over here, and I didn't know her until that day, but now I'm very glad she was there with me. It turned out that my mom didn't make it home that day, because the tornado blew something into her car as she was driving home, and they took her to the hospital, and then my dad's flight was delayed, so he didn't get home until late that night. My brother, Andrew, got home a couple hours later, but until then, it was just Katie and me in the house. I made a new friend that day, and I will always be grateful to Katie for being there." She smiled at Katie again, and noticed that her parents were smiling at her too.

"Well, our paths just kept crossing, because the next day, Katie was the person was delivering flowers to my mom at the hospital, and I saw her again. I'm not sure I ever believed in destiny before, but I think there was a reason Katie and I were destined to become friends. When Katie and I were in the basement and the tornado came, it was really scary. But then something happened that made it less scary. Katie and I both heard God speak through the storm, and then it got real calm. When that happened, I wasn't scared any more because I knew God was there and he was going to take care of us.

"I used to get the Sunday night blues really bad. I wanted to do well in school. I wanted to be athletic like my brother. I wanted to make my parents proud of me. But sometimes I just felt like I never would, and then I'd get really depressed." Annie said this quietly as she looked at her note cards.

Carolyn and Eric traded glances. Neither were aware that she'd felt that way.

"But after I heard God, I knew he cared about me. He was there in the storm, and now I know that he's there all the time. I have a lot to be thankful for now. I'm thankful for my new friend, Katie. I'm thankful that I found God in an unexpected place. I'm thankful for winning the state science fair with my friend, Kendra. And I'm thankful that I don't have the Sunday night blues any more."

Annie smiled and headed back to her seat.

The audience applauded loudly. She sat down, and her mother hugged her on one side and Katie on the other. She was glad she'd done it, but she was also glad it was over. And she was really glad Andrew had had a baseball game that night, so she didn't have to deal with his wise-cracks.

Rick stepped back up to the microphone and thanked Annie again. Then he opened up the mike to anyone else who wanted to speak. Several others shared something good that had come from the disaster of a year ago, and examples of how the community had come together to help each other. Neighbors with chain saws had cut up trees for others, people had watched each others' children so they could be with loved ones in the hospital, teenagers had organized clean-up teams and served meals at shelters. After over an hour of sharing, Rick called the meeting to a close.

"I want to thank everyone who spoke tonight. It does our hearts good to hear how this community came together in a time of need. It restores our faith in humankind's ability to share grace with one another. I also want to thank everyone who donated time and resources to the creation of this new center that we're in tonight. It could never have happened without your support, and isn't it great to know we're making a difference in people's lives and giving them hope for the future?"

People applauded and heads nodded in agreement.

"Thank you all for coming tonight, and I hope you'll join us for the reception afterwards in the dining hall. Thank you all, and good night."

The crowd began dispersing and heading to the dining hall. Annie and her family stood up, and Rick walked over to them. "Annie, what a great job you did!" He shook her hand, and said to her parents, "I'm sure you're very proud of her."

"You bet we are," Eric grinned, putting his arm around her.

"Are you all staying for the reception?" Rick asked.

"We wouldn't miss it," Eric answered.

On the other side of the room, Robin hugged the man next to her. "Dad, you were great."

"Thanks, honey. I hope I didn't embarrass you too much," Ralph said, hugging her back.

"Not at all." Robin reached down to get her purse from the floor. She looked back at him. "I'm really proud of you, Dad."

Ralph's eyes misted. "Well, I'm just sorry for all those years…."

Robin interrupted, "Don't say it, Dad, I know you are." Then she looked across the room. "Hey, I see someone over there I work with. I'm gonna go talk to him. You wanna come?"

"Sure." He followed her over to a group of people at the front of the room.

Bob noticed her coming towards him. "Hey, Robin!" He waved and she waved back. "Good to see you!"

"Hi, Bob, you too!" She turned around to her father and said, "Dad, this is Bob Griffin, a man I work with." Then turning to Bob, "This is my dad, Ralph Parks."

Bob's eyebrows raised as they shook hand. "You're Robin's dad?"

Ralph nodded. Bob looked back at Robin, "You never told me your dad was working on this center." Then back to Ralph, "It's very nice to meet you, Mr. Parks."

"Please. Call me Ralph."

"Ralph, then. Nice to meet you. You've sure done a great job here with this center, Ralph."

"Well, thank you, but a lot of people worked on it, not just me."

Katie walked up then to join Bob, and she greeted Robin. "Hi there!"

"Hi, Katie, this is my dad, Ralph Parks."

Katie shook his hand. "Hello, I really appreciated hearing you speak tonight, Mr. Parks. You are such an inspiration."

"Thanks. That's nice of you to say. Please, call me Ralph, though."

Katie smiled. "Okay, Ralph."

Robin asked Katie, "So you were the one with that little girl in the storm? The girl who won the science fair with her project?" Katie nodded and Robin said to Bob, "You never told me your wife knew that girl!"

"Guess I just forgot to mention it," he grinned sheepishly.

Katie motioned to Annie, who was looking back at them while her parents chatted with Rick. "Hey Annie, can you come over and meet someone?" Annie walked a couple steps over to join them.

"Annie, this is Robin Parks and her father, Ralph Parks," Katie introduced her. "Robin works with Bob," she explained.

"Oh. Nice to meet you," Annie said, offering her hand to Robin and Ralph.

"You gave a great speech tonight," Robin said to her.

"Thanks," Annie responded shyly. Then she said to Ralph, "I really liked your speech, too."

"Thanks. We've all been through some interesting experiences, haven't we?"

They all laughed, realizing that they'd all heard God speak in the storm.

Annie's eyes grew bigger as it hit her. "It's kinda weird, isn't it? That we all heard it, but not everyone did?" She said it quietly, not wanting her parents or others to overhear. "I wonder why that is?"

They all pondered this, but no one spoke. Each had their own theory, but it was hard to talk about, especially in a public place.

Ralph asked her about her science project, and while they were chatting, Robin kept glancing over at Annie's mother, who was still talking with Rick. She looked so familiar. How did she know her? Finally it dawned on her. She walked over to her, and when Carolyn noticed her, she stopped what she was saying to Rick.

"I don't mean to interrupt," Robin began.

"No, that's all right," Carolyn said.

"It's just that, well, I kept thinking you looked familiar, and I've just remembered where I've seen you before."

Carolyn looked at her, trying to place her.

"It was you in the car on Forest, wasn't it? The day of the storm? You were driving when something busted your windshield."

Carolyn nodded, still trying to place the woman. She didn't remember much about that day.

"I was there," Robin explained. "I was in the bar across the street, and when I came out, I saw you in your car, and I called 911."

Carolyn gulped. "You did?" She had searched her memory many times for the details of that day, but the last thing she remembered was driving with the wind blowing wildly all around her, then it went black until she woke up in the hospital.

"Yeah," Robin said, and they both just stared at each other.

Eric and Rick had been listening, and finally Eric jumped in. "Well, I want to thank you then. Thank you so much for calling 911. They told me later that you stayed with her until they arrived. Thank you so much," he said, shaking her hand with both of his.

Robin was still staring at Carolyn. "I always wondered what had happened to you. I didn't even know if you..."

"Survived?" Carolyn filled in for her. "Well, I'm glad to say I did," she said with a smile. "Largely, thanks to you."

"You had a big gash on your head."

Carolyn reached up to touch her head. "Yeah. I had twenty-four stitches and a lot of headaches for a while. No serious damage, though. I'm pretty hard-headed," she said with a smile.

Ralph was still talking with Annie, and he glanced over to see who Robin was talking with. He and Annie wandered over to them, followed by Katie and Bob. They were all standing together now.

Carolyn told Annie, "This is the lady who called 911 and helped me the day of the storm." Carolyn realized she hadn't even gotten the woman's name. "I'm sorry, what was your name?"

"Oh! It's Robin Parks," she said, offering her hand.

"Well, I'm Carolyn Stockton, and this is my husband Eric, and my daughter, Annie."

They all shook hands again, and Annie looked around, a little confused. "So, we all know each other somehow?"

They chuckled, looking at each other and trying to sort out the connections.

"Well, I guess so," Carolyn said. "You know Katie and Bob," she said to Annie.

"And I know Robin from work," Bob continued.

"And I guess now I know you guys," Robin said to Annie and Carolyn. "This is my dad, Ralph Parks," introducing him to the Stockton family. They all shook hands and began talking at once, asking each other questions.

Rick stood by himself, off to the side, watching the interaction unfold with Robin and Carolyn. He marveled to himself about his own connections with these people. First he'd known Ralph, and unbeknownst to him, he'd been counseling Ralph's daughter, Robin, when she'd come to him with her questions about hearing God. Then Annie had brought her parents to church and they'd attended most Sundays over the past year. He'd also seen Katie and Bob at church, usually with the Stockton family, but he'd never known their connection until today. Now this connection between Carolyn Stockton and Robin Parks...well, it was almost too much to even comprehend. '*The Lord works in mysterious ways,*' he thought.

His reflections were brought up short when the group's chattering came to an abrupt halt, and all eyes were on Bob.

"Katie and I have something we want to tell you," he said, directed mostly to Annie, but also including the rest of the group. "We were going to wait until later, but this seems like as good a time as any." Katie nodded in agreement.

"Do you want to tell them?" Bob asked her.

Katie nodded. "It looks like Bob and I are getting a second chance, too." Her face glowed as she took his hand. "We're going to have a baby!"

Annie screamed, "Katie!" throwing her arms in the air, and then rushing over to hug Katie. Katie returned her hug, tears quickly coming to both their eyes.

Bob beamed and Eric shook his hand. "That's just great, Bob, just great!" Eric said.

"Oh, Katie, I'm so happy for you!" Carolyn wrapped her arms around Katie and Annie in a group hug.

Ralph watched as Robin hugged Bob and Katie in turn. It warmed his heart to see this young couple so happy about their new baby on the way.

When everyone had finished hugging and wiping their tears, Katie looked at Annie and said, "Well, I guess we'll be needing a babysitter. Would you be interested?"

Annie half screamed her answer to the question, and Carolyn smiled.

Rick pulled out his handkerchief, took off his glasses, and wiped at the tears now streaming down his face. As he put his glasses back on and blew his nose, he noticed Sarah walking over to him. She put her arm around him. Yes, God was good. A year ago God had found a way to speak to the hearts of many people, even those who hadn't heard him out loud, and had formed new friendships and changed lives.

He himself hadn't heard God speak again out loud since that day in the storm with Ralph, but he felt a new sense of God's presence with him now. Even when things hadn't always gone as planned this past year building the center, they had always worked out. When he wondered if they had bitten off too much, the money would come in from some unexpected source, and they were able to continue.

He thought how much he had changed in the past year. Even though he'd been a "man of faith" before, he had a new kind of faith now. It wasn't just in name, this was a constant faith, a knowing that God was bigger than all his problems, and would make things work out, just like Paul said in the book of Romans. All he had to do was trust him, and be still enough to listen for his guidance. It seemed so easy, yet it was new for him to actually live it. He was even surprised at the changes in his congregation, who had opened their hearts and checkbooks in their commitment to the new center. Had they really changed, or had the change been in him?

He and Sarah stood arm in arm as they watched the people making their way to the dining hall for the reception. He led her over to the doors to step outside. He took a deep breath, inhaling the sweet smells of the blooming trees and bushes. Ah, the hope of spring. As they strolled along the side of the building, they overheard a conversation between a couple walking out to the parking lot.

"I can't believe you're buying into all that crap," the man said to the woman.

"I didn't say I was buying into it, I just think it's possible, that's all," the woman said.

"You gotta be kidding me. I mean, it's one thing to hear all the stories of people helping each other, but if you're gonna tell me you actually believe God spoke to those people, well, you're as crazy as they are."

The couple stepped into their car, and Rick and Sarah exchanged a glance. She shrugged her shoulders. He held her closer and they continued their stroll under the night sky, noticing the first twinkling stars and beginning chirps of the crickets. There was still plenty of work to be done.

EPILOGUE

"One year ago, in the town of Reyport, a suburb just outside of Kansas City, Missouri, an F4 tornado destroyed much of the town. But some people in Reyport say something else happened that day, something besides a tornado. We'll be right back to tell you all about it, and about how one girl's science project is now the talk of the town."

The program broke for a commercial and Annie yelled, "Mom, it's starting in a minute, come on!" Carolyn was trying to finish putting away laundry before the show started.

"Okay, I'll be right down! Are you recording it?" she yelled down the stairs.

"Yeah, it's all set!"

Carolyn closed the drawer and stopped by Andrew's room before she headed downstairs. She knocked lightly to no answer, so she opened it and saw he was wearing his earphones. He took them off when he saw her.

"Hey, are you comin' down to watch the Hailey show with us? Annie says it's about to start."

"Yeah, I guess," he said.

She left his door open and hurried down the stairs to sit next to Annie. Part of her was excited for Annie, but another part hoped that Annie wouldn't be made to look foolish on the show. She was well aware of how television shows could spin things to look however they wanted. The people with the Hailey show had all been very nice when they came to interview Annie about her science project, and they'd treated everyone in town with respect during their visit. Still, she was nervous that somehow they'd all be made to look like a bunch of deranged, religious fanatics.

Annie's eyes never left the screen as Carolyn sat down next to her, and the Hailey theme song played. A minute later Hailey introduced the show.

"One year ago last week, a tornado hit the town of Reyport, Missouri, so we took our crew there last week to visit the town and meet with some of the people affected by this tornado. Unfortunately, over five hundred tornados are reported in the United States every year, many of those in an area called Tornado Alley, which falls very close to the town of Reyport, Missouri. But this tornado was a little different than most tornados. Many people in Reyport say something else happened the day the tornado came. They say they heard the voice of God actually calm the storm.

"We're not talking about just one or two people that say this. While we were there, we found over twenty people who say they heard God speak. Now many of these people didn't even know each other before this happened, and remarkably, they all tell the same story. They say they heard God speak the same words, and then the storm ceased.

"We also visited with two girls in Reyport, whose science project won the State Science Fair, and they told us about their project and why it's gotten so much attention all across the nation."

Annie sucked in her breath, squealed a little, and looked over at her mother, who smiled back. Before turning her attention back to the TV, Carolyn noticed that Andrew had quietly slipped into the room was standing behind them. She hoped he wouldn't say anything to destroy this moment for Annie, but most of all she hoped Hailey didn't either. She realized she was holding her breath, so she consciously let it out and inhaled again, forcing herself to keep breathing.

"First we'll introduce you to Pastor Rick Davidson, who was in one of Reyport's homeless shelters when the tornado hit, and who has also been largely responsible for rebuilding the shelter into an even larger facility, which now includes a transitional housing unit for people wanting a fresh start in life. Here's what Pastor Davidson had to say."

They cut to a segment that the crew had taped when they were in town. First, Hailey asked Rick about the storm, where he'd been, what it had sounded like, and what type of damage had been done to the building. Then she asked, "So tell me, Pastor Davidson, what else happened in the storm that day?"

"I know it sounds incredible, and a lot of people may not believe it, but I was there, and many others in the basement with me heard it too, and there was no doubt about what we heard. The storm was so loud, just like what they say, like a freight train, when we heard a voice above it all, plain as day, we heard it. It wasn't a real loud voice, but it cut through all the noise of the storm."

"What did you hear the voice say?" Hailey asked him.

"It said, 'Peace. Be still and know that I am God.'" He looked at her with his transparent blue eyes, which also contained a peaceful confidence. He didn't seem defensive, or like he was trying to convince her or anyone else.

"And you believe this was the voice of God?"

"I know it was the voice of God." His smile reached his eyes.

"With all due respect, Pastor, how can you be sure?"

"Well, first off, he said he was God. Second, the storm calmed after he spoke. I don't know anyone else with that kind of power, do you?"

"Well, I guess not," she said, a little sheepishly.

The interview continued a few more minutes and then the show cut back to Hailey in the studio. "Well, it's one thing to hear something like this from a pastor, a man of faith, a believer already. But we also talked to people in the town who weren't believers before they heard this voice, but it made believers out of them. Stay with us, and when we return we'll have more of these interviews."

They cut to a commercial. "Isn't that the coolest thing?" Annie exclaimed. "Can you believe we're actually going to be on the Hailey show?"

"It's pretty cool, all right," Carolyn agreed. But she wouldn't relax until the show was over and she could see that Annie was portrayed in a positive light. She didn't want Annie to worry, though, and maybe it would all turn out just fine. The phone rang, interrupting her thoughts.

Carolyn checked the caller ID and saw that it was Eric, so she picked up.

"Hey, hon."

"Is the show on?" he asked. He was calling from work. He'd hoped to take the afternoon off so he could be home and watch the show with them, but a meeting had come up that he had to attend.

"Yeah, it's on. There's a commercial right now. So far they've shown some of Hailey's interview with Pastor Rick."

"How was it?"

"It was good." Eric shared Carolyn's fears about how Annie might be portrayed, and they'd only finally agreed to allow her to be interviewed after getting Hailey's personal assurance that she wouldn't portray Annie negatively. But could you believe show-biz people?

"Do you want to stay on the line and listen in?"

"Well, sure. Are you taping it though?" His meeting didn't start for another half-hour, and he could listen in until then. Maybe he'd get to hear the part with Annie before he had to go.

Carolyn assured him they were taping it, and turned up the volume and held the phone closer to the set so he could hear. The show returned and Hailey interviewed Ralph Parks next. He told her what he'd heard in the basement with Pastor Davidson, and shared some of his personal story about being homeless and then helping to build the new facility and directing his own life on a new path.

"What an amazing story. Mr. Parks, what is the name of this new facility you've helped develop?"

"It's called 'Second Chances.' Hopefully it will give a lot of people a second chance at a new life."

"That's terrific," Hailey nodded in agreement. "I'm sure you will serve as an inspiration to others who need a second chance, and hopefully as a reminder that it's always possible to create a new life if you really want it. Thank you for sharing your story with me today, Mr. Parks."

"Thank you," he replied. "I just hope that others won't have to hit bottom as far as I did, and that it won't take the voice of God to knock some sense into 'em, like it did me." He grinned and Hailey laughed along with him.

She continued by interviewing some of the people who had been in the basement with Rick and Ralph. They confirmed hearing the same words spoken during the storm, and the calming of the storm afterwards. A woman spoke of how her life had changed, how what she'd heard had led her to find a job and to get off the streets. A man spoke about how he'd been so afraid of life before hearing the voice in the storm, but that afterward he felt a peace like he'd never known before. His fears were gone and he, too, had been able to find employment and start a new life. He said he'd even been contemplating suicide, but that God had put hope into his heart for a better life, which he felt like he'd found.

"These are just a few of the stories we heard from those in the shelter basement that day, and each person we spoke with said they heard the same thing. A voice that calmed the storm, saying, 'Peace. Be still and know that I am God.' We'll be back in a few minutes to hear another story, from a man who claims he was an agnostic before that day of the storm. But not any more," Hailey said to the studio camera, as they faded into a video clip of the next man.

Andrew perked up. "Hey, that's Brian's dad," he said, moving into the room. Brian was one of his teammates and had been with him in the basement at school when the storm hit. "Brian didn't tell me his dad got interviewed."

"Are you sure that was him?" Annie asked.

"Yeah, pretty sure." He sat down in a chair, now more interested in the show. Carolyn chatted with Eric on the phone while they waited for the show to continue.

A few minutes later, Hailey said, "We're back, and I'm talking with Dave Ragsdale, from Reyport, Missouri. So tell me your story, Mr. Ragsdale. You were an agnostic?"

"I guess you could say that. I wasn't a person that thought much about God before this happened," the man said. "I guess I doubted there was a God, because if there was, how could he let so much bad happen in the world? If he existed and was all-powerful, couldn't he put a stop to those things? And if he could, then why wouldn't he? So until the day the tornado hit our house and I heard his voice, I guess you could say I was pretty much an agnostic."

"And now?" Hailey asked him.

"He made a believer out of me," Mr. Ragsdale answered with a smile.

"You're sure it was God you heard in the storm? Not someone else's voice, or something you just imagined?" Hailey didn't want to offend him, but she had to ask the questions she knew her viewers would be wondering about.

"No, I'm sure it was God."

Hailey paused, to let his words sink in. "So did this event change your life in any way, Mr. Ragsdale?"

"As a matter of fact, yes, it did."

"How did it change?"

He chose his words carefully. "I would say that now I'm on a spiritual quest to get closer to God." He paused. "I read the Bible, and other spiritual books. I guess I just feel more open to the idea of God now, to the point of seeking him. He made himself known to me, and now I feel him as a part of my life every day, whereas before I think I just tried to push away any thoughts of God."

"And what about church? Have you started going?"

"No, that's something I haven't done. I was forced to go to church when I was young and there were things I didn't like about it, so I never went back when I grew up. I'm not saying I never will, but right now this journey is something I'm doing on my own. I don't think a person has to go to church to have a relationship with God."

"Hmm," Hailey said, waiting for him to say more.

"I know some people still don't believe in God, and some don't believe that any of this even happened during the storm, but I know what I heard, and I know it was God," he said with a shrug.

"Why do you think some people heard him in the storm and some didn't?" she asked.

"I don't know. All I know is that I did."

The camera cut again to Hailey in her studio. "So now you've heard from someone who says hearing the voice of God made a believer out of him. I guess that might make a believer out of just about anyone, wouldn't it?" She smiled into the camera. "Next, we'll talk to some people in town who didn't hear God's voice and think it's all a bunch of hooey. It's only fair to hear from the other side too, right? We'll be right back after this."

A commercial came on, and Carolyn asked Eric, "Did you catch all that?"

"Yeah, I heard it."

Andrew got up and walked into the kitchen.

"So that guy was Brian's dad?" Annie said to Andrew.

"Yeah," Andrew answered without looking up while he poured milk into a glass.

"And Brian never told you any of this?"

"Nope," he said, setting the milk jug in the refrigerator.

"Wonder why not?"

"I dunno. Maybe he figured it was none of my business." He walked back with his milk and sat down.

Annie thought it was strange that Brian hadn't told Andrew about it. They were pretty good friends. Maybe Brian didn't believe his dad. Or maybe he worried that Andrew would make fun of him. Why couldn't Andrew be more open-minded? She hoped she didn't get like him when she got older.

The show was back. "Welcome back. Today we're talking with some people in the town of Reyport, Missouri, which was hit by a tornado a year ago, and some people there say they heard God's voice calm the storm. But other people say they didn't hear a thing, aside from the storm anyway, and they don't believe stories about God speaking to people in the storm. They think these people are either mistaken about what they heard, or that they imagined it, and some are just plain skeptical of the whole thing. Well, you can't really blame 'em, can you? After all, Missouri is the 'Show-Me' state." She smiled.

She interviewed two people from Reyport who said they didn't hear a thing in the storm. One woman said she believed some people just want to believe something so bad they can imagine it actually happened. The other person wasn't quite as gracious, saying there just a bunch of nutcases in town and everybody knew it. Then Hailey got to the part Annie was looking forward to.

"Next we'll meet two girls from the Show-Me state who will 'show us.' Miss Annie Stockton and Miss Kendra Reynolds were thirteen years old last year when the tornado hit Annie's neighborhood. Fortunately, her family's home sustained only minor damages. During the storm, Annie was in the basement with a flower delivery lady. It's true, a lady was actually delivering flowers to her house when the tornado appeared in the sky, and they ran into Annie's basement together. No one else was home with Annie at the time, and a very thankful flower delivery lady, Katie Griffin, was glad to have a place to go for cover.

"But the interesting part of this story is that Annie and her friend Kendra had just turned in their science fair project earlier that day, and their project ended up winning the State Science Fair. So what was their science project? It was a polygraph test, better known as a lie detector. Annie and Kendra developed a small-scale polygraph using a blood pressure monitor, breathing rate observations, perspiration measurements, along with a series of questions to help them detect whether someone was telling the truth or not. After the tornado hit, Annie and Kendra modified their list of questions a bit, which revealed some interesting, but probably not completely unexpected results. Here's my interview with them."

Annie squealed, and Andrew and Carolyn shushed her. The show cut to the interview conducted in their kitchen a few days ago.

"So Annie, tell me about this lie detector test," Hailey said as they sat at the kitchen table together. The only way Kendra had agreed to participate in the interview was if Annie did all the talking, and she would be there only to help demonstrate their project.

"Well, we have the measurement tools here," Annie was saying, pointing to the blood pressure monitor and facial blotting papers, "and these are the recording sheets and the list of questions. We start by wrapping the blood pressure cuff around their arm."

"Do you want to use me as your subject?" Hailey volunteered.

"I guess," Annie giggled and looked to see if she was serious. Hailey held out her arm, so Kendra wrapped the cuff around it and asked her to place her fingertips on the blotting papers. Kendra tightened the cuff.

"Okay, now what?"

"Well, we start with a few easy questions, ones that nobody would lie to, so we can record some baseline measurements.

"Okay, whenever you're ready, I'm ready."

Kendra arranged the recording sheets, checked the readings on the measuring devices and jotted notes on the first sheet. Annie picked up a pen and the question list.

"Okay, first question. What is your name?"

"Hailey McCoy." Hailey smiled a bit.

"What is your birthday?"

"August fifth."

Annie continued with questions about where she was born, what her favorite color was and her first pet's name. Then she moved on to the tougher ones.

"Do you believe in faith?"

"Yes. Yes, I do." Hailey answered, taking this more seriously.

"Do you believe in God?"

"Yes."

"Did God speak to you in the tornado on April twenty-first?"

"No."

"Have you ever heard the voice of God, out loud?"

Hailey had figured this question was coming, but she suddenly found herself wanting to tell the truth, instead of the answer she'd rehearsed. Annie watched her expectantly, elbows on the table and pen in hand. Kendra was carefully recording her observations.

"Would you like me to repeat the question?" Annie asked.

"No, that's okay." Hailey took a breath and dove in. "Yes, as a matter of fact, I have heard the voice of God."

Annie's eyes grew bigger and her jaw dropped. She forgot about her lie detector test for a minute and asked, "Really?"

"Yes. Really."

The show cut away from the Stockton's kitchen and back to Hailey's studio.

"Annie Stockton and Kendra Reynolds showed me the lie detector test they used with many people in the town, who voluntarily came to them asking to be subjects, so that others would believe what they'd heard. Annie and Kendra tested over a dozen people in town who asked to be included in their report. I can vouch for the accuracy of the test, based on my own personal experience.

"But does it take a lie detector test to prove the existence of God, or to prove that he speaks to people? Can God be confined to a set of measuring tools and devices? I don't think so. I think God speaks to us in a variety of ways, and not necessarily out loud. Maybe only those who are ready to listen are the ones that hear.

"Whether you believe they heard the voice of God or they didn't, the people of Reyport came together when it counted, re-built together, even creating a brand new place for people who need a second chance in life. And when it comes down to it, isn't that what we're all looking for? A second chance? I'm Hailey, and thanks for joining us today."

Acknowledgements

Thanks to all my early readers, who agreed to provide feedback on my first novel, and for not laughing at my many mistakes. Cora Storbeck, thank you for being a great editor, with your keen eyes and gentle suggestions. Rollane Williams, thank you for your help with grammatical, punctuation, and wording improvements. Irene Price, thank you for your suggestions on story transitions and character development. And thanks for saying it was one of the best books you'd read all year. I'll never forget that moment!

Kristi Martin, thanks for your help in making the airplane scenes more realistic. Dr. Jennifer Patterson, thanks for your input on the medical and hospital situations. Gina Kennedy, thanks for your encouragement, and for helping make the church situations more credible.

Any mistakes or oversights still remaining in this book are all mine.

Thanks to all my friends and family who kept saying they couldn't wait to read this book. Here it is. I hope you enjoy reading it as much as I enjoyed writing it.

Thanks to my mom, Beverly Rey, and to my dad, Donald Rey, who always encouraged me to write, even when some of my English teachers gave me less-than-stellar marks.   Thanks to my sisters, Lynn Wilson and Kristi Martin, for having more confidence in me than was probably ever warranted.

Thank you, Gene and Daniel, for inspiring me with your lives, and for encouraging me to pursue my dreams. I'm blessed to have you both in my life.

Finally, thanks to God, for being there in the stillness and storms of my life, and for giving me more second chances than I deserve. I guess that's what grace is all about.

Printed in the United States
218040BV00001B/4/P